STOLEN JUSTICE

A Cass Leary Legal Thriller

ROBIN JAMES

Stolen Justice

A Cass Leary Legal Thriller

By

Robin James

For all the latest on my new releases and exclusive content, sign up for my
newsletter at:

http://www.robinjamesbooks.com/newsletter/

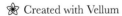 Created with Vellum

Chapter 1

Delphi, Michigan

NOTHING COULD STRIKE fear into the hearts of young lawyers quite like the steely-eyed stare of one Judge Felix Castor. Lucky for me, I wasn't that young anymore. And Judge Castor held a special place in his heart for me on account of a dragon I slew right here in this courtroom a little more than a year ago.

At least ... that's what I thought.

Castor peered over the top of his reading glasses. His scowl caused permanent creases that framed his mouth. He leafed through the pages of my brief and the defendant's. When the defense attorney cleared his throat to add a point he hadn't been asked about, Castor raised a single finger to silence him.

"Ms. Leary," Castor finally said, not lifting his eyes from the pages. "You're aware Sumner is no longer good law."

"Of course, Your Honor," I said. "But my client alleges acts of harassment within the statutory window and well into the New Year, actually."

"Your Honor," defense counsel started. He was new in town. A recent graduate of the University of Toledo School of Law. His name was David Wymer and he had a shock of red hair and rosy cheeks to match. Fresh-faced. Arrogant. Graduated at the top of his class. He straightened his tie and began to walk toward the lectern between the counsel's tables.

I winced. "The gravamen of Plaintiff's complaints stem from alleged acts that began over four years ago. As such …"

"Mr. Wymer," Castor said. He still hadn't pulled his eyes from the paperwork. "When I need you to speak I'll let you know."

Wymer sputtered. His red face turned even redder. I raised a brow as he went back to his table and crossed his arms.

"Ms. Leary?" he asked. "Your client's deposition details a handful of incidents that could arguably fall within the statutory time limit."

"Yes, Your Honor," I said. "But that really is the salient point. The defendant is free to argue to his heart's content whether those acts rose to the level of actionable harassment in contravention of the Elliot-Larsen Act. But those are material facts and they are most certainly in dispute. This matter is not appropriate for summary disposition."

Castor let the paper fall, sat back in his chair, and crossed his arms.

Wymer wasn't looking at him at first. He was busy rustling his own papers at the table. His young paralegal cleared his throat and tapped Wymer on the arm.

Castor looked at him with an amused expression. "Now, Mr. Wymer. You may speak."

Wymer stuttered.

Castor put his hand up in his trademark gesture, silencing Wymer before he really got rolling. I knew what he was doing. Felix Castor was a stickler for rules. He was harsh but he was fair. Whether David Wymer realized it or not, the judge was giving him more education in courtroom practice than he'd gotten on whatever mock trial team he'd been on less than a year ago.

"Your motion for summary disposition is denied," Castor said. "Ms. Leary is right on this one. She's raised genuine issues of material fact and it's up to the jury to hammer out. Doesn't mean I don't think this case will be an uphill battle. I trust the two of you to deal with that part. We're set for trial in six weeks. That's all."

Castor banged his gavel. There was shuffling behind me as my client murmured something to her husband. They were Ross and Livvie Becker.

Wymer gathered his things and stuffed them into his briefcase. He didn't even give me the courtesy of a handshake as he shuffled to the back of the courtroom and out the door.

Livvie rose. "What the heck just happened? Did we win?"

I waited until the sparse courtroom cleared.

"More or less," I said. "The judge agreed your case is worthy of going to trial."

"So he believes Livvie," Ross said. "He thinks she's telling the truth. That bastard's the reason she lost her job and was miserable over at the hardware store all these years."

Livvie was a forty-year-old former Miss Woodbridge County. She took a job at the local hardware store when Ross got laid off from the spark-plug factory a few years ago. Ever since, Livvie had endured crude remarks, groping hands, and finally an ultimatum from old man Harvey. If she had sex with him, she could keep her job. The trouble was, Harvey had a slew of witnesses ready to say Livvie was lying.

"The judge is only saying we get to have your day in

court. This *is* going to trial. The jury will hear your side of it and they'll be the ones to decide what happens. It's big. Harvey didn't want the details of this going public. Now, there's no way to stop it."

I didn't say the rest of it. Livvie herself was a problematic witness. Her story had shifted several times in the months since I'd met her. I believed her to the core of my soul. But a jury might not. If Harvey offered a decent settlement, I might have to strongly urge Livvie to consider it.

"It's good," I said. "A loss here today would have been the end of this, most likely. We live to fight another day."

"Thank you," Livvie said. She hugged me. Ross put a hand on her back and ushered her out.

I took a breath. The other problem was old man Harvey. He was more or less the town Santa Claus. He looked exactly like him and went to the elementary schools at Christmas to pass out candy and read stories. Castor was right, we had an uphill battle indeed.

The case was on my mind as I walked across the street and into my office. Miranda Sulier, my secretary, waited for me with a smile. She already knew the outcome of my hearing. This was Delphi, after all. Gossip traveled faster than the internet.

"Good job," she said. "I always knew there was something creepy about that old buzzard."

I set my messenger bag down. Miranda would go through it and make sense of my shorthand on all my proposed orders for the day.

"You know," I said. "I need to give credit where it's due. Tori knocked it out of the park with that motion brief. Castor cited to it at least six times in his ruling."

Tori Stockton was my newly hired paralegal. She came to me from a stint in the U.S. Attorney's office in Detroit. She was timid, sweet, but possessed a sharp intellect and stellar writing skills. Having her had been a godsend this summer.

"She's a good hire," Miranda said. She was still smiling, but there was something hollow in her eyes. "A good kid."

She was looking toward the stairs. My office was at the top of them. Tori had moved into the space right beside me.

Hiring a paralegal had been the first big sign that my little practice was taking off. For the last year and a half, I'd operated on a shoestring budget and Miranda ended up donating half of her time. But I'd managed big wins on a few high-profile murder cases and now I had a real foothold in the county.

It had come with a price though. There were still people in Delphi who couldn't forgive me for going after their home-town hero, the state's winningest basketball coach. I had no regrets. The man was a monster. The cover-up into his misdeeds had reshaped the entire school district. They still hadn't found a permanent superintendent.

"Don't suppose killing Sant-ee Claus is going to do much for your reputation," Miranda said, echoing my thoughts.

I shrugged. "Right is right. Is Tori up there? I want to tell her all the great things Judge Castor said while they're fresh in my mind."

Again, that haunted look came into Miranda's eyes. I knew she'd become something of a mother figure to Tori over the last few weeks. Tori confessed she'd lost hers just a few days before her high school graduation. Now she was working on her own law degree part-time.

"I'm worried about her," Miranda said. "She's been moping around the last couple of days. She won't tell me why. She said there was something she wanted to talk to you about."

"Hmm," I said. I sincerely hoped whatever drama had

Tori down wouldn't take her away from us. Miranda had been on at me for months to hire more support staff. I'd been reluctant. I'd gotten used to writing my own briefs again and it was hard to give up that kind of control. Now I couldn't figure out why I'd waited so damn long to take Miranda's advice. I should have known by now she was always right.

"I kind of wondered," I said. "She was dead set against coming to court with me today. It would do her some good to see the rhythm of it. Plus, Nancy and the other clerks will *love* her. Just like you do."

Miranda nodded. "She's a good kid. She's just sad a lot, I think. I was hoping her routine here would bring her out of her shell a little. I know things got rough for her in Detroit there at the end."

Rough was an understatement. Tori ended up being a material witness against one of the lawyers she worked for. It made her a champion in my mind. She'd done the right thing. But it cost her her job. Maybe not directly, but she felt the mood shift against her and buckled under it. Then she came to work for me.

"I'll go talk to her," I said. "It's been a while since I had a good old-fashioned lakeside clambake. Joe and Matty have been on me about that for a while. Summer's half over. We'll get Tori over and introduce her to some people her own age. The lake community is filled with them."

"That's good," Miranda said. "That's real good."

"And you'll come too, of course," I said.

"Betcher ass I will." She saved a wink for me as I turned and headed up the stairs.

I found Tori at her desk, her face buried in a discovery file. The Becker case. Of course Miranda would have already told her about the summary disposition hearing. Tori was two steps ahead of me, combing through deposition transcripts.

"Good job today," I said. "Judge Castor was very impressed with your brief. I'd like you to meet him next time. He's one of the best Circuit Court judges we have. You could learn a lot from him."

"I'm happy for Mrs. Becker," she said. Tori's tone was flat. She was young. Just twenty-three, but she looked even younger. She didn't wear much makeup and had fine bones and an almost translucent, pale complexion.

I took a seat on the other side of her desk.

"I mean it," I said. "You're really good at this, Tori. You wrote one of the best briefs I've seen in a while. Castor had already made up his mind before I even had to say a word."

She gave me a weak smile. Damn. She looked so tired. She had dark circles beneath her eyes and her shoulders drooped. She looked like she carried the weight of the world on them.

Why hadn't I noticed this before? Tori looked like she may have even lost weight since I first met her a few months ago.

"Tori," I said. "I don't mean to get into your business ... but is everything okay with you?"

Her eyes flicked downward. She bit her lip and shifted in her chair.

"It's fine ... I'm sorry ... I'm just tired."

I leaned forward. "Honey, you're part of this office now. I know these past few months have been rough for you. You've had your whole life sort of turned upside down. Starting a new job, everything that happened at your old office. I just want to make sure you're taking care of yourself."

She blinked hard as if she were on the edge of tears.

"Tori," I said. "What is it? You can tell me."

She shook her head. "I don't know how."

My heart skipped. Whatever was going on, I didn't need

to be a mind reader to know it was bad. Tori looked physically ill.

"Tori, whatever it is, keeping it secret won't help. You of all people should know that by now."

This time, her tears did come. They fell slow and silent down her cheeks.

"Ms. Leary," she started.

"Cass," I corrected her. "I've told you a dozen times. It's just Cass."

She sniffled. "Cass. You're so good at what you do. You know that, right? I hear what people say. They respect you. The other lawyers in town, they're intimidated by you."

It was my turn to blink hard. Ever since I came back to Delphi after a decade as a corporate lawyer in Chicago, they hadn't really rolled out the Welcome Wagon for me.

"Well, that's good to hear. But …"

"I don't have anyone else I can ask," she said. "I've tried. They slam the door in my face. They won't even take a meeting."

I tilted my head. "Who's they? What is it you need help with? Tori … I swear, if it's within my power, I'd like to help. I haven't forgotten how you stuck your neck out for my client. I know what it cost you."

"You promise?" she asked.

I opened my mouth to give her a resounding yes. Something stopped me. I had that creeping sensation up my spine that told me I may just live to regret my offer.

"I promise to listen," I said.

Tori flinched. She knew a backpedal when she heard one.

"Please," she whispered. "There is literally nobody else for him. And you're the best, Cass. I know it. I've seen that firsthand. Even if I hadn't come forward with what I knew, I think you would have gotten Ted Richards off anyway.

You're like magic in the courtroom. And you don't back down. You don't care what people say about you. I know if you take a look, if you just talk to him …"

"Tori, I need you to stop dancing around. Tell me what it is you need. Is it a boyfriend? Someone's in trouble?"

I could almost write the script. I'd watched this scene a hundred times. Was he some deadbeat? Drug dealer? Drunk driver? Had he promised Tori the moon then disappeared with her life savings?

Tori reached into her desk drawer. She pulled out a thick, dog-eared file. She opened it. Dozens upon dozens of newspaper clippings fluttered as she flipped through them. She pulled one carefully out and spread it in front of her. Every instinct in me told me to walk right back out of the room.

"He's got no one else," she said. "And he's my dad."

"What's he been charged with?" I asked. So not a boyfriend at all.

"He's been in prison my whole life, Cass. And he's dying. He won't admit it, but I can see it in his face. He has that gray look to his skin. Cancer or something. I know it."

I knew that look too. I'd watched my grandmother waste away from ovarian cancer when I was just a teenager.

"Let me see," I said, my voice sounding flat and resigned.

If the guy had been in prison most of Tori's life, it had to be something awful. A lost cause, probably.

She turned the paper so I could read the headline. My heart went from a dead stop to falling straight to the floor.

A year and a half ago, I'd managed to try the second most notorious murder case in Delphi. There, staring up at me in black and white, was the face of the number one most notorious murderer in Delphi's history.

I didn't even need to read the headlines. I recognized that face instantly. Everyone in Delphi would. In my town, at least, his name was uttered with the same disdain as Ted Bundy or John Wayne Gacy.

Sean Allen Bridges.

I sat back in my seat. It hit me like a shock wave. I'd never noticed it before. But Tori looked just like him.

Chapter 2

Sean Allen Bridges.

The name echoed through me like distant thunder. For twenty-four years, people around town had uttered it in one long, unbroken stream of syllables.

Sean Allen Bridges.

I ran my fingers over the creased, yellowed pages of the newspaper clipping Tori had given me. *The Delphi Oracle*, a paper that didn't even exist anymore, had printed a special edition in the aftermath of Bridges's conviction. The headline read, "Day of Reckoning for a Campus Killer."

Sean Allen Bridges's mug shot took up almost the entire top half. He'd been young. Lord. I hadn't realized how young. At the time, I had been an eleven-year-old middle schooler. Twenty-six seemed like fifty as far as I was concerned.

He was handsome. I saw that now. He looked a little like Brad Pitt, with a chiseled jaw and brilliant blue eyes. Tori had the same full, heart-shaped mouth. The same hooded eyelids that lent her expression a dreamy quality.

Oh yes, there could be no doubt. This man was her

father. And in the eyes of the world, this man was a cold-blooded killer.

Tori was gone now. I'd sent her home for the day. I needed to think. I needed to breathe. I folded the newspaper clipping and put it back in Tori's scrapbook. The thing was three inches thick, stuffed with more clippings, prison letters, photographs, and handwritten notes. Years' worth of them. They weren't in Tori's hand. They were scribbled in neat, tight cursive. This was old-school penmanship, not a lazy letter among them. I could ask Tori who wrote this later. For now, I needed a different kind of help.

I picked up the scrapbook and made my way downstairs. Miranda looked up from her desk. I was pretty sure Tori had still been crying when she left the building. I was surprised Miranda had left me alone with my thoughts. I started to wonder if she already knew what Tori had wanted to talk to me about.

"You might as well hear this too," I said.

Miranda grabbed a pen and her notepad. Come to think of it, I rarely saw her without them. She was the linchpin of this entire office. She kept me on time, on task, and usually stayed two steps ahead of me. Yes. Odds were she already knew exactly what was in this scrapbook.

"She just got here a few minutes ago," Miranda said, gesturing with her chin toward the office at the end of the long hallway. "I told her you might want her ear."

"Thanks," I said. I turned and headed for Jeanie's office door. I gave it a soft knock. I heard a thud as something crashed to the floor.

"Son of a bitch that corner!" Jeanie bellowed from inside. Two weeks ago, Jeanie's new office furniture had arrived. She'd been catching her hip on the desk corner pretty much daily.

Smiling, I pushed open the door. Jeanie stood hunched over at the edge of her desk, rubbing her left hip.

She glared at me with those steely eyes of hers, then pointed toward the new leather chairs on the other end of the room.

I'd given Jeanie the biggest office. She made a little sitting area with two green leather chairs and a matching couch. They were arranged in front of a stone fireplace that didn't really work. But it gave the room an inviting, homey feel.

"I've got something I need to run past you," I said.

Jeanie noticed the scrapbook. She stopped rubbing her hip. She set her jaw to the side and her eyes flicked from me to Miranda.

"Might as well break 'em in," she said, waving to the fireplace furniture.

I took a seat in one of the chairs. Miranda took the couch. Jeanie came over and sat in the other chair. When she leaned back, I noticed her feet barely touched the floor.

You can easily forget how short Jeanie Mills really is. She didn't stand a full five feet, but somehow she managed an imposing air just the same. Couple that with her short white hair with just a shock of black at the front and she had the kind of look you never forgot. She was rough. Gruff. Lethally smart. She was my greatest champion and my greatest critic. I had a feeling before this meeting was through, I'd need both.

I put the scrapbook on the table and opened it to the "Day of Reckoning" clipping.

Jeanie leaned forward and tilted her head so she could read it.

"The Menzer murder," she said. "What are you doing with all of that?"

Miranda read the clipping from her angle. She drew in a

sharp breath that surprised me. Could it be she *didn't* know what Tori was after all along?

"Tori," I said. "She brought it to me a little while ago. It turns out she has a connection to the killer."

"Sean Allen Bridges," Miranda said, her voice barely above a whisper.

Of course she knew it without me having to say it. Everyone knew that name. They knew it more than the victim's.

Heather Menzer had been just nineteen years old. A college student. If memory served, she had been studying to become a paramedic at Delphi Community College.

"It's the search I remember most," I said. "It went on for weeks, didn't it?"

The story was everywhere. There hadn't been a soul in Delphi unaffected.

Heather Menzer had been someone's babysitter. Someone else went to school with her brother or sister or something. She served someone else drinks at Mickey's Bar.

Jeanie flipped the page in the scrapbook. The next clipping profiled Heather herself. She was pretty. Not beautiful. She had big brown hair crinkled and sprayed high in a classic, mid-nineties style. Frozen in time. Forever smiling in front of a cheesy blue backdrop. A yearbook photo.

A sister. A daughter. A student. A friend. A victim.

"Days," Jeanie said. "They searched for days. Not weeks."

"That Awful Summer," Miranda said. Just like that. Capital letters. It's the way everyone talked about it even to this day. That Awful Summer. The hottest one on record in over a hundred years.

Another memory flooded back. My mother and some of the others from the neighborhood organized a water station for the volunteers. She took my rusted Radio Flyer wagon and filled it with ice and bottles of water. My brother and I went with her and took it to the park where the search focused. People were passing out from the heat as they searched on foot for Heather Menzer.

"What's the connection?" Jeanie asked. She lifted one of the clippings out of the book. It fluttered in her hand, so delicate, thin enough that the light shone through it and I could see Heather Menzer's face bleeding through from the other side.

"She says Bridges is her father."

Jeanie froze. She set the clipping down, handling it with as much care as if it were the Magna Carta. Or plutonium.

"Well, shit," she said, summing it all up perfectly. "I don't remember anything about there being a kid. She doesn't seem old enough. This was what, twenty-four years ago?"

"Almost to the day," Miranda said.

"Wow," Jeanie said. "So she was born right after. Or during." Jeanie folded her hands and stared at me. Oh, I knew that look. If I wasn't careful, she'd drop some sort of truth bomb that she knew I wouldn't yet want to hear.

"What's she expect you to do with all of this?" she asked.

"Look into it, I guess. I think she thinks he's innocent."

Jeanie raised that skeptical brow of hers. "Honey, what do you remember about this case?"

"Not much," I said. "I remember it gripped the whole town. I remember it made national news."

"*Unsolved Crimes*," Miranda said. "That show with that guy who used to be on that cop show from the seventies. I wonder whatever happened to him. Their camera people set up just across the street when they came."

"This girl," Jeanie said. "Heather Menzer. What happened to her was horrific. A lot of it didn't make it into the papers. I shared office space with Lowell Dushane. He caught the court appointment for the defense. He was

Bridges's lawyer. Cass, they tried to run him out on a rail for it."

"Hmm," I said. "I know the feeling."

Jeanie gave me a grim nod. Early last year, the town had pretty much wanted to do the same thing to me for defending the accused killer of the beloved high school basketball coach. Even after I exposed the man for the monster he was, there were some who hadn't been willing to forgive me.

"Cass, this one got as bad as they get. The girl wasn't just murdered. She was tortured. Raped. He put fourteen bullets into her one by one. The coroner says the first few didn't kill her. This guy took his time with her first. Other than being burned or buried alive, I guess, I can't think of any worse way to go."

My heart hammered behind my ribcage. Heather Menzer stared up at me from that yellowed newspaper clipping. Forever smiling. Forever dead. It was hard not to imagine the agony she would have suffered.

A monster had done this. The devil himself.

Sean Allen Bridges. No wonder his name had the same dark mythology surrounding it in Delphi as even Charles Manson or Ted Bundy's.

"And he's Tori's father?" Miranda asked, shaking her head as if to jar something loose.

"That's what she says."

"What does she have?" Jeanie asked.

"Not much more than the opinion he couldn't have done it. I think he's been telling her that his whole life. She said she's tried to get a number of other lawyers to look into it and they've all refused."

Jeanie sat back. She hooked her hands behind her head. "Can't say as I blame them. I gotta be honest. If she's wrong about it, I wouldn't want to be the one trying to help."

"But if she's not wrong, then the real monster behind this murder might still be out there."

"It's Tori," Miranda said. "She's a good kid. She doesn't really have anybody. I don't know if you knew this, but she's been staying with me for a couple of weeks. Her landlord evicted her. Wants to rent her building out to some relatives."

"Geez," I said. "Why didn't she come to me? That I might have been able to help her with."

"She doesn't like to ask for it," Miranda said. "It was like pulling teeth trying to get her to tell me that much. I damn near had to throw her in my trunk to get her to come to my place."

Jeanie let out a guffaw. "That I would have liked to see."

"I really don't think she has any other family to speak of. You know her mom's gone. No siblings. And now we know where her dad is. Before all I could get out of her on that was that he was out of town and not in contact."

"What about Lowell Dushane?" I asked. "He doesn't practice in Delphi anymore but is he still alive?"

"I don't think so," Jeanie said. "He and his wife moved down to Florida after he retired. Hell, that had to be ten or fifteen years ago now. He was old during the Bridges trial. I want to say I saw an obit in the *Free Press* a couple of years back for him."

"Can you double check? I wouldn't mind talking to him, at least," I said.

"Did you promise her anything?" Jeanie asked.

Once again, she gave me that laser-focused stare. "Er ... sort of ..."

She dropped her chin and narrowed her eyes.

"Jeanie, come on. She's like a scared rabbit. Miranda is right. I think for the moment, we're it as far as her circle of friends. Her testimony in the Richards trial this year did her some major personal damage. Now I think I understand even more why she was willing to come forward. Bad as a guy my client was, she knew he was innocent. She's apparently grown up watching her own father rot in jail for a crime she thinks he didn't commit."

"Aye, yai, yai," Jeanie said. "You've already made up your mind, haven't you?"

"I promised her I'd help her if I could. That doesn't mean I believe this guy is innocent. It just means I think we owe it to her to at least ask some questions."

"I agree," Miranda said. "I'll figure out what happened to Lowell Dushane. I used to be friends with his wife. She was his secretary too. She's dead now. Heart attack a few years after they moved down there. But she had a sister I liked. Give me twenty minutes and I'll get that old fossil on the phone if he's still breathing."

"Cass," Jeanie said. "If you do this. I mean, the minute this town catches wind you're even asking ..."

"I know, I know," I said. "It'll be the Ames trial all over again. It'll be more rocks through the window. But I was right then. I was right about Richards. And if any of us gets a bad feeling about this Bridges, we walk away."

"Any of us?" Miranda asked.

"Yes," I said. "I'll need you both. And I don't make decisions that could torpedo this firm without you. If you say no, it's no."

Miranda had her eyes on Jeanie. She could throw her own laser stare. Jeanie shook her head.

"Dammit all to hell. I can't take on the two of you."

"The three of us," Miranda said. "Tori's part of this operation now too."

Jeanie nodded and threw up her hands. "Fine," she said. "I double check on Dushane. If he's alive, I'll get his withered ass on the phone. I'll talk to him. He had a thing for me a million years ago."

I couldn't help but smile. I was learning half the town had a thing for Jeanie Mills back in her prime.

"What about you?" she asked.

I flipped to another page in the scrapbook. A more recent mugshot of Sean Allen Bridges stared back at me. This one had been part of a prison transfer.

"After you track down Lowel Dushane," I said to Miranda, "can you get me on the visitors' list at Handlon Prison? I need to talk to Sean Allen Bridges face to face."

Chapter 3

THE NEXT MORNING, Saturday, I woke up to the sound of my brother's jet ski zipping along the lake.

I pulled the room-darkening shades last night and for a moment, had no sense of time. It was already stifling hot on the second floor. The small window air conditioners I used would never be able to keep up today if it hadn't gotten below seventy degrees last night. I threw on a bathing suit and swim cover-up, my summer uniform here on the lake, and headed downstairs.

Matty did a donut right in front of the dock, sending a wall of water straight at it. My brother Joe had a pole in the water and dodged the worst of the blast. He managed to flip Matty off in the process.

Matty pretty much had the lake to himself at the moment. Last weekend was the Fourth of July and campfires burned up and down the lake for days. All the weekenders and vacationers had gone home. Now it was just us.

Joe pointed to a cup holder on the pontoon docked beside him. Bless him. He'd brought down my coffee in my favorite stainless steel mug.

"Not much else to do today besides sit in the water," he said, wiping the sweat from his brow.

Joe zipped his line back across the water with such dexterity you'd think the thing was part of his arm. He was deeply tanned. His normally light brown hair had bleached almost white on top. The local weatherman predicted it could get close to a hundred degrees today.

"Yeah," I said, picking a spot on the back of the boat beneath the shade of the bimini. "Katy and Emma coming out today?"

A look passed across my brother's face. He and his wife Katy had hit a bit of a rough patch of late. He'd had some turbulence from his ex, Emma's mother. It opened old wounds between them.

"Emma's working," he said. "One of the other waitresses at the Sand Bar came down with mono or something. She's getting tons of hours."

"Good!" I said. The Sand Bar was a popular bar and grill on the south end of the lake. It was only open between Memorial Day and Labor Day. My niece Emma cleaned up in tips every weekend.

"Vangie said she's going to try to come over with the baby after lunch," he said. "I told her I'd take a look at that water damage in her back bedroom."

My younger sister Vangie had just rented a house on the other side of the lake. The *baby* in question was her seven-year-old daughter, Jessa. Things hadn't gone as smoothly for my sister since she'd moved back here permanently a few months ago. She was having trouble finding a job that paid as well as her bartending gig back in Indianapolis. I was trying to convince her to let me pay to send her back to school. So far, her stubborn nature won out and she refused to take me up on it.

Matty zoomed back toward the dock. He beached the jet

ski and climbed off. He shook the water off the ends of his dark hair, reminding me of a big dog. He had a bright smile as he hopped up on the dock and joined me on the pontoon.

"What about you?" I asked. "You staying through the weekend?"

It was code. Matty had his own issues with his estranged wife, Tina. For the past two months, he'd been living with me. I didn't mind having him around, but feared it was only putting off the inevitable. He and Tina had been going round and round for the better part of two years. I didn't like how she strung him along even if a lot of their problems were Matty's making. He inherited our father's legendary alcohol problem but luckily not his meanness. For the moment, he had it under control.

"Can I ask you something?" I said. Joe reeled his line in and stuck the pole in a holster he'd built beside the dock. He reached in and grabbed his own coffee from the holder next to the captain's chair. The boat swayed in the water as Joe stepped on and swiveled the chair so he could face me.

"Yep," he said.

"Do you remember the summer Heather Menzer was killed?"

Joe froze mid-swallow. He narrowed his eyes in confusion, then set his cup back down.

"That nursing student?"

"Paramedic, I think," I said.

He shrugged. "Right. They caught the guy who did it, didn't they? You know, I sometimes work with a guy who used to date her."

"Sean Allen Bridges," Matty added.

Bridges's name echoed through me again. Even Matty knew it. The summer of the murder, he had only been four years old.

"Yes, on all counts," I said.

"Freaked Mom out," Matty said. "She wouldn't let you go anywhere by yourself."

A memory jarred. He was right. I hadn't even been allowed to ride my bike two streets over to a friend's house without Joe by my side. It had been like that all through town. Even after Bridges was arrested, the brutality of it all shook the town to its core.

"That Awful Summer," Matty said. "Guys in the shop still talk about it like that."

Awful. Horrific. A nightmare.

"Dad was on the search party," Joe said. "I begged him to let me come too. He said no. I went anyways. It was me and a few other buddies from the neighborhood. It was like that movie *Stand by Me*. We walked the railroad tracks out by Beach Road."

"God," I said. "Jeez, Joe. I never knew that. What the hell would you have done if you'd been the ones to find her?"

"I don't know," he said. "Jimmy Stover said we'd be famous. He was such a dumbass."

"Still is," Matty offered.

"I'm just surprised Dad paid attention long enough to even have an opinion," Joe said.

I went silent. That Awful Summer. There was something else bothering me about it, tugging at the loose corners of my memory.

"He was sober," I said.

Matty grabbed a towel off the back of the boat and wrapped it around his waist. Joe stared out at the water. He took another sip from his cup.

"I don't remember that," Matty said. "I don't ever remember Dad when he was sober."

"You wouldn't," Joe said.

"But he was," I said. "For ninety days. I counted."

Joe nodded. "He tried meetings for a while. I guess they helped."

The wind lifted my hair. I tied it back with the hair tie I had around my wrist.

It was something we rarely talked about. There had been hope in the house for those brief few weeks. The yelling stopped.

"We had a Fourth of July party here," I said. "Remember, it was just after Grandma Leary had her hips replaced. Uncle Patrick had that big, ridiculous boom box and he ran an extension cord all the way down the dock. He was playing Steely Dan and that southern rock they all liked."

"Figures," Joe said. "It's a wonder he didn't electrocute us."

"They danced," I said. "Mom and Dad. I'd forgotten about that. I mean, it was just so weird. They were laughing and he twirled her. Grandpa yelled at him because he damn near tripped and fell into the fire."

"It really is a wonder any of us survived into adulthood," Matty said.

"Yeah," Joe said. He hadn't met my eyes. He just kept staring out at the lake.

"It's silly, I know. But everyone around here always calls it That Awful Summer." I made air quotes around the words. "It wasn't like that for me."

Joe chewed the inside of his cheek. He was acting weird. Pensive. I knew he remembered the same things I did.

"Yeah," he said. "But then it was fall."

He drained the last of his coffee cup and rose. The boat rocked as he stepped off it and pulled his fishing pole back out of the holster.

"How'd she get him to do it?" Matty asked. "You know how many times I begged him to go to A.A.? And how is it I never knew that?"

"Like I said," I answered. "You were what, four years old? You didn't even know what drunk was back then, Matty."

"Yeah," Joe chimed in. "He just thought it was normal."

"You know," I said. "At the time, I remember thinking I could see what Mom saw in him. He was so funny. Charming. Handsome."

"He was a charmer, all right," Joe said.

I let out a breath. The conversation was going nowhere. If anything, it seemed to anger him. No sooner had I thought it before Joe reeled his line back in and turned to me.

"Why are you bringing up Heather Menzer and that summer?"

He gave me his patented, withering stare. I knew that look. It's the one he used to see straight through me. My brother knew me far too well. We were a year and a day apart but a lot of people thought we were twins. Growing up the way we did, in constant turmoil, we understood each other better than everyone else did.

"Nothing," I said, but it was already too late.

"Bullshit, I know you. I know that look. Are you planning on stirring something up again?"

Sweat started to bead his brow. It wasn't even ten o'clock in the morning yet and the temperature was north of eighty. There wasn't a single cloud in the sky.

"Never mind, Joey," I said.

He set his pole down.

"Let me guess," Matty said. "Somebody asked you to file an appeal for Sean Allen Bridges."

Apparently Matty had inherited enough of Joe's mind-reading DNA. There was a limit to what I could say to them. But Sean Allen Bridges wasn't my client. Not yet, anyway.

"I've been asked to look into it, that's all," I said. The

truth was, if I did go further with this, there would be absolutely no way from keeping it out of the press. The minute I went to even meet with Bridges, the gossip mill would start to grind. No doubt some corrections officer would mention it to another, and he'd be the brother or the friend of someone else in town. Matty would know. Joe would know.

"He's a monster, Cass," Joe said. "I mean, I bet if you said the name Sean Allen Bridges all the way out in California, people would know who he was."

"I said I've been asked to look into a few things. That's all. I haven't even decided whether I want to."

"Right," Joe said. "Except if that were true, you wouldn't have even bothered bringing it up at all. I know what you're doing. You're trying to handle me. You want me to say I think it's okay."

I gave him my own withering side-eye. "Really? Since when have I been in the habit of submitting my career choices for your approval?"

"Two thousand and never," Matty answered for me.

"You think he's innocent?" Joe asked.

"I have no earthly idea." It was an honest answer. "Probably not. I don't remember a lot about the case on the face of it. I know the cops were damn sure they got their man. They've been wrong before, of course. And it's been twenty-four years. So, this is really and truly going to be about me doing something for someone who had nowhere else to go. A favor. That's all. The only reason I'm telling you is so that you don't hear it from someone else."

Joe turned back to the water. Another jet skier whipped by. Joe raised his hand in a wave.

A car door slammed behind me. Vangie had just pulled up. My niece Jessa tumbled out of the back seat. She was already in her life jacket and barreling toward the dock.

She was smiling. Happy. Her pigtails bounced behind her

as Vangie followed with armfuls of gear. Beach towels. Sunscreen. Plastic toys ready for Matty to blow up. Oh, he'd bitch about it, but he'd do it. My brother was positively smitten with Jessa.

Vangie got to the end of the dock. Joe side-stepped as Jessa flew past him.

"Cowabunga!" she yelled as she jumped off the end. She made a big splash and popped up like a cork. She flailed her arms and legs and did an awkward backstroke.

"Uncle Matty," she hollered. "Will you come in and throw me?"

Matty dropped his towel and stepped off the boat. He moved past Joe and executed a cannonball that sent a column of water shooting straight in the air.

Joe smiled at them, but it didn't reach his eyes. He looked back at me.

"Will you lighten up," I said. "This isn't the apocalypse or anything. Jeez."

He rolled his eyes. "Right. You say that all the time. And then it is."

"I haven't even …"

"Save it," he said. "So when are you going to visit this guy?"

I let out a sigh. There was no point trying to hide a single thing from him.

"Soon," I said. "Probably this week."

While Matty and Jessa splashed their way further out, I put my arm around my older brother.

"Why do I get the feeling this is gonna be another long, awful summer."

Jessa's scream of delight echoed as Matty threw her high in the air.

Chapter 4

I MADE the two-hour drive to Ionia, MI alone. Jeanie wanted to come with me, but I needed her to handle a few hearings I couldn't reschedule today. Plus, I wanted my first impressions of Sean Allen Bridges to come unclouded by anyone else's. To put it simply, if I got the slightest bad vibe from the guy or his story, I would go back down US-127 with a clear conscience that I could leave this case behind.

I stood in the visitors' holding area gripping the handle of my messenger bag with both hands. I held it in front of me almost like a shield. Handlon Correctional Facility had that same dank, dark smell all prisons had. You could feel bits of your soul draining away as you breathed in the stale air.

I'd been searched. Lectured. Judged. Two corrections officers stood still as stone gargoyles at the entrance to the conference room I'd been given for this meeting.

Someone had pulled some strings. Jeanie, probably. I expected to be meeting Bridges in a common area surrounded by dozens of other inmates greeting sad, desperate loved ones for a few fleeting minutes before they were sent back to their cells.

"You can have a seat at the table," one of the officers said. His face held no expression. No judgment either. I was glad of it.

"Does he get many visitors?" I asked.

The officer shrugged. "He's got a kid. College-aged, I guess. Years ago, his mom used to make the trip. She stopped coming. She was always old. I suppose having a son like him would do that to a person. Anyway, I think she passed on."

I nodded. These were things I already knew. Sean Allen Bridges had spent the last two and a half decades getting shuffled around through the Michigan State Prison system. But he'd been housed in Handlon the longest. Eight years. If things stayed the way they were, he was never, ever getting out.

A deafening buzzer went off behind me. I tried not to jump.

The officer opened the door and gestured toward the conference table. He flicked a switch and the fluorescent lights came on with a headache-inducing buzz and flicker.

Other than the table and four ancient metal chairs, there was nothing else in the room but high windows. They let in what little natural light there was from the gray sky above. It had been storming all day. It would only kick the humidity up another ten degrees by evening.

"We'll be right outside," the officer said. "We can see everything from the window. Your conversation is private though."

"I appreciate that."

He took sentry by the door as the other officer stepped away. I went to the table, sat my messenger bag on top of it beside me, and waited.

I folded my hands in front of me and crossed my legs.

Tiny beads of sweat formed between my shoulder blades. With the high ceilings, the acoustics in the room were unforgiving. I swore they could probably hear my pounding heart.

I don't know why I was nervous. I'd met plenty of potential clients this way. Hell, I defended one of the country's most notorious serial contract killers earlier this year. But somehow, Sean Allen Bridges stirred some primal fear inside of me. His crimes touched people I knew. It had reshaped the history of my hometown.

The door opened behind me and Sean Allen Bridges walked in.

I rose.

They kept him cuffed, in leg chains that circled his waist and bound his wrists. He wore a dingy blue jumpsuit with orange patches on the shoulders.

Sean Allen Bridges was only fifty years old. He looked about ninety.

He seemed almost birdlike. His cheekbones protruded below dark, hollow circles beneath his eyes. His blond hair had gone mostly white. He regarded me with the palest blue eyes. They were the only thing that matched the pictures of him I'd seen from twenty years ago, only the light and fury had gone out of them.

Bridges shuffled to the table. He raised his arms in an awkward attempt to shake my hand. His skin felt dry as sandpaper and tissue thin. I noted a few fading prison tattoos on his forearm.

He sank into his seat. I did the same.

"Mr. Bridges," I said. "My name is Cass Leary. I'm an attorney down in Delphi. Your daughter Tori has been working for me for a little while."

A bit of the light came back into the man's eyes. He managed a weak smile that deepened the creases in his face.

"She told me," he said. His voice was so low, I had to strain to hear him.

Bridges had a grayness to him. If there were such things as auras, his was clouded, mottled. No trace of brightness shining through.

"Are you all right?" I asked. "Do you have what you need in here?"

He paused for a moment. "Is that what Tori sent you here for?"

I sat back, a little stunned. Had she not already told the man what she asked of me?

"Among other things," I said, "your daughter is a warrior. A champion, in my eyes. She's not afraid to speak out when she sees an injustice. Even when it costs her."

His expression stayed glass-like. "She's young," he said. "Give her time."

"You're aware she gave state's evidence against some powerful people this year?"

Bridges raised his hand and scratched his chin. "Like I said, she's young."

"That she is. She's also incredibly smart and talented. She's going to make a good lawyer someday if she wants it."

"Well," he said. "Thanks for looking out for her then. She's pretty much had to do that alone her whole life."

"She asked me here to look into your case," I said.

Bridges froze. I still couldn't get a good read on him. I realized I might never be able to. This man had spent half his life in an institution. His survival instincts would be finely honed by now. I was new. An outsider.

None of that mattered though. I was only interested in the truth.

"Then I'm sorry you've come all this way," he said. "You've wasted your time."

"Tori says you've been telling her her whole life that you're innocent."

He curled his lips in the first hint of a smile. "Look where I am," he said. "I mean ... we all say that, don't we?"

"I'll be honest. I haven't even dug into your case fully. I only know what I read in the papers. I told you I'm from Delphi. Born and raised."

He scratched his chin again, regarding me. "What are you? Thirty? Thirty-five? I'm a little before your time ... Cathy, did you say?"

"Cass," I said. "Cass Leary."

A flicker of recognition passed through his eyes.

"Leary," he said. "Eastlake."

"Yes."

"I went to school with a Willie Leary. King of the burnouts. Brother of yours?"

"Cousin," I said.

"Let me guess," Bridges said. "He's in the system now too?"

"He was," I answered. "Now he's not. He died when I was a teenager. Drug overdose."

"Sounds about right."

Was he trying to bait me? As if there were nothing more separating us than this metal table.

"But you got out," he said. "Or you could have. A lawyer?" He whistled low.

"Yeah," I said. "I got out. For a while, anyway. But here I am. And here you are, Mr. Bridges. If you're trying to make me feel bad about my family name, you can save yourself the trouble. I know who I am and where I come from. I've also faced up to much bigger and badder than you. But like you said ... here I still am."

I leaned forward and folded my hands together. I gave

Sean Allen Bridges, convicted killer, the iciest stare I could muster.

He was a shell of a man. Hollowed out. Gutted. Skinny. Physically weak. But there was strength in the way he stared back.

"You gonna ask me?" he said.

"Ask you what?"

"Come on. It's what you're here for. I know how this goes. I already had my day in court. This is my life now. Mine. You get me?"

"I'm not sure I do."

"You don't need me. If my kid is begging you to start kicking rocks over, I don't even matter. You need some technical hook. You'll spend your life in trial transcripts. It doesn't matter what I say. So, you came to try and figure me out. See if I'm worth the grief. So ask me."

"Did you do it?" The words spilled out before I could stop them. It wasn't like me. He was right about the rest of it. Technically, I could get most of what I needed from court archives. None of this mattered at all if there wasn't some reversible error in the trial court record or new evidence that would have changed the outcome of the case. This long past his conviction, it would be like looking for a needle in a stack of more needles.

"No," he said gritting his teeth. The word seemed to cost him. It shuddered through him, bringing the first sign of color high into his cheeks.

"No," he said again. "I didn't kill Heather Menzer. I barely even knew her."

"But you did know her. You had contact with her. Tell me what you think the cops got wrong."

He waved me off. "What difference does it make now? Even if I prove it."

"I think it matters to your daughter. She's grown up

believing your innocence. She now lives in the same town that utters your name with the same hate as Lee Harvey Oswald or Mark David Chapman's."

"Then she should have moved," he said.

"Look, you're right about what you said. Even coming here today will probably cause me a ton of aggravation I don't need. But I owe your daughter. If she hadn't come forward for me, a different killer would be walking free right now."

"I'm not a killer," he said. "But you don't get it. In here … it's better if I am."

"Look," I said. "I can't begin to know what your life is. How you've survived twenty-four years in here. That tells me you're strong. Ruthless. But I also know it seems to matter to you that your daughter thinks you're innocent. So you can't have it both ways. She deserves more than that. You may not have been directly involved with raising her, but she's grown into a righteous young woman. If nothing else, she deserves to see you be just as strong as she is."

"What do you want from me?"

"Your story. Let's start there. Where were you the night Heather Menzer disappeared?"

"Home," he said. "And no one saw me. I was alone. No alibi. I'm a liar, Ms. Leary. Can't hide that."

"Just tell me the truth now. I'm good at what I do. If you're lying to me, I'll figure it out."

He tapped his fingers on the table. I could feel his need as if it were a palpable, tangible thing. He wanted to tell his story. They all do. But this man also knew hope could come back to bite him in the ass.

"I wasn't a good man," he said. "I was a bullshitter. A hustler. I thought I was smarter than everyone. For a while, I was. Until I wasn't."

"But you're not a killer," I said. "That's what you want Tori to believe. So, convince me."

"I was a drug dealer," he said. "I made my living off of pretty, rich, white girls. College kids. Pot. Pills. Whatever they needed. Who knows, maybe I am a killer. Somebody was bound to OD off shit they got from me. I don't know."

"But what about Heather Menzer?"

He narrowed his eyes. "Well, she was a pretty, rich, white girl."

"You sold her drugs?"

"Maybe," he said. "Probably. She looked familiar to me when they showed me her picture. She looked like a hundred other girls."

"You sold on campus? At Delphi Community College? Where she went?" I asked.

"Hell, yeah."

"You sold to her?" It was easy enough to verify. My wheels were already spinning. There would be toxicology reports.

"I looked like one of them," he said. "Back then ... I had the swagger. The charm. They weren't threatened by me. It was cool to know me."

I knew what he meant. Even in his twenty-year-old mugshot, Sean Allen Bridges looked like a teen heartthrob. I could pretty much write the script for how this played out. He probably got invited to all the frat parties. The most popular non-student around campus. He probably made a fortune for a while. But it didn't necessarily make him a killer.

Could it be as simple as that? A case of mistaken identity? He'd been in the wrong place at the wrong time with the wrong girl?

If I agreed to take this case, this would only be the first

of many meetings with him. For now, I wasn't sure whether I believed him.

"Was Tori's mother one of your customers?" I asked.

His face fell. "Nah. Mary was ... well, she had trouble of her own before I even met her. If I could go back ... she's the main thing I regret. All this, it almost killed her. I didn't even know she was pregnant until way after she had the baby. I was already behind bars by then."

"I want to believe you," I said. "For Tori's sake. You know she's approached a bunch of other lawyers to try and get them to look at your case."

He closed his eyes and let out a sigh. "I wish she hadn't. She just doesn't get it."

"What doesn't she get?"

"This," he said, raising his arms. "You said she was right-eous. It's only because she's still young. She's got this fantasy about saving me. She thinks this will play out like some movie. *Shawshank*. I don't know."

"But we both know better," I said.

His eyes snapped open. "So you get her to understand that. That's what you can do for me. I know how this works. I know how damn hard ... no ... impossible it is to get a murder conviction overturned. Hell, I probably know it more than you do. I've read the case law. The statutes. There won't be any new witnesses. No new evidence. I'm fucked because I thought I was smarter than everybody else. I've got to live with that. The cops pegged me as a liar and they were right. Just about the wrong thing. But it's too late to change it. Even if I won ..."

He set his arms down with a thud. He had faint lines over them.

"You're using," I said, pointing to the track marks. "Does Tori know?"

He ran his hand over the inside of his arm. "It's not what you think."

I raised a brow. "Still running a con, are you?"

"You don't get it. Let me ask you something. This meeting. What I say in here. Even if you decide not to get involved, you can't talk about what I said, right?"

I let out a hard breath. "Right. Whatever you tell me is confidential."

"'Cause I can't pay you."

"It doesn't matter. Even in an initial consultation like this, I'm bound."

"These are track marks," he said. "But I'm not using. They're from my last round of chemo."

My heart sank. His grayish pallor made sense. The prison surroundings had numbed me to it. But I'd seen people with that look before.

"Pancreatic cancer," he answered before I could ask. It was another hammer blow.

"Tori doesn't know," I whispered.

He shook his head. "She suspects. I've lost weight. Forty pounds in the last six months."

"How long?" I asked.

"Doc says I'm lucky if I'm still here at Christmas."

"I'm so sorry," I said.

"So, like I said. It doesn't matter. Even if you find some bombshell. I'm not getting out of Handlon on my feet."

"I think it does matter," I said. "It matters to your daughter."

"You like lost causes, Cass?"

I couldn't help myself. That got a laugh out of me. The minute I started, it changed something in Bridges's eyes. For the first time since he sat down, he smiled.

"Mr. Bridges," I said. "Lost causes are my specialty."

His face turned serious again. "I'm not a good man," he said.

I went silent. I considered what he said. He was right about all of it. Without new evidence, his case would be impossible to overturn. It had been twenty-four long years since his conviction. The chances of finding anything useful were virtually nil.

But there was something about his eyes. Something about his stark honesty. He didn't read like all the other criminal defendants I'd represented over the years. He made no excuses. He hadn't even really blamed the cops or the system.

And there was one other thing that weighed in his favor with me. There was Tori. She believed in her father. So far, I hadn't known her instincts to be wrong.

"Mr. Bridges, for your daughter, I'm willing to at least look into your case. But I can't offer you much hope. Just an open mind."

He blinked hard, taken aback with what I'd just said. It occurred to me I'd probably just offered something he hadn't known for most of his life.

"What do you want from me?" he asked.

"Nothing. Just the truth. And if I get into this and find there's no point continuing ... if I find any part of your story is a lie ... I walk away. I'm done."

"Why?" he asked. "Why would you even bother?"

"Well, this might sound ... I don't know ... trite. Call it a gut feeling. Maybe it's because of who I am. *My* name. I'm used to people jumping to conclusions about me too."

"Man," he said. "I don't know what that kid of mine did. Whatever it was ... it got your attention."

"It did. And my respect. So for her ... I'll do this."

He reached across the table and shook my hand. His seemed

so frail. I was afraid if I squeezed too hard, I would break it. But his eyes stayed clear and focused. He knew exactly how much of a long shot this whole thing would be. Though I couldn't bring myself to say it, any victory I achieved might be posthumous.

I rose from my seat and motioned to the officer at the door.

I said my goodbyes and squared my shoulders. The cold look the officer gave me would only be the first of many. When the town found out I was taking this on, I'd make new and deeper enemies.

As the door clanged hard behind me, I knew I was Sean Allen Bridges's only hope. And he knew he was running out of time.

Chapter 5

"It's just the two folders. I brought both. The rest of this is just a bunch of stuff somebody else was too lazy to put back."

Nancy Olsen, Woodbridge County's deputy court clerk, stood with her hand resting on an ancient metal pull cart. Before I could move to help her, she heaved the thing over the bump in the floor where it switched from tile to ugly maroon carpet.

Nancy had been here as long as I could remember. I'd learned more about civil procedure from her on the first day of my internship fourteen years ago than in my entire three years of law school.

I was lucky. Nancy liked me. Her sister had been the principal at Delphi High way back when and told her I was one of the good ones, despite my family name. I liked Nancy immensely too. She was tough. Fair. Efficient. I didn't know how the building would even stand when it came time for her to retire. Hell, it was far past that time. But this place was in her blood.

"Thanks," I said. "Might as well dig in."

"If you'd asked me for this six months from now, it would all be on PDF. We're finally working our way through the eighties and nineties backlog."

Six months from now. Sean Allen Bridges might not be here. I couldn't tell her that. I couldn't even tell her why I was asking for the State vs. Bridges trial file.

"It's okay," I said. "But why only two folders?"

"Most of it's evidence exhibits," she said. "He never appealed so there weren't any transcripts generated."

"He never appealed?" I asked, incredulous. I hadn't bothered to ask Sean that. It stunned me.

"Nope," Nancy said. She put the two faded green folios on the desk in front of me. All criminal files in the Wood-bridge County Circuit Court were coded green. Domestic relations were coded red. General civil was yellow.

"Pleadings in the first one. Exhibits in the second," she said. She pulled a bulky, oversized manila envelope off the cart. She opened it and four VHS tapes slid out.

"It was recorded?" I asked. "I didn't think Judge Castor allowed cameras in his courtroom. Not even then."

"Oh, he didn't. Still doesn't. Trial TV tried to get an order. They wanted to broadcast it as their daytime highlight. I think those are copies of the police interviews. At least the one of Bridges. If memory serves they admitted them in their entirety. Jury saw the whole thing."

"Thanks," I said. I picked one up. "I'm going to end up needing copies of all of it."

Nancy didn't bat an eye. "That'll take a minute. But I think I can pull a string or two and move this file to the top of the food chain with the records interns up there. If you give me until tomorrow afternoon, I'll have the tapes trans-ferred to DVD for you."

"I'd really appreciate that, Nancy. Thank you."

She smoothed her hand over the thicker of the two folders. "Can't believe it's been almost twenty-five years since That Awful Summer."

I rested my chin in my palm. It was going to be a long afternoon.

"Oh, honey, what was I thinking? You lost your mom that summer too, didn't you? She was in that car accident."

I lifted my chin. "What? Oh. No. Not that summer, no. A couple of years after that."

"Huh," she said. She had a curious, confused look on her face like she was about to ask me whether I was sure. Then it evaporated into a smile.

"It was so hot that year. The air conditioners in the building couldn't keep up. We blew the circuits every afternoon by four. Damn near sweat my tits off every day. We were so worried about that girl out there in the heat ..."

Her voice trailed off. She still had her hand on the thicker of the two files, the one with all the documentary evidence in it. No doubt she was only a few pages away from the more grisly crime scene photos. That poor girl, indeed.

"I really appreciate all this," I said. She smiled.

"No problem, kiddo. I'll give you some peace and quiet. For a minute anyway. I'm about to send one of those dingbats down here to clean up their mess."

On the other table in the corner, coffee cups and snack-sized chip bags were strewn everywhere. One of said interns had presumably not cleaned up after themselves.

"Thanks," I said. I grabbed the first of the two folders.

Nancy paused for a moment at the door, but she didn't ask me any other questions.

The file for the State vs. Sean Allen Bridges, File No. 95-FC-1048, was organized chronologically.

I skipped past the charging document and went straight to the warrants. Sean was arrested two weeks after Heather

Menzer's body was found half submerged in a creek deep in Shamrock Woods.

When the police initially went to question Sean, he told them he'd been out of town the night Heather disappeared. Security footage in the parking lot of his apartment contradicted that along with statements from several witnesses who placed him at a party not far from Mickey's Bar where Heather worked. At least one of those witnesses swore she saw Sean talking to Heather and she seemed upset, though he'd hotly denied that all along.

After he blew the deeper interrogation, it was enough to get them a warrant to search Sean's car. They found Heather's blood on the passenger seat and smeared across the inside of one of the back windows. Finally, hairs matching Sean's were found on the shirt Heather was wearing when she died.

They had physical evidence. They had a witness who saw them together. They caught Sean in several lies about his alibi.

I flipped through to the pleadings. Lowell Dushane filed a motion to suppress the blood evidence from the car. He argued the statement of the witness who claimed to see them together wasn't enough to give them probable cause for the search warrant. He might have been right. But the hairs on Heather's shirt were even more damning.

"You were lying to them, you dumbass," I said. What might have happened had he simply told the truth about being in town that night?

I flipped through to the prosecution's witness list. There were over one hundred people on it though he'd likely only called a fraction of them at trial. I would need the transcripts for all four days of trial. I would get Tori on to tracking down those who might still be alive. That was *if* I decided to keep going with this.

The evidence folder loomed in front of me. My pulse kicked up a notch. I squeezed my eyes shut. Heather's smiling yearbook photo swam in my mind. Once I started looking at the evidence file, I knew I would never be able to see her like that in my imagination again.

I took a breath and dove in.

Jay McMurtrie had tried this case for the state. Winning it helped elect him mayor of Delphi five years later. He served two terms and retired to the Florida panhandle.

I could almost hear the notes of his opening statement echoing through the building. The rhythm of his case came through with the order he entered exhibits.

First, there were Heather Menzer's school records. She was two semesters from earning her paramedic license. She had plans to enter the army the following spring and work as a medic. She was a straight-A student. A member of a sorority.

Her time card at Mickey's Bar showed her clocking out at 11:02 a.m. the night she disappeared. Every second after that would throw this town into turmoil for six whole days until her decomposing body was found just a few hundred yards from the baseball diamonds where just about every kid in Delphi once played for Community Ed.

The crime scene photos were gruesome, jarring. The stuff of nightmares. I steeled myself as I turned each page.

She was barely recognizable as Heather Menzer. As human even. Her skin had turned almost black.

The police photographer documented her wounds in exacting detail. Eight bullet wounds to her legs, four in each thigh. One shot in each buttock. She'd been shot twice in each shoulder. One shot shattered both her wrists as though she'd been forced to clasp them behind her.

One shot grazed her hips. Another grazed her right

cheek. Finally, two bullet wounds were found in her head; the worst took off the top of her skull.

This girl had been brutalized, tortured, and raped. The coroner theorized that only the head wounds were fatal. She had most likely been alive through each, agonizing pull of the trigger.

It took everything in me not to stop. Not to close those files forever and simply walk out of that courthouse basement and never look back.

The lab reports were conclusive. Unimpeachable. At least at the time anyway. That was Sean's hair on Heather's shirt. Her blood in his car. And Nancy had just delivered perhaps the killing blow to this case. Sean Allen Bridges had never filed an appeal.

Even if I found some issue with the warrant or the forensics, it was far too late to bring it up now. His appeal window had long since closed. Without new, compelling evidence that would change the outcome of the trial, this was the deadest of ends.

"What the hell am I even doing down here?"

I picked up one of the VHS tapes. Everything else in the court file had not come as a surprise. There was just one last thing I wanted to see. I wanted to see Sean in his own words. I wanted to believe him the other day. But he had almost twenty-five years to prepare for that meeting. How was he when he was caught off guard?

I decided I'd at least withhold judgment until after I viewed the tapes. I closed the file and grabbed my messenger bag. I'd only made a handful of notes. I had more questions than answers.

I left the files where Nancy's interns could find them, and headed for the elevator. I was almost to the Main Street exit when I heard my name called by a voice that made me smile.

"Detective Wray?" I answered, turning to face him.

Detective Eric Wray was tall, dark-haired with a pair of sharp blue eyes that glinted when he smiled. He was smiling now. He walked toward me with purpose. It was good to see that too. Not so long ago, he'd taken a bullet in the shoulder that was meant for me. It put him on medical leave from the Delphi Police Department for most of the year.

He was back at work now, sporting a crisp gray suit with a red tie. His detective's badge shone on his belt loop.

"You look good," I said.

"I know," he smiled. I faked a punch to his shoulder. His good one.

"Just got done testifying up in Castor's court."

"How did it go?"

"Good."

"Always get your man, do ya?" I teased.

"What are you up to?" He looked me up and down. I wasn't dressed in my usual courtroom attire. I came casually in a pair of jeans and a fitted tee. I didn't know how dusty the bowels of the Woodbridge County Archived Records room would be.

"Just here doing some research," I said. I thought about changing the subject. As soon as Eric figured out I was sniffing around the Bridges case, I knew he wouldn't like it. Just like my brothers, Eric Wray had made it his personal mission to not mind his own business when it came to me.

"So listen," I said. "This is Delphi. It's probably only a matter of time before your spidey senses start tingling about me so I might as well just clue you in. As long as you promise to save me the lecture."

He let out a hard breath and narrowed those sharp blue eyes.

"Sean Allen Bridges," I said. He reared back for a split second, then his face hardened again.

"What about him?"

"Probably nothing. And mostly stuff I can't even talk about. But I know I'm not going to make it all the way across Main Street before your cop network finds out I visited him at Handlon."

"Jesus," he said. He touched my elbow and guided me toward the exit. We walked through the security door into the harsh light of the sun.

"God, it's hot," I said. Sweat immediately broke out on my brow. I should have tossed the jeans and worn shorts.

"Why are you visiting Sean Allen Bridges?" He stopped and turned to face me.

"You know I can't ..."

"You brought it up. And you're right. I was going to find out anyway."

"You've met Tori?" I asked.

"Your paralegal?" he said. "You know I have."

"Well, turns out she's his daughter."

He let out a long whistle and shook his head. "You're something. Christ, Cass. You're like a disaster magnet. Haven't you had enough turmoil in your life lately? I know I have. Let me guess. He's been telling Tori that he's innocent."

I didn't answer.

"She wants you to prove it."

I still didn't answer.

"And there's not a damn thing I can say or do to keep you from launching yourself head first into this."

I opened my mouth to say something. He put a finger on my lips to silence me. It left me staring, cross-eyed, down my nose.

"Listen," he said. "Don't talk. That Awful Summer? I was fourteen years old. Todd Menzer was my age. He went to Luna but we were friends. We played Pop Warner football together."

"Eric …"

"No. Let me finish. I'm not going to tell you not to do this. I know it won't do any good. But that girl? That case? Cass, it's what made me want to be a cop. Todd and I looked for her. Dammit. Did you know we were this close to being the ones who actually found her? We were about twenty yards away."

"God ... Eric …"

"Talk to him."

"What?"

"Todd. Heather's brother. He still lives in town. Hell, he still lives in the house they grew up in. He bought it from his mom a few years ago. She lives there too. He takes care of her."

"I'm sorry," I said. I meant it. I had no idea how personally connected he was to the case. I should have known. This was Delphi after all.

"I'll set it up," he said.

"What?"

"Todd. You. I want you to talk to him. Before you decide anything. Will you?"

I clenched my jaw. Eric wasn't lecturing. He wasn't judging. He was pleading with me through those clear blue eyes. I exhaled.

"Of course," I said. "And thank you."

He shook his head. "Don't thank me. Not yet. When you see him ... I want you to be at his house. Heather's house. There's something you need to know."

With that, Eric turned. I wanted to ask him what he meant but he was already across the street leaving me staring after him.

Chapter 6

I FOUND Tori sitting in the second-floor library, elbow deep in discovery materials on the Becker sexual harassment case. I wanted her to put together another settlement demand letter in light of our victory on summary disposition. I had no idea whether Livvie Becker would even entertain settlement at this stage, but she needed to understand her options.

"You know," Tori said as she held up a page from Old Man Harvey's deposition. "I really think this was the tip of the iceberg. I think if we get creative, I bet I can find you a dozen more women with the same story over the years."

"Maybe," I said. "But it won't matter if their stories are more than three years old."

She put the paper down. "I don't know. Maybe they won't be eligible for recovery, but just being heard might be worth something to them."

She sat cross-legged in the middle of the floor, papers spread in neat stacks all around her. Tori worked like I did, in controlled chaos. To anyone else, this room would look like a disaster zone. But Tori knew where everything was and she had her own method of organization.

She was smart. Capable. She had a wide-eyed optimism that I hoped this job wouldn't grind out of her too soon. Unfortunately, I feared it was the very thing clouding her thinking about her father's case.

She looked up and must have seen something in my eyes. Tori put the paper down and slowly got to her feet.

"You saw my dad?"

"I did," I said. "Sit down. We need to talk."

Tori dusted her pants off and tucked a strand of her straight blonde hair behind her ear. Her eyes flicked over me and she kept folding and unfolding her hands as she rested them on the table top.

"You think he's guilty?"

"I don't know." It was the most honest answer I could give her.

"But you've seen him. You saw what I did. He's not well. I know it's something bad. He won't tell me."

This was an odd tightrope. Tori was my paralegal. Technically, I could share what Sean said to me without violating attorney-client privilege. But if Sean wanted his daughter to know about his condition, he would have told her himself.

"There was physical evidence tying him to the victim," I said. "Both on her body and in his car. His alibi had more holes in it than lace, Tori."

"I know all of that."

"I know you do. And I also know how hard it is for you to be objective about any of this. I can't imagine the hell it's put you through."

"No," she said. "Don't do that. I don't want sympathy."

"Tori …"

She leaned far forward. "Cass … I know all of this. I know what it looks like. I know how horrible a crime this was. But I also know my dad had no one back then. He still has no one except for me. And I know this town … the whole country decided he was guilty and wrote him off. Nobody listened to him. Not even his own lawyer. The only real advice he ever got was pressure to plead out."

"I do have a ton of questions still. But Tori, you're not a layperson. You're not naive. You know that taking a plea would have been good advice under the circumstances."

"I'm not asking for a miracle," she said. "I'm just asking you to do the thing nobody else has been willing to. I just want an objective look at this case from someone whose judgment and skill I trust."

I smiled. "You're good at this."

"I'm not trying to kiss your ass, Cass. You forget, I know what you're capable of. What you did in the Richards trial …"

"What *you* did," I said. "If you hadn't come forward, we wouldn't be sitting at this table talking right now. You'd probably still be working at the U.S. Attorney's office or somewhere even bigger."

"I don't just mean the trial," she said. Her voice got quiet. "I mean what came after. You're a superhero in my eyes."

I looked out the window. Not even Tori was supposed to know what really happened with Ted Richards after the last trial. Sometimes I swore I could still feel his blood on my hands. But that was over. I needed it to stay dead and buried.

"Just keep digging," she said. "If you look at the evidence, the interviews, the witnesses …"

"If I comb through all of that and think your father got a fair shake and there aren't any more stones to turn …"

"Then that's it," Tori said. She clenched her jaw so hard a nerve jumped in her cheek.

"You sure about that?" I asked.

"I'm sure. It doesn't mean I'll believe my dad's guilty. But

I'll accept there's nothing legally to be done about it anymore."

"Okay," I said. "So now I need to ask you some questions. Whether you like it or not, you may very well be one of the rocks that needs turning over."

"I'm not scared of this," she said. "I'm only scared of what might happen if I never pursue it."

"Tori, you have to understand ... it's far more likely I'm going to find even more reasons why your dad is guilty. You might learn things that hurt you."

"I'm ready for that. I promise."

I stopped myself from saying that no one is ever ready for that. But I respected Tori. I wouldn't patronize her.

"Okay," I said. "Tori, what did your mother have to say about all of this? I mean, she's the one who told you Bridges was your father."

Tori folded her hands again. "She wouldn't ever talk about the murder. I mean, she told me the basic facts. What he was in prison for. But anytime I tried to ask her for more details, she'd shut down. She said I didn't need to know everything."

"She encouraged you to have a relationship with him?"

"I don't know if I'd say encouraged. I think it mattered to her that I knew the truth."

"But she took you to visit him?"

Tori shook her head. "No. My grandmother used to do that. Dad's mom. She's also the one who made the scrapbook. But my mother didn't get in the way of it."

"Do you think your mother thought Sean was guilty?"

A faraway look came into Tori's eyes. It took her a few agonizing seconds to answer. "I think my mom wouldn't let herself come to a conclusion on that. I think if she could have afforded it, she would have packed me up and moved me as far the hell away from Michigan as she could. But that was never an option. She was broke most of my life. She had no real family on her side. She had no contact with her mother or real dad. There was a story there. A dark one. She wouldn't tell it and I stopped asking. She had a stepdad she was close to for a while, but he passed away by the time I was in kindergarten. He was the only grandfather I remember on either side. My Grandma Bridges was pretty much the only support she had. We even lived with her for a while. By the time she died, I was already in high school."

"I'm sorry," I said. "That must have been hard. And then you lost your mom not long after that."

"He's the only family I have left," Tori said. "And I know how this all looks. I know you must think I'm just grasping at straws."

"I think everything is messy when it comes to family and you're trying to be a good daughter. And there's also a chance you might be right. So, you have to take that chance."

"Would you?" she asked. "I mean ... if you were in my shoes. If you believed in your heart there was something wrong about your family story? Does that even make sense?"

My family story. My father was a fall-down, mean drunk. My mother did her best to keep it all together in spite of it. Then she was gone and I was just left with the fall-down, mean-ass drunk and little brother and sister who had nobody but Joe and me to keep it all together.

"Well," I said. "My family story is far more boring,"

Tori found a weak smile. "They never are though."

I smiled back at her. "Trust me. Mine's as boring as they come. Now, let's go figure out the truth about yours. If you're brave enough to handle it."

Tori didn't have to answer me. I could read it in her flinty stare. She was more than brave enough. She was going to have to be.

Chapter 7

"THIS BETTER WORK," I said.

Two days later, Nancy Olsen sent the Sean Allen Bridges interrogation tapes to my office on a DVD. I held the shiny jewel case in one hand. My other hand hovered over the landline intercom. Tori and Jeanie were downstairs in Jeanie's office going over interrogatory requests on a new custody case Jeanie was handling.

I pressed the button. "Jeanie?" I said. "If you're at a point you can take a break, there's something I think you and Tori should watch with me."

I debated whether I should watch the interview alone first. I decided against it. Tori had made it clear the other day she was ready for whatever might come of this case. She wanted the truth as much as we could reconstruct it. There could be nothing truer than how her father handled the interrogation. I knew at its conclusion, a warrant was issued for his arrest.

I took the disc downstairs. Jeanie had her laptop hooked to a twenty-seven-inch monitor. I handed the disc to her and she popped it in the drive.

Tori saw the case number written in bold black letters on the jewel case. She sucked in her breath and moved her chair so she could see Jeanie's monitor better. I sat beside her and mustered some form of a smile.

The grainy picture popped up. The camera was pointed straight at Sean's face. The detective, Rick Runyon, could be seen in profile on the other side of the table. It was a tiny room, designed to make a witness feel like the walls were closing in on him.

Behind the detective's shoulder, Bridges would have seen the only way out. A heavy metal door with a small window that cast harsh light from the hallway fluorescents. The tape was twenty-four years old. The interrogation rooms at the Delphi Police Department still looked exactly the same.

Runyon had short-cropped gray hair. His wide shoulders strained against his ill-fitting brown suit.

Bridges wore a polo shirt. His tanned biceps filled out the short sleeves. His blond hair was slicked back with hair gel. His bright-blue eyes stared straight at Runyon.

Sean was handsome. You could see it even in his decades-old mugshot. But here, it was easier to see why someone like Heather Menzer or her peers would gravitate toward him. He had Ken-doll good looks. For a brief moment before the sound kicked on, Sean smiled straight at the camera he knew was there. Straight white teeth. A dimple in his cheek. A charmer. A killer?

Detective Runyon kept his tone conversational. The lawyer in me wanted to scream at the monitor. Keep your mouth shut, dummy.

"Sean," Runyon said. "I know Officer Pruitt and Officer Billings came out to talk to you. I want to ask you some follow-up questions to flesh out what you told them. You want to look over that card I gave you? You understand your rights?"

"We're cool," he said.

No, Sean. You are not cool. You are a young, dumb kid and you have no idea what you are up against.

"Okay ... just so I have clear notes. Tell me again what you told them."

Great, I thought. He was getting Sean to recommit to whatever evasive answers he gave the canvassing officers.

"Whatever, man," he said. He leaned back, draping a casual arm over the back of his chair. He thought he was in control. He had no idea the trap he was about to walk into.

"July 8th," Runyon said. He rifled through papers, a notepad or something. "Wait, no. July 9th. You told them you were where?"

It was all an act. Runyon was a seasoned homicide detective. He would have known exactly what night he needed to pin Sean down on.

"Out of town," he said. "I had a friend in a band in Detroit. I was going to go hear him play."

"What band?"

Sean waved his hand. "The Icy Hots or some dumb name. I don't know. It ended up falling through."

"What bar in Detroit?"

Sean shrugged. "I don't even know."

"So you were definitely out of town on the evening of July 9th?"

"Yep," Sean said.

"When did you get back in town?"

"Morning of the 10th, I think it was. Was that a Sunday? Yeah. I don't know, maybe ten o'clock in the morning."

"Where did you sleep that night?"

"Didn't sleep."

"So you weren't at a party on Logan Street the night of the 9th?"

Sean shook his head no. He started to pick at his thumbnail.

"So if someone said they saw you at that party on Logan Street, that's not true."

"I can't control what the hell people say," Sean said.

"Logan Street is near Delphi C.C.'s campus, right?"

"I don't go to D.C.C."

"Right. That's not what I asked you."

"You want me to draw you a map? Yeah. Logan is near D.C.C."

"So, if two people came in and told me they saw you at this party on Logan Street, are they lying or are they just mistaken? I want to make sure I've got the facts."

"Where again?" Sean sat a little straighter in his seat.

"Logan. There's a couple of fraternity houses there. You familiar with it? I can draw you that map if you want."

Sean waved him off. "I've been down there. Yeah. Guy I went to high school with. I think he's in that frat."

"What's his name? You want to write it down for me?" Sean took the pen from Runyon and wrote a name down. He flipped the pad around and slid it hard across the table.

"That the asshole who said I was there?"

"No," Runyon said. "Different asshole. But this helps, thanks."

"Who said I was there?"

"What kind of car do you drive, Sean?"

"Red F-150."

"So, if someone saw your car parked on Logan Street on the evening of July 9th, they'd be mistaken. Because you were on your way to Detroit. To see your friend's band. Right?"

"Look," Sean said. Some of the bravado left his tone. "That weekend was kind of a blur, okay? I didn't leave town until later."

"So you might have been at this party and just got your dates wrong?"

"Yeah. Maybe."

"Tell me where you live?"

"You have all this. I told all this to those two cops. I live in Tanner Woods apartments over on Bowman."

"Right," Runyon said. "You like it there?"

"It's a shithole. I'm going to buy my own place in a few months."

"You're right. It's a shithole. They've had a lot of break-ins over there."

Sean dropped his foot on the floor with a thud. "I don't know about any break-ins. Is that what this is about?"

"Well, they've got security cameras in the parking lot. You ever had anyone try to break into your truck?"

"Last year," Sean said. "They smashed the back window. I got that fixed."

"They smashed your window in the parking lot? You ever ask your landlord to check out the security footage?"

"No," he said. "I usually park in the west corner. Far enough out so nobody dents the thing."

"So they just smashed out your window instead."

Sean grew silent.

"Sean," Runyon said. "Cut the crap, okay? I'm trying to help you. I checked the tapes the night of the 9th. Your red F-150 is seen coming and going three times that evening. You left at eight. You came back at nine. You left at nine thirty. You came back again at eleven. You left again at one thirty in the morning. Then you came back around five a.m."

Sean was quiet and still as stone.

"You were at the party on Logan. That's one of the places you went. But you didn't stay there very long. You came back. You left. You want to level with me now?"

"So what?" he said. "I told you that night was a blur."

"You go out drinking? Partying?"

"Maybe."

"Maybe you did? Maybe you don't remember? Which is it, Sean?"

"Yeah," he said. "Maybe I went out partying."

"You never went to Detroit, did you? Come on. It's just us talking. You got some girl you didn't want checking up on you? Believe me, I know how that is."

"Nah," he said. "I don't answer to her like that."

"Sure. Got it. Why'd you tell Pruitt and Billings you weren't there?"

Sean didn't answer. Of course *now* he got smart and started to clam up.

Runyon leaned out of frame. When he straightened, he slid a photograph across the table. Even from this angle with the grainy resolution, I recognized Heather Menzer's yearbook photo.

"You ever seen this girl before, Sean?"

He looked sideways at the photo. His eyes flicked back and forth. He slid the photo back. It was clear as day, Sean Allen Bridges was trying to figure out what kind of lie would get him in the least amount of trouble.

"I don't know," he said. "I might have seen her around."

"Where?"

"I don't know. Is she the one who said I was at that party? Maybe I saw her there. It was crowded. I don't know for sure."

"Think hard," Runyon said. "Look again, Sean."

"I told you. I don't know."

"You ever give her a ride somewhere?"

"No way," Sean said.

"She was never in your truck?"

"Hell no."

"But you think she was at the Logan Street party?"

"Maybe. Yeah. Maybe. I think she's one of those sorority chicks. She probably dates one of the Delta Smegmas."

"The what?"

Sean smiled. "It's just a joke."

"Got it. That's clever, Sean. So you *did* see her at the party?"

"Yeah. Definitely."

"Did you talk to her?"

Sean shrugged. "Maybe in passing. But I talked to a lot of people."

"Sean, where were you going all those times your left your apartment and came back?"

"Just out."

"You carry a beeper, Sean?"

"Yeah. I do."

"Did you get paged that night?"

"I don't remember. If that chick paged me, I don't know how she got my number. I didn't give it to her."

"You think she paged you?"

"I don't know. I said maybe. I said *if*."

"Would you have a problem if we looked at your pager from that night?"

Sean rubbed his bottom lip with his thumb. He knew he was caught. He just didn't know by what.

"I don't see why I should let you do that. I went to a party. Big deal. Lots of people were at that party. Are you hauling all of them in and asking about that?"

"Yeah, Sean," Runyon said. "We are."

"Well, I don't remember that girl. I told you she looked familiar but I don't know from where. I don't have anything else to tell you."

"I'll ask you again, was this girl ever in your truck?"

"I told you. I don't think so."

"No, you said no way."

Sean squirmed in his seat. He looked at some point over Runyon's shoulder. No doubt he felt those walls closing in.

"Sean, you can help yourself out here. Why don't you just let me search your truck?"

"For what? Who is this girl? What the hell is she saying I did to her?"

"Come on, Sean," Runyon said. "You're a bright guy."

"Wait," he said. "Is she saying I raped her or something? Is that what this is all about? The hell with this. I'm done."

"Sean, this is Heather Menzer. That's her name."

Sean went deathly still. He reached across the table and picked up Heather's picture. He might as well have had a thought bubble appear above his head. This interrogation took place ten days after Heather disappeared. Four days after her body was found. She had been in all the papers, on the news, on national television.

I watched with a pit in my stomach as a twenty-six-year-old Sean Allen Bridges looked up, met Runyon's stare, and finally pulled his head out of his ass.

"No way. No fuckin' way!"

"Sean," Runyon said. "You've been lying. You lied to Pruitt and Billings about where you were the night of the 9th. You lied about being at that party. Now you're lying to me about knowing who Heather Menzer is. You do know, don't you?"

"No," he said. "I never knew that girl. She was just some ... she wanted ..."

"What, Sean? She wanted what?"

"I don't know. Speed. Pot. Something. A lot of girls here like taking shit to get them over the edge on exams ... I don't know."

"Did you give her speed or pot?"

Sean looked left and right. He scooted his chair back.

"I'm done. We're done. I don't know anything. I didn't do anything. I want a lawyer."

"Sean …"

"Fuck you!" Sean yelled. He looked straight at the camera. "I. Want. A. Lawyer!"

"God," Tori whispered beside me. "It's too late, Dad. It's too late!"

"Sean, stand up," Runyon said, his voice a flat monotone. "Turn around."

Like a robot, Sean stood. He turned.

"You're under arrest for the murder of Heather Marie Menzer …"

Runyon's voice droned on as he read Sean his rights a second time. There was a struggle. Runyon pinned Sean down, pressing his cheek to the table. Four other uniformed officers quickly charged in.

Runyon got cuffs on Sean. He peeled him off the table and shoved him forward toward the door. Sean gave one last, desperate look at the camera as he was led away.

Chapter 8

"Runyon had you lying left and right, Sean," I said. He barely had a chance to sit down before I laid into him. I'd played the interrogation tape so many times, I could almost recite it by heart.

"I didn't kill that girl," he said. His voice was ragged. He had medical tape covering his arm. When the guard brought him in, he moved a wastebasket close to him. Sean started to cough and for a moment, I was certain he might pass out.

"I'll be all right," he said. "It's always the worst on the third day."

Chemo. He'd had his second to last round of chemo.

"I'm lucky," he said with a wry smile. "I've still got my looks." He ran a hand over his head. His hair was all gold-and-silver stubble.

"You lied about where you were the night Heather Menzer disappeared. Why? And don't lie to me. You're already in here."

"Right," he said. "What's the worst that could happen?"

"The truth."

He let out a great sigh. After another round of dry coughing, he sat up a little straighter in his chair.

"I was an idiot. That's the best explanation I can give you. I thought I had it made. You don't understand how it was back in those days. Weed, speed, Ritalin. That's where I made the most of my money. Delphi C.C. was my territory."

"You were coming and going from your apartment that night," I said. "Those were all drug deals."

"Yeah," he said. "I told you. I was an idiot. Runyon had me believing I was in there because of my business. They were tightening the screws on my main supplier. I'd been warned."

"Who was he?" I asked.

"Doesn't matter," Sean answered.

"It does. Every single thing matters. And it matters to Tori."

"I didn't snitch then and I won't do it now. Even twenty-some-odd years later, word would get out. I wouldn't survive the week. Hell, I might not anyway, the way I feel."

"Do you even want me to take a look at your case?"

He folded his hands on the table, rattling his wrist chains. "Tori wants me out. That kid believes me. Other than my mom, she's the only one who ever has. And I know you don't. I know you're just doing this for her."

"Sean, if you're innocent, I want to prove it. That part has nothing to do with Tori."

"I told you," he said. "It doesn't matter now who my supplier was."

"How do you know he wasn't behind what happened to you? Or someone close to him. You said Delphi C.C. was your gold mine back then. How do you know they weren't trying to get rid of you?"

"He's dead anyway," Sean said. "He's been dead for over fifteen years."

"You're telling me you lied to Runyon because you thought he was trying to bust you for dealing dope. Were you using at the time?"

"Nah," he said. "I mean, I smoked some weed every now and again. But I never touched anything harder than that."

"Speed, Ritalin. You sold it to college students."

"Yeah. Exam week was when I made serious bank."

"What about Heather Menzer? You told Runyon she looked familiar to you. Have you ever figured out from where?"

"Maybe," he said. "I don't know for sure. There were a group of girls. Sorority girls. I made a few deals. Heather might have been with them but I can't remember for sure. It's just the best I can come up with after all these years. Believe me, I've tried."

"Where?" He shifted in his seat and started to sweat. His color turned a little green. But Sean managed to stay upright. I had a feeling he'd spend the rest of the day curled up in a fetal position. I needed him sharp right now.

"There was a car wash on Fletcher Road. Not that far past Shamrock Park. One of those self-serve places."

"I remember," I said. "It's vacant now."

"Yeah, well, that's where I did a lot of my business. I remember pulling up there. The girls came together in a pack. I didn't like that. It wasn't how I liked to do things. I liked to know exactly who I was dealing with."

"What did you sell them?"

"Just like I said. Pills," he said. "Ritalin. Some weed."

"How many times?"

"Twice," he said. "I didn't like the vibe. I didn't like that there were so many of them. Exponential risk."

"No," he said. "And I'm telling you. I'm not even one hundred percent sure she was one of them. But I think so. She *looked* like the rest of them. Familiar enough, anyway.

But I never talked to her. I never knew her name. She was never someone I dealt with directly."

"Do you remember the names of any of the other girls? Could you figure that out?"

"No," he said. "I never would have even known Heather's except for what happened. And it took me a long time to remember even that much. I've had a lot of time to think about it. I tried to tell the cops after the fact. I tried to tell my lawyer. It just wasn't enough. By then, I think they'd pretty much made up their minds about me."

"I'll be honest. There are holes in the police timeline. It's never even been conclusively established whether Heather went to that party on Logan Street. There were just some witnesses who said they thought they saw her there. And others who said they saw *you* there for sure. The only thing we know with certainty is that Heather worked at Mickey's that night until eleven and then she never came home."

He shook his head. "I really don't remember if she was at that party or not. She could have been. I wish I could tell you."

"Sean, I actually believe you about your alibi. I believe you'd have tried to lie to Runyon about all of that. But what the hell was your hair doing on Heather Menzer's shirt? Her blood was in your car. The lies were bad enough, but the physical evidence is what got you convicted. You know that. You have no explanation for it. In the end it doesn't even matter whether you and she were at that party at the same time. They can put her in your truck and they can put you in contact with her."

He curled a fist. He'd had twenty-four years to come up with a plausible explanation. Instead, he just pounded that fist to the table and met my eyes.

"I swear to God, I don't know."

"Those girls were never in your car at the car wash or any other time?"

"No," he said. "That isn't how I worked. They came up to me. I didn't get out of my car. I never put Heather Menzer in my car. I never got near her. Somebody framed me," he said. "Somebody planted that evidence."

"Sean," I said. "That makes for a great movie. But it's not that easy to plant evidence. It's not plausible."

Sean turned his palms up in a gesture of defeat. "I don't know. That's the honest-to-God truth. I don't know. I've gone over it and over it."

"You got about a minute left," the guard poked his head in.

Sean's breathing had become more labored. His color had gone from green to sheet white. I had more questions, but it would have to wait until another day.

"You should let Tori come and see you," I said.

"No," he said. "Not yet. Not until I get clear of the worst of this."

"You should tell her what's really going on with you. She deserves to know. You said yourself she's the only one who's believed in you all these years."

"She's had it rough," he said. "Her mom ... she was a good kid. Pretty. Smart. But she couldn't get out of her own way. Of all the things I regret, Mary's the biggest. Not Tori ... I mean, we didn't plan her. But ... it turns out she's the best thing I ever did. I'm the one who first turned Mary on to weed. After everything with the trial. And her finding out she was pregnant by me ... that happened right after I was arrested. It was all too much for her. She started using harder shit years later. It ate her from the inside out. Then Tori was left with nobody. My mom did what she could. But she was broken too. I did that. Not because of Heather Menzer. But because of all the mistakes I made leading up to it. Those women have been serving a different kind of life sentence. All because of me. Mary was ... she tried hard. She wanted to be good. Maybe she would have been if ..."

"Time's up, Bridges."

The guard loomed like a mountain at the door. "I'll be in touch," I said. "I want to look at the police reports. I'm sure I'll have more questions."

"Thank you," he said. Sean grabbed my hand as he rose. The guard stiffened and started to move. I put a hand up to stop him.

Sean Allen Bridges was wasting to nothing. The chemo wasn't going to work. And yet, he had a vice-like grip on my arm. I felt very much like he had just reached out to grasp the last hope he would ever have to see the sky again.

Except I still hadn't decided whether he was a killer or not.

Sean let go. I hoisted my messenger bag over my shoulder and nodded to the guard.

Chapter 9

By the time I got back to the office, it was after seven. Tori was still there. I walked into the conference room and found her setting up the whiteboard in the corner. She had cleared out all of the discovery materials from the Becker case and had her father's trial file spread out in neat stacks.

She'd only been with me for a few months, but Tori Stockton's mind worked a lot like mine did. She stood with her back to me, a red dry-erase marker poised in her right hand. At the top of the board, she'd made the heading, "Witnesses." On the left side of the board, she'd begun writing down phone numbers and addresses.

The floorboards creaked as I walked in. She jumped and turned.

"Sorry," I said. "I didn't mean to scare you."

"Did you see him?" she asked, breathless.

"I did," I said. I held my messenger bag, two-handed in front of my legs. I wanted to tell her the kind of shape he was in. But Sean hadn't given me permission. Not yet.

"There are twenty-two people to track down," she said.

"I've had luck with about fourteen of them." She tapped the board with her marker. "These eight are AWOL."

"Twenty-four years is a long time. Let's start with the full police report. I'll put in a FOIA request in the morning."

"Already done," she said. She lifted a paper off the table.

I let out a whistle. "Well, I guess that cat's about to come out of the bag."

"Sorry, should I have waited?" Tori asked.

"No," I waved her off. "Not at all. It's just ... this is Delphi. I'm surprised I didn't cause more of a stir getting the trial file. I've got the transcript ordered. It'll take a couple of weeks for the court reporter to get that to me."

Tori nodded.

"Thank you," I said. "For getting a start on organizing this. There is a lot to go through."

"I don't mind," she said. "Cass ... I swear, I've been going through it in my head for years already. I *know* there's an answer for that physical evidence."

"And you know that's the biggest hurdle to all of this," I said.

"I do."

"Okay ... it's late. You better get on home. Miranda will have my ass if you don't eat something for dinner."

"I hate imposing on her," she said.

"Are you kidding? She lives for this stuff. And she loves you, Tori. You're becoming part of the family."

She blinked rapidly. Tori forced a smile. She was clumsy as she gathered her purse.

"Okay," she said. "I'll get out of your hair. Are you going home too?"

"In a bit," I said, looking around the room. "I just want to sit with all of this for a few minutes."

"Can I help you?"

"No," I said. "I mean, not right now."

"Got it," she said. "You need the quiet. I get that. I'll see you tomorrow?"

"Absolutely."

Tori's next smile was genuine. She slung her purse strap across her body and waved as she went downstairs.

I put my bag down and sat at the head of the conference table. I was surrounded by the Heather Menzer murder case. Tori had taped her smiling picture to one wall. I knew instantly why she did it. It was a show of respect. Though she believed her dad was innocent, that couldn't change the fact that this poor young woman suffered a brutal, horrific fate. None of us could ever lose sight of that.

Still, I had questions. Why didn't the police pursue the other women Sean said were with her when they made their first buy from him? It was a small enough town. Someone would have started talking. I didn't remember seeing anything in Heather's toxicology report about Ritalin or any other substance she wasn't supposed to have. Was he lying then or was he lying now?

I pored over my notes and the trial exhibits again. When my phone rang, I jumped. I'd lost track of time. It was after ten o'clock.

I saw the caller ID and let out a sigh. News in Delphi surely traveled fast.

"Hey, there," I answered.

"Hey, yourself," Eric Wray said. "A little bird told me your office has filed a FOIA request on the Menzer murder file."

"Ah, Delphi and its birds."

"Cass, I meant what I said. I need you to talk to Heather Menzer's family."

"I know," I said. "And I will. I promise. I want to."

"Good. Because I've already set it up. I'll take you to Todd Menzer's house. Clear your schedule."

I smiled. "You work fast, Detective Wray."

"It's important," he said.

"I know …"

I was about to launch into a speech about how I didn't want him to worry about me. I knew how to take care of myself. I never got the chance.

A loud thump shook the building. In the alley behind me, I heard a crash and what sounded like running footsteps.

My heart raced. Someone was out there.

"Cass?" Eric said. "You okay?"

"Uh … yeah … it's just …"

"Just what?"

I kept the phone to my ear and walked over to the window. There was another crashing sound and a bang against the back door. There was absolutely no reason for anyone to be in that alley at this time of night. There was no access to it from the street. It was blocked off by a gate.

"Cass?"

"I'm here," I said. "It's just … I heard a noise."

"On the lake?"

"No," I said. "I'm still at the office." From the second-floor window, I had a partial view of the alley. There was definitely something moving down there.

"What's the matter?"

"Probably nothing. It's just … um … I think I might have a prowler in the alley abutting Clancey Street."

"Stay inside," he said. "I'm like five minutes away."

"Eric … you don't have to …"

"Cass," he said. "I mean it. I know you. You attract trouble. If I know about you poking into the Menzer murder, everyone else does too. And there are still a lot of people in this town who haven't forgiven you for taking the Drazdowski case."

I kept myself from reminding him about his role in that

case. It didn't matter now. The truth was, enough had happened to me over the last two years to trip my own spidey senses.

There was zero doubt in my mind someone was trying to break into my back office door.

"Yeah," I said. "Maybe you'd better get here."

From the other end of the phone, I could hear Eric talking into the police radio he always kept with him.

Glass shattered. My heart jumped straight into my throat.

I peered out the window. There was another dash of movement. Then a sound pierced straight through me.

It was a plaintive wail. Whoever was trying to get in must have tripped or cut themselves.

Unless …

"Cass?"

"Eric,' I said. "I'm heading downstairs. I'm pretty sure Tori left the back door unlocked."

"Cass!"

I was already down the stairs, pulse racing. I had visions of the knob slowly turning as I approached the back door. I passed the front door on the way. The deadbolt was engaged.

I went through the kitchen and got to the back door. The screen door caught the wind and thumped against the frame.

I dove for it, ready to slam the door and lock it. But as I got there, something made me stop.

Two beady eyes glowed at me in the dark. I heard a whimper, then a whine.

"What the ever loving hell?"

I opened the screen door and stepped outside. There, cowering near the dumpster, was a small brown-and-white dog with floppy ears. It held its front leg at a crooked angle against its body. It was hurt.

I squatted down.

"Hey, there, little guy," I whispered.

The dog licked its paw. I put my palm out. "Did you get stuck?"

The dog whined. It was shaking. "Let me get you out of there."

It looked like it had become stuck in some chicken wire someone tried to toss into the dumpster and missed. I reached for the dog, careful to watch whether he ... or she ... growled.

It didn't; instead, it sniffed the air and started licking my hand.

Then I heard another whimper, higher pitched than the first. The dog wasn't alone. And she was a she.

Curled in the corner, I saw what had her in distress even more than the chicken wire. She had a puppy. A tiny dark-brown-and-white-spotted thing, no bigger than a hamster, lay tucked against the dumpster where its mother could best protect it.

"Don't worry," I said. "We'll get you sorted out."

Then she cried out as a flood of light hit the dumpster, making her eyes flame green. I shielded my own eyes.

"Cass!" Eric came at me, his hand reaching to grip the nine-millimeter handgun he had holstered in his belt.

"It's okay!" I said. "I think I found my prowler."

I moved so Eric's light shone at the two dogs. He straightened and instantly moved his hand away from his weapon. He moved his Maglite so the light wasn't shining so harshly.

"Watch them," I said. "And make friends. I'll go find a box and some blankets."

"Hey, there, little guy," Eric said in baby talk.

"Look again," I said.

Eric's eyes widened as he saw the puppy. Then he melted as he dropped to his knees. The mother dog started licking his hand.

Chapter 10

THE NEXT MORNING, Miranda, Tori, and Jeanie crowded in the kitchen, shoulder to shoulder. Jeanie Mills, tough-as-nails female lawyer pioneer, was reduced to unintelligible cooing as she scratched the mama dog behind the ear.

"She's so gentle," Miranda said. "I'm surprised she didn't try to rip your arm off when you went for her baby."

The baby was busy nestled against Mama, nursing. I'd found a good-sized box, cut down the sides, and layered it with towels. A quick call to Miranda, and Tori had come in with a big bag of dog food and a water bowl.

"I think she knew she needed help," I said.

"No tags? No collar?" Miranda asked.

Jeanie started sneezing again. Reduced to baby talk, she was still terribly allergic to pet dander. Keeping them here couldn't be a long-term solution.

"I'm going to take them into the vet later this evening. They'll check for a chip."

Mama dog whined and looked straight at me as if she understood what I said. Was it the word vet or chip that set her off? Then I realized I was losing my damn mind.

"Someone will take them," Jeanie said. "She's just too darn sweet."

The mother dog gave a yawn and curled up as her puppy moved to snuggle himself against her chest.

"I can't figure out what she is," I said. "She's got beagle markings but pointed ears like a terrier."

"American mutt," Miranda said.

Jeanie started to cough.

"All right," Miranda said. "Enough with you. You go on back to your office and stay out of the kitchen."

"You sure you're okay with keeping them here until I get back?" I asked. I'd been cagey about where I was going. For some reason, I wasn't ready to let Tori know. Within the hour Eric was picking me up to take me to Heather Menzer's mother's house. I didn't expect it to go well. How the hell could it?

"We'll be fine," Tori said, smiling. "If Jeanie can't stop sneezing, I'll take the box up to my office. It's a floor away and on the opposite corner of the building."

Jeanie blew her nose into a paper towel, sounding like a strangled goose. The puppy stirred and the mama dog let out a keening whine.

"Okay, okay," Jeanie said. "I'll quit scaring the animals."

She and her hacking cough moved through the kitchen and back to her office. No matter what else happened, the dogs would need to be out of here tonight. After her own scare with breast cancer last year, Jeanie was back to full steam. I didn't need her sidelined by allergies. With another assurance from Tori and Miranda, I left the dogs in their care and gathered my things.

Eric showed up right on time. I met him at the corner of Clancey and Main, right outside the office. Tori's office window faced the other direction. She wouldn't see me leave.

"How're the dogs?" he asked. Eric too had been reduced

to a puddle of mush when we carried the dogs into my office last night.

"So far so good. I'm going to try to figure out who they belong to after we get done today."

Eric gave me a grim nod. "I've already put the word out at the office and said something to one of the county deputies. So far, nobody's reported a dog missing like that mama. That puppy looks to be a couple weeks old though."

"She's a good mama," I said.

Eric grew silent. He drove west out of Delphi. The Menzers lived one town over in Luna. As small as Delphi was, Luna was half the size. Pure farm country. Their local high school had maybe one hundred students in the entire building, all grades included.

We drove through the deepest corn fields on a back country road that went from pavement to gravel to pitted dirt. Finally, Eric turned down a winding drive surrounded by woods. Heather Menzer's house was a little ranch-style with warped white siding and black shutters.

A bloodhound came barreling toward us as we parked the car. Eric stepped out and I followed. The dog stopped and sniffed my legs, scenting my new office mascots.

"Bosco!" a male voice boomed. Its owner clapped his hands as he came out from around the back of the house.

"Hey, Todd," Eric said. Todd Menzer was tall and skinny. He wore faded blue jeans, work boots, and a grungy tee shirt with an auto parts store logo on it. He had sandy-blond hair with his bangs cut short and spiked up with a bit too much hair gel. But he had kind brown eyes and a warm smile as he reached out to shake my hand.

"You're the lawyer?" he asked.

I was floored. I hadn't expected such a warm reception. I wondered if Eric had fully explained what I was doing here.

"Uh ... yes. I'm Cass Leary."

Bosco retreated to the woods with a howl. Todd went to Eric and the two of them engaged in a hearty "bro" handshake that left them slapping each other on the back.

"Good to see you, man," Todd said. "Been too long."

"It has," Eric said. "Your mom holding up okay?"

Todd's face fell a little as he looked back toward the house.

"She sleeps a lot," he said. "Her Parkinson's has gotten pretty bad. Her mind's not too good anymore either. She thinks I'm my dad a lot of the time. She ... uh ... she talks to Heather more."

"I'm sorry about that," Eric said. "She's sure been through a lot in her life."

He looked from me to Todd Menzer. I hated if any part of my visit brought pain to this family. I wouldn't be here at all if Eric hadn't insisted. I narrowed my eyes at him, hoping to convey that very thought.

He made a downward gesture with his hand. It's all right? Calm down? I hated walking into meetings without knowing what to expect.

"Come on in," Todd said. "I got the A.C. working. It's too damn hot to stand outside."

We walked in the front door straight into the living room. It was like stepping through a late seventies, early eighties time machine. Wood paneling everywhere. Floral printed furniture. There was even an old console television in the corner.

"This is Mom's part of the house," Todd said. "It's better for her if I don't change too much. I live in the addition off the back."

"I really appreciate you taking the time to meet with us," I said. "I don't want to take up too much of your time."

"Heather's room is this way," Todd said. My heart

lurched as he led us down the narrow hallway off the living room. I could hear a television on in one of the back bedrooms tuned to a daytime talk show.

I shot a look at Eric. He made that downward gesture again, then put a hand on the small of my back, leading me after Todd.

At the first bedroom on the right, Todd reached up and picked something off the top of the doorframe. It was a small, long gold piece of metal. He popped it into the door lock and turned the knob. Eric stood in the hallway as I followed Todd Menzer into his murdered sister's bedroom.

I tried not to gasp. I tried not to react at all. The room was neat, clean, dust free. A pristine time capsule for a girl that would never sleep here again.

She had a compact disc player in one corner, the discs stacked neatly in an S-shaped holder on the wall. The walls were painted peach. The bedspread had peach blossoms and roses on it. She had an old white clock radio on her nightstand and blue varsity jacket on a hook near the door.

But none of that gutted me the way her corner desk did. She had a Macintosh LC computer on it, an anatomy textbook open, and a notebook with neat cursive beside it.

"It's okay," Todd said. "You can touch stuff."

"Oh, I wouldn't even …"

"She was so smart," Todd said. He sat on the edge of Heather's bed. "Never got anything lower than an A-minus in her life and she'd lose her damn mind if she did that. She really wanted to be a doctor. She was thinking the army would be a way to get there."

There was an army recruitment poster hanging on the wall next to the computer.

"She'd have left for basic that next spring. Mom was hopping mad about it. I mean, at the time it was no big deal.

We weren't in a war. But Ma had a brother who served in Vietnam. Came back messed up. My grandparents threatened to disown Heather when they found out. So stupid. Disowned from what? They never had a pot to piss in."

"I'll leave you two to talk," Eric said out of nowhere. I turned and glared at him.

"Eric," I started.

"Just tell him what you told me, Cass," he said. Then before I could stop him, he turned on his heel and left me alone with Todd.

"I'm so sorry about it all," I said after clearing my throat. "I can't really imagine what something like this does to a family."

"Destroyed it," he said, not missing a beat. "Dad couldn't deal. He hung on for a couple of years, but then it got too much. They fought about this room. He wanted to tear it all down. But it brings my mom some comfort. It's gone now, but for years, it still had Heather's smell. I mean, I couldn't tell. She swore it up and down though. Until one day she said it was gone."

I turned and went to the desk.

"Ma still comes in here every other week or so. To tidy it up. But Heather was always really good about it."

"I can see that," I said. Heather had her pens color coordinated in a coffee mug on the right edge of the desk. She took notes using a fat, multi-colored pen, the kind you have to click to get a different color to pop down.

"I used to do that," I said, lifting the pen. "In law school."

I carefully set the pen back down exactly as I found it.

"She prays in here," Todd said. "I do too sometimes. I mean, at first I thought my dad was right. It was kind of morbid leaving it all like this. Some shrine. But over the years, I've changed my way of thinking. You get a sense of her in here. We had her cremated. I mean, she's still got a headstone and everything. That was another huge mess of a fight in the family. But my dad just wouldn't have it any other way. He didn't want to bury her with all those bullet holes, you know?"

"Ugh. My God. Todd ... I shouldn't ..."

"So, this is where I come to pay my respects. When Ma goes ... I don't know ... maybe I'll box it all up and put it in storage. Not yet."

He rose from the bed and went over to his sister's closet. He opened it. The door stuck in the track. He jiggled it and slid it all the way open.

"I'll have to fix that," he said. "But see what I mean. She was neat."

Sure enough, Heather's clothes were perfectly spaced on their hangers and arranged by color from light to dark. Blouses, polos, jackets, each of them meticulously cared for. Todd ran his hand along the row, making the shirts and blouses swing.

"She used to iron her tee shirts," he said, pulling one out. The shoulders were creased now from hanging so long, but otherwise there wasn't a wrinkle in it. He put it back with the others and closed the closet door.

"Todd," I said. "I don't know what Eric's told you about my interest in your sister's case. I'm afraid you may have the wrong idea."

"You're Sean Allen Bridges's lawyer," he said. There was no hard edge, no malice in his voice.

"Um ... yes ..."

Todd nodded and folded his arms. An awkward silence settled.

"You're thinking of appealing the conviction?" he asked.

My mouth dropped open. "Well ... I mean, it's a little

more complicated than that and you have to understand, I'm limited by my attorney-client privilege."

Todd moved past me and went to Heather's desk. He opened the top drawer and pulled out a small, black, leather-bound book. He held it to his chest as he sat back on the edge of the bed.

"He's never admitted it," Todd said. "Not once. Did you know one of those tabloid papers paid some other prisoner to try and get him to?"

"What? No. I didn't know that. When?"

Todd shrugged. "It was years and years ago. Didn't amount to anything. I only know because they came here too. But nobody really cares anymore. Heather is old news."

"Why did you agree to see me?" I asked. "You have to hate Bridges. You think he killed your sister. Destroyed your family."

Todd grew silent. He opened the small book he'd been holding and flipped through the pages. It had gold-leaf paper. I assumed it was Heather's prayer book.

"Because I think maybe I believe him," Todd said, stunning me.

"What?"

"It's just a feeling. I don't know. It sounds crazy. Do you believe in ghosts?"

I let out a breath. "No. I'm afraid I don't."

"Yeah. I guess I don't either. But I believe in spirits. I believe sometimes the people you love and lose, they stay with you. It can be little things. A song coming on the radio at just the right time. Or sometimes it's like you can hear them say something, some reaction that's just so perfect for what they would have said if they'd been standing right next to you. Or you feel them still ... loving you. Heather was almost five years older than me. She looked out for me. I sucked as a student. Had a hard time with math and reading.

Heather was mostly the one who helped me out with all of that. We were close. And ever since she died, after the trial and all of it. I've never felt like it was right."

"What do you mean?" I asked. "What you heard at trial?"

"Yeah. I don't know. Heather was smart. Book smart. But street smart too. This guy was a drug dealer. She never would have been dumb enough to get in a car with him alone. She never walked around on campus by herself. Nobody has ever made it clear to me how the hell he got her alone. Her car was parked on the side of the road half a mile from her apartment. The keys were still in the fucking thing. Sorry. She would not have just pulled over for that guy. I don't understand it. I feel like somebody has to know more. And everybody's offered me a ton of different explanations. Some of them make sense. But I still feel Heather telling me they're wrong. I know how nuts that sounds."

"I appreciate this," I said.

He stood and held the book out to me. "Take this," he said. "Maybe it'll help."

I took the book. I flipped open the front cover and my heart dropped to the floor. "Todd …"

"It's Heather's journal. The cops already went through it. They didn't find anything, but maybe you can. People she talked to. Whatever. I just want the truth. If Sean Allen Bridges really did kill her, then I know he'll rot in hell. He's already behind bars. She got her justice then. But if he didn't … if he's been telling the truth. If this stupid vibe I've had all these years is right … then that means either somebody else did this and he's out there. Or somebody else is lying. Either way, I'm not afraid of the truth."

"Thank you," I said. "That's all I want as well."

"Keep it as long as you need," he said, pointing to

Heather Menzer's diary. "But don't lose it. And promise me you'll bring it back."

"I promise," I said, swallowing past a lump in my throat.

"You better go now," he said. "Ma's shows are about to be over. She doesn't like strangers in the house."

I thanked Todd Menzer one last time, then left Heather's room with a dead girl's diary clutched against my heart.

Chapter 11

HEATHER MENZER SPENT the beginning of That Awful Summer trying to find a way to deal with her mother. Her diary was filled with page after page detailing how frustrated she was that she wasn't getting support at home.

Just like Todd had said, most of the friction centered around Heather's decision to enlist in the army the following spring. Her mother and father tried, without fail, to convince her otherwise. When that didn't work, they wielded the single bit of power they had over her. They took away the keys to the car she'd been using. It was titled in her father's name even though Heather made the insurance payments.

"She was trying to get out!" I found myself screaming at the yellowing pages.

I sat under the boat's canopy, sipping lemonade and trying to stay cool. The air conditioning died in the office. We were all working from home.

Up in the yard, Vangie and Jessa played with Mama dog and her puppy. Other than a slight strain to one of her paws and a nasty tick embedded under her ear, both Mama and baby got a clean bill of health from the vet. I was still no closer to finding out who they belonged to. The mother wasn't chipped and no one had yet responded to the posters and online postings we made.

Jessa squealed with delight as the puppy made an erfing noise and wiggled in my niece's arms.

"His tongue's all scratchy," she said.

"Just be careful how you hold him," Vangie warned. "You keep him in your lap. I don't want you to drop him."

The sunlight caught my sister's hair, turning it into spun gold. She smiled from ear to ear as she watched Jessa's joy.

Some days, that was hard to come by. Vangie and Jessa's story was a complicated one. They'd only recently been reunited under circumstances so tragic it squeezed my heart to even think of it. But they were both safe and whole now and finding their way back to each other.

Jessa laughed and fell backward as the puppy tried to crawl up her chest.

"Be careful, Little Bean," Vangie warned and my breath caught.

Little Bean.

I'd almost forgotten. That was our mom's nickname for Vangie.

I set the journal down and walked up the dock. I took a shortcut to them through the shallow water. It felt cool and good, rising up to my ankles.

"I'm about to put a suit on," Vangie said. "It's too dang hot not to be in the water."

"I was just thinking the same thing."

I stopped short. Vangie's laughter, Jessa's squeal of delight. It was like walking through a time portal. I could be looking at my mother and Vangie. Almost anyway. By the time Vangie was Jessa's age now, Mom was already dead.

"What's that look for?" Vangie asked.

"Just, nothing ... you ... you just reminded me of Mom. She called you Little Bean."

Vangie canted her head to the side. "She did?"

"You don't remember? I thought ..."

"No," she said. "I mean ... not deliberately. Wow. I've been calling Jessa that since she was a baby. That's from Mom?"

"Yep. You were Little Bean. Matty was Turbo. He would never sit still."

Vangie smiled. "He still won't. Have you been thinking about her a lot?"

I came out of the water and sat on the grass beside my sister. The puppy had already worn out, like puppies do. He curled up in Jessa's lap and yawned. The mama dog kept a watchful eye on him, but seemed content to stretch out in a sunspot on the grass.

"Some," I said. "It's this case I've been working on. It's just reminded me of some things about that summer."

"That Awful Summer," Vangie parroted. "I don't remember."

"You were two years old, of course you don't."

"I just don't want this case to eat into you," she said out of nowhere.

"They all do, a little. And it's okay. Or it will be. Don't worry about me."

I reached over and rubbed the puppy's round belly. He yawned again, his pink tongue curling up into a perfect "C."

"Are you keeping them?" Jessa asked.

"Well," I said. "They belong to someone else. Later today, I was hoping you'd help me put some fliers up at the end of the street."

Jessa's face dissolved into a pout. In that, she looked just like her mother at that age once again.

"Come on," Vangie said, carefully lifting the puppy from

Jessa's arms. He stayed fast asleep. Mama dog's tail wagged and she eyed Vangie with concern.

"It's cooler in the house for now. We'll have some lunch and Uncle Matty will be here in a while. He'll take us out to the sand bar," she said. "You too." She gave me a stern look that reminded me of the mama dog's.

Laughing, I went back to the boat to gather my notes and Heather's journal. Vangie made peanut butter and jelly sandwiches. Right after, Jessa conked out on the couch with both dogs. After we cleaned up, I had the journal and my notes spread out on the kitchen table.

"You're not going to stay buried in that all afternoon, are you?" Vangie asked. "I mean it. You should come out with us to the sand bar. Joe and Matty are determined to get Jessa up on skis today. It's the perfect day for it. The water's like glass."

"I don't know," I said, my voice already trailing.

Vangie pulled up a chair beside me. "At least tell me what you're looking for," she said. "Maybe I can help. I never told you, but I spent a summer working in a law firm in Indiana."

My eyes snapped to hers. Vangie had lived away from Delphi almost as long as I did. She had a life I'd known nothing about. I'd been too absorbed in my own.

"You did not," I said.

"Most boring three months of my life. I don't know how you do this day in and day out."

She turned the diary so she could read it. I supposed there was no harm in it. Heather Menzer wasn't my client.

"What are you looking for?" she asked.

"A clue. Something. Nothing. Right now I'm beating my head against the wall."

"What's this?" she asked, picking up one of my legal pads. I'd started to write the names of everyone mentioned in Heather's diary. So far the list wasn't long. She used it mostly to rant about her parents. I told Vangie that.

Vangie picked through the trial file. I'd begun to organize it with sticky tabs. My sister zeroed in on the witness lists.

"Well," she said. "Why don't you go put a suit on? Jessa will be out for a while. The lawyers I worked for used to have me summarize depositions in like ten different ways. Chronological. Factual. What I called the cast list."

"The what now?"

"Like in a play. I'd write up a cast of characters. Whatever people the deponents talked about. Then I'd make a chart with a few bullet points about who they were, what they could testify about, where they lived."

"Ah," I said. "Actually, yes. That'll help. But it's what I pay Tori for."

Vangie raised a brow. "She isn't the most objective observer on this, is she?"

"She's good, Vangie. Extremely sharp. She's worried about her dad, but she's not naive about where we'll probably end up."

Vangie was already making notes on a blank piece of paper. She scanned the diary with her finger, stopping every time she came across a name. Then she started leafing through the witness lists.

I held up my palms. "I'll leave you to it then."

"Mmm," Vangie said, already lost in thought.

I went to the living room, put a light kiss on my niece's head. Mama and puppy were snoring. The heat sapped their energy too. I cranked down the thermostat. Grandpa Leary would have had a stroke if he saw me. Days like this, he would have made us all take chairs and stick them in the shallowest part of the water. Grandma Leary would go back and forth, bringing us lemonade and popsicles. We'd have peace for a while, until my father showed up and chaos reigned.

My brothers showed up about an hour later. Jessa woke up disoriented, but her face lit up as Matty leaned down to kiss her. The mama dog growled at him, but she soon fell under his spell too.

I changed into a suit and threw on a cover-up. I nearly ran into my sister as she met me in the hallway coming out of my bedroom.

Her face was knit with concern. She held the legal pad she'd co-opted in one hand and the diary in the other.

"Did you find something already?" I asked.

She brushed past me and went into my room. She set the pad and diary on the bed and stepped back as if she needed to literally see it from another angle.

"Vangie?"

I moved and looked over her shoulder.

"Maybe nothing," she said. "But she keeps talking about some friend named 'Em' in the diary. I can't find her or him on the witness lists. Emily? Emma? There's nobody. She keeps saying Em is on her way over. She says she's worried about her. I found that three or four times. And in her second to last entry, she says Em won't listen to her anymore about the Dee."

"Let me see that," I said.

"I looked through the index of the trial transcript," Vangie said.

"I should be getting the full version in a couple of days. The police report too. Tori filed a FOIA request."

"Good," Vangie said. "Because there was nobody called as a witness who sounds like an Em. They only called two of Heather's friends. Stacy Avalos. Jenny Regan. Unless she had some nickname for one of them, they don't sound like an Em. Or a Dee. What do you think it means?"

"I don't know," I said. "Probably nothing." Which was most likely true. Still, the hairs prickled on the back of my neck. I had an appointment to review the police case file Monday morning. It was all I could do not to try and pull some strings to get a look at it then and there.

Chapter 12

MONDAY MORNING, I walked into the Delphi Public Safety Building. My presence drew a few dirty looks. As I did mostly defense work these days, to a lot of the cops in here, I was the enemy.

Not to all.

As I waited in front of the desk sergeant's window, Eric walked toward me.

"She's with me today, Ramos," he said to the sergeant. Ramos made a noise, more of a grunt, actually. Then Eric gestured with his chin for me to follow him. He was silent as we entered the elevator. I always hated the smell of these things. No amount of antiseptic cleanser could mask the smell of body odor and desperation. As the doors closed, I noticed a dent in the steel. I decided not to ask about it.

The records department was housed in the bowels of the Safety Building. It was dank, dark, and claustrophobic. With space at a premium, they used the hallways for makeshift storage of old office furniture.

"You can set up in here," he said. "I'll get Bonnie. She'll bring in the boxes."

"Eric, wait," I said. I hadn't had much of a chance to talk to him after my meeting with Todd Menzer. I didn't know what to say to him. As soon as I collected my thoughts, he'd gotten called away on a case.

"I didn't really get a chance to thank you for setting that meeting up for me. Todd was …"

"He's an odd duck," Eric said. He stood in the doorway.

"You believe what he believes?" I asked.

Eric was quiet for a moment. "I respect what he believes. And there were some unanswered questions about what happened to Heather. But … there always are in cases like hers. There's no such thing as closure. And I don't believe in ghosts."

"But you took me out there. Why?"

Eric's nostrils flared as he contemplated his answer. "Because I *do* respect his beliefs. And if there's even a shred of a chance we overlooked something, I'm not afraid of finding that out."

There were footsteps in the hall. Eric nodded. A middle-aged woman with stunning white hair came to the doorway carrying a cardboard box in her arms. Eric took it from her and the two of them stepped inside.

"Bonnie Tate, this is Cass Leary. Bonnie's our civilian records clerk. She'll log you in."

"Hello," I said, extending my hand to shake hers as she put the box on the table in front of me. It was marked with evidence tape and Heather Menzer's name. A chill went through me.

"You supervising or do you want me to get Clayton?" she asked Eric.

"I'll stay," he said.

Bonnie took a clipboard she had resting on top of the box and wrote something. She handed it to me to sign my name.

"The paper files are all on this flash drive," she said, handing a slender black stick to me. "That's your copy. You're lucky. We just got through digitizing the nineties cases about six months ago."

"Thank you," I said. "That's pretty much what they told me at the county courthouse too."

"That'll have all the written reports and supplements," she said.

"Really, thank you. This is great."

Bonnie gave Eric a look. He nodded and Bonnie took a box cutter out of her pocket. She sliced through the tape and opened the box. She slipped on plastic gloves. Eric stepped forward.

My throat got tight as Bonnie started removing the physical items one by one.

"Not much of this," she said. "Most of what you'll probably want is in those reports."

Still, it got hard to breathe as Bonnie Tate carefully laid out Heather Menzer's personal effects.

Her jean shorts were vacuum sealed in plastic. The bullet holes jarred me. She wore white Reebok tennis shoes that night. The scent of mildew hit me.

"Half of her was in the creek when they found her," Bonnie said. She was slow and methodical as she removed the rest of Heather's clothes.

She laid out the shirt Heather had been wearing. That alone had damned Sean Allen Bridges to his fate. There was a second, smaller bag taped to it. The hair samples.

"May I?" I asked. Bonnie handed me a fresh set of latex gloves.

"Don't try taking anything out," she said.

"No. No. Of course not."

I ran my hand over the plastic. Heather had worn a red

polo shirt with Mickey's Bar & Grill embroidered in white stitching over the left breast.

"Hell," Bonnie said. "They still wear those same ones, don't they?"

Eric came closer. "Yeah. I guess so."

"Classic look," I said. I took out my phone and photographed the shirt and shorts.

Bonnie went back into the box and pulled out the last of it. She was right. There wasn't much here. No murder weapon. Just Heather's clothes.

"That's what they found on her," Bonnie said. "Here's what they found in her car."

Her car had been found by the side of the road, less than a mile from her apartment. Bonnie had Heather's purse. It was a small, purple leather bag. There wasn't much inside of it. This was before cell phones. Heather had just loose change, a tube of lip gloss, a few pens, her school ID and two credit cards. In a separate bag, Bonnie pulled out Heather's keys. They had been found still in the ignition.

"This is what Todd's been so confused by," Eric said as Bonnie set the keys down. Heather kept them on a chain with a pink-haired troll doll dangling from it.

"He said it wouldn't have been like her to just leave her car like that."

"Right," Eric said.

Bonnie opened the wallet. It was more of a pocketbook. Heather kept a checkbook inside of it. I took another picture with my phone.

"Is there something specific you're looking for with this stuff?" Bonnie asked.

I ran my finger over the plastic protecting her Mickey's Bar shirt again. I hadn't worked at Mickey's. But I'd worked at the Sand Bar one summer when I was nineteen. Just her age. I could still see the faint outline of her initial written in black marker on the tag.

"I don't know," I said. "Not until I know. You know?"

Bonnie gave me a grim nod. I took a few more minutes and snapped pictures of everything. At my request, Bonnie carefully removed the contents of Heather's wallet. I was looking for anything. A note. A phone number. Anything.

"Can you flip up the check register?" I asked. At the time, it had been a new book. Heather had only two pages of it filled out. It was still a time when people wrote more checks instead of using a debit card. She wrote with a sloppy, almost indecipherable hand. Her expenses were for mundane things. Checks to the grocery store. The campus bookstore. She was paying her own car insurance. I found that slightly odd since the car was in her father's name. I noted it and thanked Bonnie.

With cold efficiency, she put all the physical evidence back in the box and resealed it. She made a note in her clipboard and had me sign again. Eric signed too. Then Bonnie walked out carrying the aging, grisly remnants of Heather Menzer's last few hours on earth.

"She's a good egg, Bonnie," Eric said once her footsteps faded down the hall. "But she's the biggest gossip in the building. If there's anyone in town who doesn't yet know you're interested in this case, she'll take care of it."

"What about you?" I asked. "She's also going to mention that you were down here with me. She's gonna know you facilitated all of it."

"You filed a FOIA. Anybody can do that."

I raised a brow. "Come on."

"I can take care of myself. And I'm not afraid of what anyone thinks of me. Anybody I care about knows what kind of cop I am."

"Mmm. Not the kind who'd go over to the dark side and fraternize with the enemy, huh?"

Eric's face grew serious. "You're not the enemy."

I palmed the little black flash drive. Later this afternoon, I'd have Tori print it all out and dive in. Something flashed through Eric's eyes as he focused on the drive.

"You've already looked through what's on here, haven't you?" I said.

"More of a skim," he said.

"You know I'm going to want to talk to the cops who worked this case."

He chewed his bottom lip and nodded. He reached into his jacket pocket and pulled out a folded piece of paper. A devilish smile lit his eyes.

I shook my head and laughed. "You already made notes for me."

"Just saving myself the trouble of the phone call I know I'm going to get from you." He was teasing. He jerked the paper away at the last second when I reached for it. Then he gave it to me.

"We were an even smaller department back then," he said.

I opened the folded paper and read the names he'd written. Beside each, Eric had put an address and phone number if he had them.

"Rick Runyon was the lead detective," I said. "I watched his interrogation."

"He retired a long time ago," Eric said. "He was outgoing in the Bureau as I was incoming. Decent enough guy. Kind of a blowhard. One of those 'back in my day' types. Hell, I guess I'm one of those now. This new generation of cops coming up ..."

I couldn't help but laugh a little. Eric had no address listed for him.

"He lost his wife a few years ago," he said. "She had cancer. We did some fundraisers for her through the union. Spaghetti dinners, that kind of thing. He was a good, old-school cop. For you? I doubt he'll be much help. Like I said, blowhard."

"And I don't suppose he's too keen on defense lawyers of any kind," I said.

"You would be right."

"You respected him though," I said.

"I did."

"You've only got three officers listed," I said. I recognized two of the names: Pruitt and Billings.

"Like I said, we were a bit smaller back then. Those are the cops who filed supplementals when Runyon asked for it. Witness statements and things like that. Pruitt's still around. He works in property crimes now. Billings went to another department a few years after the Menzer case. Not sure what happened there but he's working over in Toledo now. Rent-a-cop. I think he hurt his back or something. Delwood, the last guy, he died of cancer in '07."

"Eric, thank you. Really. I know helping me isn't going to make you popular."

"I've never been worried about that," he said.

It was true. I'd known Eric back in high school. He had been a hotshot jock. He may not have ever worried about popularity, but that's because he always had it.

"I've gotta say. I'm a little surprised. I thought you'd be the first one to give me crap about sticking my nose in this one. But you've been the opposite."

Eric's gaze on me lingered. There was a deep history developing between us. He'd saved my life once. He always managed to be there when things became the most dire. And I knew some of the darkest secrets he kept. Things I swore to never mention to him again. But along with that history was a new awkwardness. I spent some time with an ex earlier this year and I knew it bothered Eric. He would never say anything. Point of fact, he didn't really have the right. He still wore a wedding band around his finger. He caught me looking at it and dropped his hand to his side.

"Well," he said. "I guess I know by now there's no stopping you once you've set your mind to something anyway. I figure my best course is to try to clear things to keep you from getting hurt."

I tilted my head, regarding him. "Yeah? How's that working?"

He rolled his eyes. "Damn shitty, actually."

"Well, I appreciate it anyway." I slipped the flash drive and Eric's notes into the outside compartment of my messenger bag. Eric held the door for me then we made our way back upstairs.

He was right. Bonnie Tate's penchant for gossip became apparent. I got nothing but cold, hard stares as I walked past Sergeant Ramos and back out into the world.

Chapter 13

FORMER OFFICER BRIAN D. BILLINGS agreed to meet with me four days later. But only if I came to him. Though I questioned the wisdom of it, he picked the parking lot on the north side of the old North Towne Mall in Toledo, Ohio. All of the anchor stores had moved out years ago. An hour south of us, I remember my mom brought me here when I was little. It was easy to get to from U.S. 24. Now it was an asphalt graveyard except for a car dealership that used what was left of the parking lot for their fleet.

That was Brian's job now. He trolled around in a private patrol car, shooing away drug dealers, prostitutes, and vandals.

It was seven o'clock in the morning. The sticky heat had me sweating before the sun was even fully out. I spotted Billings's car right away. He flashed the lights and I pulled up alongside him. Tori wanted to come, but I'd killed that idea. Now this felt creepy as hell.

Billings got out of his car and walked toward me. Well, it was more of a strut. I'd only seen the department's archived picture of him in uniform in the mid-nineties. I could still see remnants of that twenty-something kid, but he'd gone completely bald and had a spare tire around his middle. He gave me a warm smile and a wave as he came to my car. I rolled down the window and killed the engine. In about fifteen minutes away from the air conditioning, I would sweat right through my blouse. Billings's white uniform shirt was already pretty soaked.

"Ms Leary?" he asked.

"That's right," I said, smiling. I reached out of the window and handed him my card. "I really appreciate you meeting with me. You know, it's hotter than hell. How about you let me buy you a cup of coffee at the McDonald's just down the street?"

He looked to the southwest where I'd pointed. "It's okay," he said. "You said you wanted to ask me some stuff about the Heather Menzer case. It'll be a pretty short conversation."

"Right," I said. "Then I'll get right to it."

"What's your interest in it?" he asked.

"A friend of the family asked me to look into it. I hope you'll forgive me, I can't really talk too extensively about my client."

"Right," he said.

"I've read the case file from the Delphi P.D. You were one of the officers on scene when Ms. Menzer was found?"

He nodded. "Me and my partner Mark Pruitt found her. Well, Mark did anyway. I wished he hadn't. I know it sounds bad to say that, but I wish she'd been one of those cases where they never found her, you know? It would have been easier on her family."

"You think so?" I said. "Don't you think the not knowing would be even worse?"

He considered my words, then firmly shook his head.

"Not if you'd seen her. She was like ground hamburger, what they did to her."

"They?"

Billings shrugged. He leaned down into my window, giving me a slight whiff of his body odor.

"They. Him. Whatever. A monster got her. That was all new to me at the time. I'd been on the job I think a year. Not much more than that. Didn't think I'd ever see something like that. You know, in Detroit or even here in Toledo, sure. But Delphi? No way. Didn't think they had real boogie men like that."

"Oh," I said. "I think you'll find there are boogie men wherever you go."

His face froze. Billings shifted his weight. "Yeah. I suppose. That one though. It messed me up."

"How so?"

"Gave me nightmares. They warned me about this job. You see some stuff. But that was the worst. At the time anyway. Later, you see stuff happening to little kids. It changes you."

"Officer Billings, in the report, you were the one, along with Pruitt, who interviewed the campus community. Do you remember how quickly Sean Allen Bridges became a suspect?"

Billings took a toothpick out of his breast pocket and started to chew it. "Pretty quick. Hell, before we even got over there, he said something to me about how he figured Surfer Boy might be involved."

"Surfer Boy? That's what he called Bridges?"

"Yeah. Or maybe it was Party Boy. Sumpin' like that. We knew he was a pusher. Pruitt had some run-ins with him before. What do they call it, Big Man on Campus. That was Bridges."

"But he wasn't a student," I pointed out.

"No? Yeah, I don't remember that. He was the hook-up though. Kids used to get their weed and whatever from him. He was connected. Command wanted to know to who. Whom? Yeah. We had our eye on him for a long time. He was slick though. He could talk his way out of crap. Did it all the time. Pruitt was pissed about that. He was pretty much making it his personal mission to catch that fucker. We figured it was only a matter of time before some girl got killed. We thought it would be from bad blow or something. Never would have thought it would be more ... uh ... direct ... you know?"

He kept shifting from his left foot to his right foot as he leaned into my window.

"Anyway," he continued. "I told Mark that. Or he told me. I don't know. One of us said it. That guy. Bridges. Headed for trouble, no matter what."

"Was there ever a time you considered any other suspects?"

Billings jerked back. "You serious? Who'd you say was paying you again?"

"Officer ..."

"It's just Billings. Or Brian. I'm not a cop anymore. I do this." He stood up and spread his hands wide, gesturing to the expanse of overgrown parking lot.

"I'm just trying to piece together the flow of this investigation. You were a big part of it, you and Pruitt. If it weren't for you, I doubt the prosecutor could have secured a conviction."

"Well, Runyon ran the show," Billings said. "That was clear from the get-go. Pruitt brought up Bridges to him. He knew Pruitt was the liaison with the Delphi C.C. cops. Cops ... that's a joke. They weren't cops. They didn't even carry guns back in those days. Just pepper spray and Maglites. If there was ever anything even mildly serious, they'd call us in double quick. One time I heard they called Delphi P.D. to deal with a cat stuck in a gutter. Useless."

"So Pruitt is the one who brought up Bridges to Detective Runyon?"

"Yeah. That's right. Then it was go time. It went down quick after that. He lied to us in his interview. Said he was home all night or something. As soon as those campus jocks figured out what we were investigating, they set us straight real quick. There was a big frat party. Bridges probably made a fortune that night. Probably twenty people saw him there and told us so. Bridges was slick. But he was a lousy liar."

"There was some conflict in the interviews," I said. "Some people said they saw Heather at that party and that Bridges might have been talking to her. Do you remember anyone telling you that?"

Billings looked over the top of my car, squinting. He puckered his lips and shook his head. "I don't know. Maybe. Whatever it was I would have written it down in my supplementals. Didn't really matter though. All that blood they found in Bridges's car."

"I don't think it was that much blood. Drops."

Billings looked at me. "It was enough, right?"

"Do you remember any boyfriends or talking to anyone Heather Menzer might have been seeing?"

Billings snarled a bit and shook his head. "Nah. I think she thought she was too good for Delphi. She wasn't the type to go slumming with anyone around here."

"You knew her?"

Billings quickly shook his head. "Nah. She just seemed like the type. There were a million sorority girls like her. Rich kids. That's what Bridges preyed on. Wasn't she headed off to some big fancy college? "

"The big fancy army," I corrected him. "And Heather was far from rich. She grew up in Luna."

"Huh," he said.

"Were you on board with Pruitt's hunch about Bridges?"

"What do you mean?"

"I mean, did it at any point ever occur to you to rule out any other suspects?"

Brian Billings's face changed. He went from a dopey grin to a snarl of contempt.

"Is this a cross-examination, Ms. Leary?" He lingered over my last name. So it *did* mean something to him. He'd been away from Delphi for years, but I could almost see the thought bubble form over his head. Would he be bold enough to call me white trash to my face?

"I just want to get a clear picture of how this investigation unfolded. That's all."

"Case made national news. You think you're the first person who's ever breathed down my neck over it? Reporters came to my house back in the day. Pruitt even got reprimanded for getting rough with a photographer. Guy got in his face once. You don't do that to Mark Pruitt without getting clocked."

"Do you still keep in contact with Mark Pruitt?"

Billings looked skyward. "Nah. Haven't talked to him in years. I took a job in Chelsea after Delphi. He started having kids. You lose touch."

"Sure," I said.

"It's funny what you remember though. I mean, I couldn't tell you what the hell I did out here the last few nights. But I remember how things were in Delphi, what, twenty-five years ago? Your family lived out past Trumbull Street, right? East side of the lake?"

It was a dig. Everyone from Delphi knew the east siders were trash.

"Yeah," I answered. Billings's expression turned smug.

"Uh huh. Took a couple of domestics out there. Pruitt warned me about those too."

I straightened my back. "My father had his issues."

Billings tilted his head. He twirled the toothpick between his teeth. "Yeah. Your daddy was a bastard. I got warned about him too when I joined the force. Don't remember him being the one to cause the trouble though. How's your mama doing these days?"

It was such an odd thing for him to say. The Delphi P.D. and Woodbridge County records archive probably had enough incident reports about my father to fill up a novel. I was beginning to think Brian Billings's memory was no good at all.

"My mother passed away a couple of years after Heather Menzer did," I said.

Brian Billings looked truly shocked at that. "Huh," he said. "Must have been right after I left. Too bad. Pretty thing she was. Looked a lot like you?"

"Not really, no."

Billings shrugged. "Can't say as I couldn't have seen that one coming a million miles away. Sorry for it though. Must have been rough on you."

"It was rough on her being married to my father," I muttered, hating that I gave this idiot that much of me.

"Hmm," he said for the second, infuriating time. "Well, if you say so. Can't say as that's how I remember it."

"Is there anything else you'd like to tell me about the Menzer murder?"

Brian Billings shook his head. "Nah. I think I've helped you enough. Say hello to Pruitt for me if that's where you're headed next."

Then Brian Billings twirled his flashlight, slipped in his holster, and turned his back on me.

Chapter 14

FORMER DELPHI P.D. DETECTIVE RICK RUNYON lived in an old farmhouse on the outskirts of town. It took me forever to find it. He'd let the driveway go. All that marked it was just some dead, beaten-down grass. You couldn't see the house from the road, but my GPS and his rusted-out mailbox standing at a tilt in the road let me know this had to be the place.

The man refused to answer any of the eleven phone calls I tried to make. This was probably a fool's errand but before I could close the book on this case, I had to get Runyon to talk to me at least once.

My cell phone rang, jarring me as I made the turn up the overgrown path. It was Wray. I put the car in park and answered.

"How did it go with Billings?" he asked.

"He's not the sharpest knife in the drawer, I don't think." I was careful. Instinct told me to leave out the part where Billings basically threw Runyon and Pruitt under the bus as far as widening the field of suspects. Pruitt was my next stop.

That would be even dicier as he was still working for the D.P.D.

"Yeah," Eric said. "He washed out here."

"You able to find out why? I mean, for sure? His story is that the Menzer case turned him off. Not sure that's the whole truth."

"I've made a few calls," he said. "Where are you now?"

"Canyon Road," I said. "Runyon's place."

Eric let out an audible sigh. "I wish you would have told me. I would have gone with you."

"No," I said. "You've gone over and above with this. I know it's not doing much for your popularity within the department. I know what kind of straws I'm grasping at. I can handle Rick Runyon."

"He's an old-school asshole, Cass. Don't be surprised if he slams the door in your face."

"He wouldn't be the first. And I'm sure he won't be the last," I said. "It comes with the territory."

"Yeah. Well ... Sean Allen Bridges was the biggest feather in Runyon's cap. And he's one of those guys who hung on too long. He could have retired when he hit his thirty years. He kept on going until he hit thirty-eight and was basically forced out. I asked around. He promised his wife he'd take her to all the places she wanted to go. He kept working. Telling her one more year. One more year. Then she got her breast cancer and died."

"Ugh," I said. "I really appreciate the heads-up. I'll tread lightly."

"Just let me know if he won't come out or tries to throw you off his property."

"Thanks," I said. "But I really think in light of all that, you need to steer clear. Runyon may be retired, but if he was on the job that long, he's still got friends there. He can make more trouble for you."

"I keep telling you I can take care of myself," Eric said.

"No doubt," I said. "And you know I can too."

I put the car back in drive and headed up the path. I hung up with Eric just as I passed a trail camera Runyon had bolted to a tree.

"Great," I muttered. "He's probably got the place booby-trapped."

The house itself was rundown. The garden overgrown, the lawn gone to seed. I wondered how much of the maintenance had been Mrs. Runyon's job. It was sad, really. It couldn't be easy being married to a cop. Rick Runyon's wife hung on, expecting a payoff he could never deliver.

I parked the car, grabbed my notebook, and headed for the front door. The wooden porch steps sagged and creaked under my weight. The doorbell made no sound. I knocked on the wooden frame of a crooked screen door and waited.

I heard a round of coughing from deep in the house. I steeled myself for whatever stream of obscenity Rick Runyon might spew when he found out who I was.

Finally, after two full minutes of knocking, the old detective appeared.

He walked with a slow shuffle, his back hunched. He trailed an oxygen tank behind him. Still, his hazel eyes were clear and sharp as he looked me up and down through the screen door.

"Detective Runyon?" I said, holding my notebook in front of me like a shield. "My name is Cass Leary. I'm sorry if I disturbed you, but I've been trying to call."

"I know who you are," he said, then erupted in another fit of coughing. Rick Runyon was only in his mid-seventies. But nearly forty years on the force and the loss of his wife had put decades on him he hadn't yet lived.

"I'll cut to the chase then," I said. "I'm looking into the

Heather Menzer murder file. I know you served as lead detective …"

"You're a defense lawyer," he said.

"I am. Yes."

He curled his lips in disgust. "You're a Leary."

"I'm that too," I said, stiffening my spine.

"Your old man still in jail?"

So it would go like this. "I honestly have no idea," I answered. "Haven't spoken to the man in years."

"Hmm. Meanest drunk I ever saw, that one."

"Me too. Mr. Runyon. I promise I won't take up much of your time. Is there somewhere we can talk? So you can sit …"

"Talk right here," he insisted. "What the hell do you want?"

"There are just some things I want to understand about the investigation into Sean Bridges."

"Bad liar, that one," he said. "Thought he was slick. A con artist."

"Yes. He was all that. He's also dying."

I was skirting an ethical line big time, letting that out. But I gambled it might buy me some time with Runyon. What would it matter answering a few of my questions if Bridges was headed for hell anyway?

Runyon's face changed, registering what I think was shock. It was hard to tell. He shifted his weight and gripped the doorframe.

"I've spoken at length to Todd Menzer," I said. "Heather's brother. You know, he doesn't think Sean is guilty."

It was a stretch, but worth trying. Runyon said nothing. His scowl deepened. He hadn't yet slammed the door in my face so I decided to take that as a good sign.

"He can't figure out why Heather would have pulled her

car over and gotten out of it that night. She left her purse behind. Did you ever ask Bridges about that?"

"Everything out of that kid's mouth was a lie," Runyon said.

"You're right," I said. "It was. I made a promise. As I said, the man is dying. I don't know how long he's got. Weeks. Months at most. He's got a daughter. She works for me. I promised to ask the few remaining questions the family has. Both families, as it turns out. The Bridges *and* the Menzers."

He stayed still as stone.

"Look, let's not pretend you don't know who I am. Who I *really* am," I said. "You may not like what you've heard about me, but you have to know I'm thorough. I'm also not afraid of ruffling whatever feathers I have to for answers."

His eyes were cold, hard, penetrating. He gripped the doorframe in a vise grip.

"Detective, Todd Menzer gave me Heather's diary. You've seen it, haven't you?"

I pulled the diary out of my messenger bag. There was an indexed copy of it in the police file. I knew he'd seen it. He'd probably memorized every line. I opened the book to a place I'd earmarked.

"Em," I said. "I've been through the police file. The court file. The transcripts. Did you ever find out who Heather's friend Em was?"

Runyon shrugged. "It's what, twenty-five years. What do you expect from me?"

"Detective," I said. "Bridges says he didn't do it. He's been consistent about that for almost twenty-five years. He said he sold drugs to Heather or her friends. He said he never killed her. You're right. He's a liar. I'm not naive. You know what? At the moment, I'm pretty sure you got the right man too. But like I said, Bridges is dying. I made a promise to his daughter. She's a good kid. Honest. Hard working. She's overcome a lot to get where she is. She's putting herself through law school."

"Didn't know Bridges had a kid. Since when did Handlon start allowing conjugals for murder convicts? He sure it's his? Maybe somebody's been lying to him too."

"Her mother was dating Sean that summer. It was before Sean went to prison. Her name was Mary Stockton."

Runyon's eyes narrowed. He opened his mouth to say something, but erupted in a new round of coughs. It got so violent, I put my hand on the screen door, ready to open it if he keeled over.

Runyon gripped the stand holding his oxygen tank and his cold eyes slowly rose and settled on me. It was a clear warning to stay back.

"Did you ever look at anyone other than Sean Allen Bridges? I'm just trying to understand how the theory of this case got developed. That's all."

"I know who you are," he said. "I know what you do."

"Yes," I said. "And so you also know I'm good at it. Very good at it."

"So am I!" he shouted.

"I know that."

I also knew he really hadn't answered my main question. I asked it again.

"Em," I said. "Can you at least tell me who she was? Or he? Honestly, that's not even clear from these diary entries."

"You should leave it all alone," he said. "You think that girl is going to find peace? Closure?"

I wasn't sure which girl he meant. Heather? Tori?

"No," I finally said after a pause. "Not really. I don't think that's even possible. Not with what happened to that poor girl. I've seen the file. The whole file."

He waved a hand. "You've seen pictures. It's not the same. What happened to her ... what he did ..."

"You've seen horrible things. The worst in people. I can't even imagine. And I promise I'm not here to question your methods. I'm just trying to get answers to a few lingering questions the families have. That's all. If you could just tell me what you remember, I'll be on my way. I've spoken to Brian Billings. I'll speak to ..."

"Billings?" he asked. "You telling me he's questioning what we did? That little ..."

"No," I answered. "Not at all. He basically said you were the one to talk to, of course. He respects you. So do I. And mainly, I'm just trying to find this one witness. And, Detective, I'm not giving up on this until I have those answers."

Runyon straightened. His face changed again, going slack. I didn't know him well, but it seemed some of the bluster had gone out of him.

I felt like a complete jerk for standing out there grilling him. He was old. He was sickly. No matter what else he was, this man deserved whatever peace he'd carved out for himself.

"Wait here," he said after a beat, stunning me. "I have something you might want to take a look at."

"Thank you," I said. "I promise I won't take up much more of your time."

Runyon turned. He shuffled back down the hall and into the shadows where I couldn't see him. He opened a door further down the hallway. I heard the floorboards creak as he walked. My pulse quickened. What on earth might he have kept from the Menzer investigation that I hadn't already seen?

I heard more shuffling as if he was moving something heavy across the floor. A door slammed. Then silence.

I waited. A minute went by. Then two.

Runyon started coughing again. This time, even worse than before.

"Detective?" I called out. Had he fallen over?

No answer.

I waited another moment and then tried the screen door. He'd locked it from the inside. I could see from where I stood it was just one of those cheap hook and latches. It gave when I pulled on the door. It seemed odd that a former cop would rely on such flimsy front-door security.

Then Rick Runyon's shout jolted my heart.

"Fuck!" he shouted. His voice was odd. Panicked.

I pulled on the door, ready to break the latch.

Then a single shotgun blast shattered the air, rocking me to my core.

Chapter 15

ADRENALINE TOOK OVER. The blast still echoed in my brain as I pulled on that rickety screen door for all I was worth. It might not have been the smartest thing. Maybe I should have waited. But I'd played this scenario out over and over in my head since I was five years old. I just always assumed I would be running down the hall to find my father.

I raced down the hall toward the source of the sound. I knew what I would find. I knew it would sear my soul for the rest of my life. I went anyway. Maybe I was wrong about it all.

Except I wasn't.

I froze in the doorway of Rick Runyon's first-floor bedroom. It didn't seem real at first. It looked like someone had thrown a jar of dark jelly against the wall.

Rick Runyon's body slumped to the ground, his back against the wall. He still gripped the 12-gauge shotgun against his chest. His head was gone. The man ... was gone.

His portable oxygen tank lay on the ground beside him, half under the bed. It's a wonder the thing hadn't exploded.

I couldn't breathe. The air turned thick. My heart turned

to fire in my chest. My arm shook as I lifted my wrist and spoke into my smartwatch.

"Call 911."

The sound of the dial felt almost louder than the shotgun blast before the dispatcher answered.

"911, please state your emergency."

"My name is Cass Leary," I said. "I'm calling from 1532 Canyon Road. A man has shot himself. He's gone. Please tell the responding officers it's Detective Rick Runyon."

"Okay, Ms. Leary? How do you know this man is gone? Is he breathing? Can you check?"

"He's gone," I said. "He ... his head ... there's nothing left of it."

"Okay. Stand by. I have your location. Are you alone in the house?"

I answered her questions. I couldn't tear my eyes away from what was left of poor Rick Runyon. What in God's name had he been thinking?

The dispatcher assured me she was sending help. Help. For what? She urged me to stay on the line but I couldn't. I let the call drop.

I stood against that doorframe, finally tearing my eyes away from Runyon. The room was sparse. He slept in an unmade hospital bed. He had four green oxygen tanks lined up against the wall. There was no artwork on the walls. Just one tall dresser and a nightstand. He kept a picture of himself and I assumed his wife beside his bed. She had been pretty. Deep dimples and gleaming white teeth. In this shot, she rested her head against Runyon's broad shoulder. They sat on a boat with the lake and sunset behind them.

It was Finn Lake. Not far from my house. I recognized the shoreline.

Runyon's closet door was off the track. My heart

clenched. His wife's clothes were still hanging neatly in rows, her simple heels lined up on the floor.

I took a tentative step into the room. He had a beer stein with loose change on the dresser. The drawers were stuffed with his clothes and didn't completely close. It looked like he threw everything in there without folding it. A stark contrast to the way his wife maintained her closet. Eric said she'd been dead for years.

I turned to face the bed. The nightstand drawer was open. I took a hesitant step toward it. He kept his pill bottles inside it, lined up in a cardboard box. Besides that, I could make out the tarnished outlines of old handcuffs, his leather badge clip, and a nine-millimeter handgun. Probably his service weapon.

He hadn't used it though. Why the shotgun? Why the hell did it matter?

Just before the shotgun blast, I'd heard him move something heavy across the floor. I scanned the room now. There was something poking out beneath the bed. I squatted down. Runyon had a large footlocker under there. I could see a rectangular shape in the dust where he'd moved it from.

"What were you trying to hide?" I whispered.

In the distance, I could hear the sirens. Curiosity burned through me. What the hell was in that trunk?

Slowly, I rose to my feet. Whatever secrets Rick Runyon took with him, I couldn't obstruct justice to find it. Even if it meant helping Sean Allen Bridges, if that's what this was about.

I backed out of the room and made my way to the front door just as an ambulance and two black-and-whites roared up the driveway. I shielded my eyes with the back of my hand against the lights and walked outside to greet them.

Chapter 16

Hours later, I sat in an interview room at the Delph Public Safety Building. It was odd, sitting on this side of the desk. It happened to be the same room Runyon brought Bridges to all those years ago. The paint had faded. It probably hadn't gotten a new coat since those days either.

The door opened and Eric walked in, his face ashen.

"You okay?" he asked.

I flipped my hand and shrugged. "Yeah. I guess. I don't even …"

"Did they offer you anything? Water? Something to eat?"

"Eric, I'm fine. I just want to go home and sleep for a hundred years."

He closed the door behind him and sat opposite me. He had a small, leather-bound notebook. He flipped it open and clicked his pen.

"I don't have anything to add from what I told you and Detective Lewis at the scene," I said.

"I get that," he said. "And you know you're not obligated to stay here. I appreciate that you have. This whole thing is … complicated, to say the least."

"Are you running this investigation?"

He clicked his pen closed. "It's a mess is what it is. I'm going to have to act as a witness too. We were on the phone a few minutes before Runyon ..." He struggled for a way to put it.

"Yeah," I said. "Eric, I need to know what's in that footlocker beneath Runyon's bed. I need you to make sure nothing happens to it. I have a bad feeling about all of this."

"What are you talking about?"

I wiped a hand over my face, trying to stave off the wave of exhaustion I knew would come. The adrenaline drained from me.

"This wasn't a coincidence. I didn't just happen to roll up on Rick Runyon just as he was planning to off himself."

Eric's face was shadowed with stubble. He looked haggard. Maybe he was just as tired as I was.

"He was your friend," I said.

Eric let out a breath. "I knew him. I told you. He was heading out just as I was coming on. He was a legend in this building."

"Because of the Menzer murder," I said.

"That and a lot of other stuff. Rick Runyon was a good detective. He trained me ... hell, he's trained every detective working in this house right now."

"I'm sorry," I said. "I really am. This whole thing is a nightmare. But I already told you. Runyon acted strange when I started asking about Bridges. I showed him a page from Heather Menzer's diary. I asked him about this mysterious friend of hers, 'Em.' I told him I'd already spoken to Brian Billings and was about to try and talk to Pruitt. That's when he shut down on me and told me to wait for him. Next thing I know, I hear that shotgun blast."

Eric slammed a fist to the table. "You shouldn't have gone in that house. God ... Cass ... if he ..."

"If he what? You think he would have blown my head off?"

"No!" he shouted. "It's just you have a hell of a knack for walking straight into danger. Something could have happened to you. If it had, you think I could live with that?"

His eyes were wide with fear, the pupils black as night against pale blue.

"I sent you there," he said, his voice dropping to a whisper.

"It's not your fault," I said. "It's not my fault. We'll never know the kind of demons Rick Runyon was facing. But Eric, he was hiding something. I'm sure of it. Nothing else makes sense. I saw his eyes change when I asked about Heather's diary."

"We'll never know that."

It was my turn to slam a fist to the table. "And I'm not going to stop looking!"

"Do you realize how bad this is going to get?" he asked.

"I just want the truth."

"You have the truth," he said.

"Really? Are you bailing on me now? You're the one that took me to Todd Menzer. You *know* what he thinks. I told Runyon that too. About Todd's concerns. I know it in my bones there's something to that diary. Something Runyon didn't want to talk about. I'm sorry he was important to you. I don't doubt he was a good man and a good detective. But we're in this now. You and me."

"This will ruin him," Eric said.

"Runyon? Eric, he's dead. His wife is dead. They had no children. He's left no one behind to hurt."

As soon as I said it, I realized how wrong I was. Rick Runyon had left someone behind. He was sitting right in front of me. I looked over Eric's shoulder. Through the window, I could see a half a dozen officers walking by. They didn't need to be there. They were like looky-loos driving by a car crash.

I was the car crash. I had no doubt every person in this building already knew what I'd been doing on Rick Runyon's front porch. They already knew I had pulled the Heather Menzer murder file. From the looks I got, it wasn't hard to deduce every cop in the building would think I might just as well have pulled the trigger.

I looked back at Eric. His haggard expression took on a new meaning.

"They're going to blame you too, aren't they?" I asked. "They all know you've been helping me delve into this case."

"The evidence against Bridges is overwhelming, Cass. I don't care if Runyon was sloppy. And I'm not even saying he was."

"Then why did you take me to Todd Menzer's? Dammit, Eric, you've had a bad feeling about how this went down too. You might as well admit it."

He stayed silent. But he slowly dropped his gaze.

"Terrific," I said.

"Cass."

"No," I said, rising. "You can't do this halfway. And you know I can't. I get it. You weren't expecting this case to lead me right to your own house. But it did. I'm going to find out why. So you better tell me right now. Are you planning on standing in my way?"

His eyes traveled up to meet mine. He paused for a beat. Then another. Then he let out a sigh that made his shoulders shag. Finally, he uttered one word that summed up the entire day.

"Shit."

I straightened my back. "Exactly."

I slung my messenger bag over my shoulder. I meant to

storm out, but something stopped me. I didn't know how this was going to turn out. But I felt very clearly that Eric and I were about to cross to different sides of the ocean on this. I wanted to say something. Instead, I just patted Eric on the arm as I left the room.

Chapter 17

I woke to sandpaper licks and puppy breath. Not a bad change from the last twenty-four hours. That, and the scent of strong, freshly brewed coffee assailed my senses. If it weren't for the heavy heat weighing me down, I'd think this was heaven.

I brushed the fur off my teeth and headed downstairs with the puppy under my arm. His mother followed close at my heels with a jaunty wag of her tail.

Joe was in the kitchen, flipping pancakes in my grandmother's hundred-year-old iron skillet.

"I love you," I said as I plopped down in one of the kitchen chairs.

I set the puppy down. He was way too little to have made it onto my bed unassisted. Vangie and Jessa were already out on the pontoon. One of them must have put him there to wake me up.

"It's late," I said. "I've got time for a quick cup then I need to head into the office."

Joe turned. "Forget it. I already talked to Jeanie. You're taking the day off."

I raised a brow. "Since when have you become the boss of me? I've got work, Joe. I've got a trial four weeks away on Becker if it doesn't settle."

"The hardware store?" he asked. "Yeah, I always thought that Lou Harvey was a creepy old lech. Glad somebody finally had the guts to say so in court."

"Just making sure the town has more reason to love me," I said, sipping my coffee. It burned the roof of my mouth but it was a small price to pay for the much-needed jolt of caffeine.

The mama dog started barking and did a Scooby-Doo slide around the corner as the front door opened. Matty walked in and scooped her up. He got slathered with a tongue bath for his efforts.

"Fine watchdog she makes," Joe said. "Any luck finding out who she belongs to?"

"Nope. No chip. No collar. Nobody has called from the signs we put up."

Joe nodded. The puppy was busy tugging at Matty's shoelaces. He nearly tripped over him as he reached down and picked the little guy up. He sat at the table beside me.

"You going to keep them?" Matty asked.

I ran my finger over the rim of my coffee mug. "I haven't decided yet. I'm not home very much lately."

"Aw," Matty said. The puppy was busy trying to wriggle his way out of Matty's arms. Finally, he surrendered and fell asleep in an instant, the way puppies do. Two seconds later, he was snoring against Matty's chest.

"There's plenty of us in and out," Matty said.

"I've noticed," I said.

There was a squeal and a splash outside as Jessa did a cannonball off the end of the dock under her mother's watchful eye.

"Well," I said. "Miranda's got cats that don't like dogs. Jeanie's deathly allergic to pet dander. Vangie and Jessa are still figuring out their own routine. I don't see either of you volunteering."

"Katy is still deciding whether she wants *me* back in the house," Joe said.

Things had been strained between him and his wife. "I don't even want to try bringing two dogs into it. One of whom is still piddling on the carpet." He pointed his spatula at the puppy and got a sleepy grunt in response.

"Don't look at me," Matty said.

"Right," I said. "You're still between homes."

If Joe and Katy were estranged, Matty and his wife Tina were downright enemies lately. He slept in my guestroom more than his own bed these days.

"I think Marbury's doing great," I said. "He only had one accident yesterday."

"Marbury?" Joe said, turning. He flipped two pancakes on a plate with expert skill and put them in front of me.

"Er ... yeah," I said. I pointed to the puppy and then the mama dog. "Marbury and Madison. You know ... seminal case establishing judicial review?"

I got blank stares from both my brothers. "Come on," I said. "High school civics class?"

Still nothing.

"Man," Matty said. "You are such a nerd."

Marbury woke up and trained one sleepy side-eye on Matty.

"Well," Matty said. "I can see whose side *you're* on."

Madison curled up at Matty's feet. I knew she'd stay there until he put her baby down. Ever the protective mama.

"So," Joe said. He finally turned the stove off and took a seat at the table with us. "You going to talk about it?"

I got up and poured myself another cup of coffee. "What have you heard?"

"I heard Rick Runyon blew his brains out in front of you. And I heard the cops think you had something to do with it."

He shot a glance to Matty. It didn't come as any shock that the two of them had planned to corner me with their concern. I loved them for it. Sometimes though, I missed the privacy I had when I lived in Chicago.

"Well, you're mostly right. Though he didn't do it in front of me. I was standing on the porch. I didn't see it. Just ... the aftermath. And no, the cops know I didn't have anything to do with it. Not directly anyway."

"I never liked that guy," Joe said. "I mean, I never had any personal run-ins with him but I think Dad did."

"That doesn't surprise me," I said, sipping my coffee.

Vangie came in with Jessa. She had her stand on a towel by the door so she wouldn't drip on the floor.

"That was a killer cannonball," I said. "In a little while you'll have to get Uncle Matty to show you how to do a backflip."

"Can you?" Jessa asked. Madison ran to her. Jessa erupted in little-girl laughter as the dog licked her knees. Matty set Marbury down. The puppy scrambled after his mother and Jessa sat on the floor to play with them. Vangie joined us at the kitchen table.

"You okay?" she asked.

"I am. Still trying to wrap my head around everything. But yes. I'm okay."

"Did this have anything to do with the case you're working on?" Vangie asked. "The Menzer murder?"

It was hard to know what to say. "It might," I said. "I was there asking questions about the investigation. That doesn't leave this table, by the way."

"You think Runyon shot himself so he wouldn't have to

answer them?" Joe asked. He lowered his voice at the end so Jessa wouldn't hear.

"I don't know," I said. "I really don't. The timing was suspicious, to say the least. I gotta be honest. Until yesterday, I was almost ready to give up on the whole thing and tell Tori I'd hit a dead end."

"So," Joe said. "You ask a couple of questions about what he did back in the day. He turns around and blows his head off. What the hell are the cops saying?"

"Not much," I said. "It'll take some time to piece it all together. They'll run his phone, his computer if he had one. Find out who he was talking to in the last few days ... other than me."

"You don't really expect they're going to say he did anything wrong," Matty said. "Cops look after their own."

"Just like Learys," I said.

"You just said," Vangie chimed in, "you hit a dead end. How do you know that guy doing what he did had anything to do with you? He had to have already been depressed. I mean ... you don't just ..."

"Who did what, Mama Vee?" Jessa asked. We all froze. Jessa herself had witnessed the worst tragedy of all when her adoptive parents died not long ago.

"I think we should talk about this later or not at all," I said under my breath.

Vangie nodded and put on a smile for her daughter. Jessa climbed on to Vangie's lap. Joe got up and put a heaping plate of pancakes in front of her.

"You did the Mickey ears!" Jessa shouted.

Sure enough, my brother had fashioned the pancakes to look like a Disney-worthy version of the big mouse.

"Mom used to do that," I said. "God. I forgot all about that."

Matty passed the syrup to Jessa. Vangie helped her pour

it on. Soon, Jessa's chin and fingers were sticky with the stuff. If I knew Matty, his solution would be to let the puppy take care of that when she finished eating.

Vangie moved Jessa over to the bar so she could better supervise the mess.

"There was something else I wanted to talk to you about," I said to Joe. In all the chaos of the last few days, I hadn't yet had a chance to talk to him about my strange interview with Brian Billings.

"Before I talked to Runyon, or tried to anyway, I went out and met with another cop who worked on the Menzer case. He was a patrol officer at the time. Brian Billings. That name ring any bells for you?"

Joe considered my question. "Cass, you're talking over twenty years ago. I was twelve when those murders happened."

"He's not still with Delphi," Matty offered. "Because I never heard of him."

I shot my little brother a look. I didn't have to ask why he'd be in a position to know that. Unfortunately, Matty had plenty of run-ins with the local cops over the years. Usually on account of the numerous bar fights he got into when he'd had too many down at Mickey's.

"No," I said. "He left town a year or two after Heather was killed. He's a rent-a-cop out in Toledo now. Runyon ran the case for the homicide bureau. There were two beat cops who did most of the canvassing. Billings was one. The other was a guy named Pruitt."

"Mark Pruitt, I know," Matty said. "Kind of a dick."

"Uncle Matty?" Vangie gave my brother a stern eye. He put up an apologetic hand and smiled at Jessa. She was still busy working through her Mickey Mouse pancakes. Marbury and Madison waited at her feet for her to drop something.

"He's on my list to talk to next," I said. "Though I have a feeling the Runyon situation will make him less willing to meet with me."

"So what did you want to talk to me about?" Joe asked.

"Well, Billings. He didn't really impress me much. Seemed like your typical disgruntled former employee. I got the impression the rent-a-cop status wasn't something he chose, you know?"

"They usually don't," Joe agreed. "Not former cops, anyway."

"Well, he kept saying he knew me. Not me, but stuff about the family."

"That surprise you?" Joe said. "You act like you're new to this family."

"No. Not that. It was Mom, actually. He talked about Mom."

Vangie's ears perked up at the bar. She gave Jessa a kiss on the head and an admonishment not to touch anything but her fork. She went back to her seat at the table.

"What the heck did he say about Mom?" she asked.

"Well, it wasn't so much what he said. It's what he left out. He kept talking about domestic disturbance calls he'd made to the house. He kept implying Mom was some kind of troublemaker. It was weird. I corrected him and told him it was probably Dad he was thinking of. I don't know. I just didn't like the look he kept giving me. Do you know what he was talking about?"

Joe stared into his empty coffee mug. "Who the hell knows. People like to think they know crap about us they don't," he said.

"Yeah. I know all that. I'm in this family too. It's just ... I don't know. He was giving me that I-know-something-you-don't look."

"He was just trying to rattle you and make himself feel superior," Joe said. He rose from the table and turned his back on me. Then he started clearing the plates and loading the dishwasher.

I didn't like it. It felt like a blow off. Whether he realized it or not, Joe had just given me the same know-it-all look Brian Billings had just before turning his back on me.

I didn't get a chance to press him. There was a knock at the door. Marbury and Madison scampered to it wagging their tails.

"Yeah," Matty said, rising. "Not the most fierce guard dogs."

Matty got to the door ahead of me. Tori stood on the porch, her face ashen.

"Come on in," I said. "Get out of the heat. I take it you heard what happened when I tried talking to Detective Runyon. I was going to call you today."

Tori gave Matty a weak smile. She leaned down to pet the dogs and said hello to Vangie and Jessa.

"Yeah," she said. "It's all over the news."

There was something off about the way Tori looked at me. Her eyes darted from me to the others. The hairs rose on the back of my neck.

"Tori?" I asked. "What's the matter?"

Matty caught my gaze. He cleared his throat and excused himself, taking the dogs with him.

Tori looked about ready to fall over.

"Sit down," I said, my pulse jumping with alarm.

"I'm okay," she said, breathless.

"Then what?"

Tori lifted her eyes to mine. She'd been crying.

"It's my dad," she said, her voice breaking. "Cass, I just got a call from the prison when I was on my way here. He collapsed at breakfast. They won't tell me how serious it is. They just told me I need to hurry."

I looked at my brothers and Vangie. "Give me five minutes," I said to Tori. "I'll drive you."

Chapter 18

BRIDGES LAY on his side facing away from us. I had to move heaven and earth to get permission to bring Tori back to see her father. His condition was grave enough he'd been transported to a local hospital. We waited just outside his room together.

Tori stood to the side as the doctor came to talk to her. "He's developed pneumonia, in both lungs" he said. "It's weakened him and I'm not happy with his iron levels and a few other things. He had an episode where he couldn't breathe and wasn't moving enough oxygen. They brought him here."

As the doctor tried to gently explain the severity of the current crisis, I went in Sean's room and came to his side, leaving Tori in the hall. He looked up at me. His color was a strange mixture of yellow and gray. I wondered about his liver on top of the rest of it.

"Have you told her?" he asked, his voice a ragged whisper.

"Told her what?"

He contorted into a round of dry coughs. I realized he meant his diagnosis.

"Sean," I said. "You're my client. You told me that in confidence. Sure, she works for me, but there's a line even I can't cross. But you have to tell her. And you have to tell her today."

The doctor and Tori walked in. He had a comforting hand on Tori's arm. I got the distinct impression that he too had been given strict orders to skirt the bigger issue with Sean's health. It was ludicrous. Tori wasn't stupid. She took one look at her father and she knew.

"I've heard some rumors," Sean said after he finally recovered.

I pulled up a wheeled stool to the side of the bed so I could lean in close to Sean's face. If gossip from Delphi had already reached him in here, there was no point in sugar-coating anything.

"Rick Runyon's dead," I said. "He shot himself more or less right in front of me. There are still a lot of questions I can't answer, but for me, there's no doubt he didn't like what I asked him."

Tori came to the other side of the bed. She leaned down and kissed her father on the head. He closed his eyes and brought a shaky hand up to her cheek.

"Hey, pumpkin,' he said.

Pumpkin. I don't know why it struck me. But it occurred to me my own father had never once called me by any term of endearment. Only my mother and grandparents had. Baby doll.

I caught Sean's eyes. I gave him a solemn nod. Tori waited.

"I'll be all right," he said softly.

Tori shook her head. "No, you won't. You've tried to keep me in the dark but I can see it, Dad. I can smell it. You forget, I was with Grandma until the bitter end. It was the same with her. Tell me the truth. It's cancer."

Sean wheezed. Tori looked at me and I tried to keep my face neutral.

"Pancreatic," Sean finally said. Tori's expression stayed hard. She'd been bracing for this for months. She might not have known the source, but she could see her father wasting away right in front of her.

"I can leave you two alone to talk," I said.

"No!" Both Tori and Sean said it together.

"No," Tori said. "They're not going to let us stay here long. Dad needs to know what you know."

Tori knew her father well, in spite of everything that had kept them apart. It finally dawned on me. This investigation ... my help ... had been the thing keeping Bridges going.

I settled back on the stool. One of the nurses quietly closed the privacy curtain. A police officer stood near the door and Bridges was cuffed to the bed. This was as good as it would get.

"Runyon," Sean said, coughing.

"Runyon," I answered.

"What triggered him?" Tori asked. "I mean ... ugh. Poor choice of words."

"I don't know for sure," I said. "I brought a copy of Heather's diary, the one her brother gave me. I asked him about her friend Em and wanted him to connect the dots for me. There was nobody in the police report or the trial witness lists who was an obvious match to that name."

"'Em,'" Tori repeated. "I've been racking my brain. I can't find anything either."

"That's the last thing I asked Runyon before he ... did what he did."

"He had it in for me from the beginning," Sean said.

I hated that he was sick. I hated that I didn't have more

to go on than Rick Runyon's desperate last act. Still, it would do none of us any good if I walked on eggshells with this.

"Sean," I said. "You lied to him from the very beginning. You were your own worst enemy at every turn. I don't know what Rick Runyon was trying to hide. But he had a good reputation. He was a well-respected detective. His actions alone will not be enough to blow this open again."

"You said Billings made it sound like Runyon had my dad in mind from the downstroke," Tori said. "Like they had tunnel vision as soon as they knew he was at that party."

"Maybe," I said. "Detective Pruitt is my next conversation if I can get him to talk. I'm not optimistic though. He doesn't have to without a subpoena and I can't get one without a case to attach it to. I don't have nearly enough to file any kind of motion yet."

"What do you want from me?" Sean asked.

"Your memory," I said. "Sean, I need you to think. Hard. You've said you didn't know Heather. That she might have been just one of the girls that hung around with your other clients. I need the names of every single other one. I'm not convinced Runyon was thorough in his interviews. I need to figure out who this 'Em' person was. I think it matters that they never tracked that down."

"He's a liar," Sean said. "And he was guilty of something. There's no other reason why he would have gone and done what he did. He knew you were going to figure this out."

"I appreciate your confidence in me, but I have to be brutally honest. Up until he pulled that trigger, I was getting ready to tell you I can't help you. I have no hook to file a motion for a new trial. And right here, right now, I still don't."

Sean started to cough again and seized up. A nurse came by to check his IV lines. She carefully lifted Sean's arm to make sure the medical tape holding the lines in place hadn't come loose. Sean's skin hung from his bones. The man was nearly six feet tall and I wondered if he weighed even one hundred and thirty pounds. The flesh of his right wrist bore an ugly, reddish-purple distinct band beneath the handcuff.

"Is there no way you can loosen those?" I said to the corrections officer. "He's not going anywhere. He can barely breathe, let alone walk."

"It's not as bad as it looks," Sean said. I backed down. Instinct told me if I pressed, it could cause even more trouble for him.

"Pumpkin," he said to Tori. "I'd really like something fizzy. Can you maybe see if they'll let you bring me a pop or something?"

It seemed an odd request. If Tori thought so too, she didn't let on. She merely kissed her father again and set off to find what he asked of her. The moment she left the room, Sean Allen Bridges locked his eyes with mine.

"Just leave it," he said, shocking me.

"Leave it?"

"Tori doesn't need any more disappointment. That's all I've been for her."

"She loves you. She believes in you."

Sean blinked. "Do you?"

I looked toward the door. There was no sign of Tori.

"I wasn't sure," I said. "I like your daughter a lot. She deserves to know the truth, no matter what that is. And until Rick Runyon put a 12-gauge under his chin, I figured that truth would be the thing she's been afraid of all along. That you're guilty and you've been lying to her. But now, my gut's telling me Runyon wanted to be dead more than he wanted to be around when I figured something out about this case. I don't know what that is. But I'm in it now. No matter where it leads."

There was a flicker in Sean's eyes. Just a small thing. A tell. My heart sank.

"What haven't you told me?" I asked.

"I've told you the truth," he said. "I didn't kill that girl. I swear to God. I swear on my daughter's head and she is the only thing that's good about my life. She's the only reason I haven't given up in here in all these twenty-four years."

"And yet," I said. "You haven't told me all of it. As sure as I am about Runyon, I'm sure about you too. If you didn't do it, then maybe you're protecting someone. Who?"

Bridges slammed his head deeper into the pillow. His eyes glazed over as he opened them. "Tori," he said. "I'm protecting her the only way I can."

It wasn't an answer. But I knew it was all I'd get for the day. Sean started to fade.

I leaned in and whispered in his ear. "You're not allowed to die yet. Do you hear me? You hang on. You do exactly what these doctors tell you to. Because I *will* find the truth. That's a promise. But not to you. It's a promise to her. You're not done yet, Sean. Not by a long shot."

He opened his eyes and gave me a slow nod. Tori came back into the room carrying a Styrofoam cup with a paper straw.

"You need to make your goodbyes," the nurse said as she came back around the privacy curtain. "Your father needs rest and we need to get him started on some breathing treatments."

I squeezed Bridges's arm. Then I stepped around the bed and left him his last few moments with Tori.

Chapter 19

THREE DAYS LATER, the night before Rick Runyon's funeral, Jeanie and I sat on the floor of the conference room. We'd taken Runyon's full report apart piece by piece.

I arranged it by witness. Either Runyon, Pruitt, or Billings had spoken to Heather's classmates, the other tenants who lived in her building, her co-workers down at Mickey's that summer, her family, her friends. There was no Em. There was no reason for her to get out of her car that night. There was nothing to point in any other direction but the web of lies Sean Allen Bridges told.

Jeanie picked up one of the crime scene photos as I pored through the index page of the report. She rotated it, studied it. Then she put it down in frustration.

"They all say he was a charmer, a con man," Jeanie said. "We've got a parade of girls who say they had a crush on him. Couple of them even claimed to go out with him."

"Right," I said.

"And not a single one of them has ever said he got rough with them. Not once. That just doesn't track."

"And the coroner couldn't establish whether the sexual

147

assault took place before or after her death. The submersion made that hard to determine," I said.

Jeanie put her wrists behind her as she looked at the photo, simulating how Heather might have been bound.

"Where's that statement from the gun expert?" she asked.

I sat back on my heels. "Uh. That should be the last one. That's pile fifty-nine," I said. We'd arranged the supplemental statements by number and put the circle of physical evidence associated with each one beside it.

Jeanie rose and started counting. "It's fifty-eight," she said.

"No," I said. "It's fifty-nine." I held up the index. Runyon had listed each supplemental interview and footnoted it to the main report.

Jeanie walked around. She counted out loud. When she got to fifty-eight, she stopped.

My heart stopped with her. Adrenaline raced through me. It was right there. Like an image in the water but with the slightest breeze or disturbance, it shimmered away.

I looked at the index. I looked at the piles. Jeanie stood frozen as I repeated the same count.

Fifty-eight. There were fifty-eight written interview statements. I looked back at the index. It didn't track. The last one was missing.

"Son of a bitch," I muttered.

"Say it," Jeanie said. She'd already worked it out in her own head.

"One's missing," I said. I went back to the box we'd brought the copy of the police report over in. I pawed through it. I checked again. I counted again. I got the same answer four different times.

"He redacted one," I said, my hands shaking as I handed the report index to Jeanie. "Runyon references fifty-nine statements. We only have supplementals for fifty-eight."

"Christ," she said. "It's got to just be a math error. Right?"

She met my eyes. The truth pulsed through each of us. I heard the echo of the shotgun blast that ripped through Rick Runyon.

There was no mistake. The answer was literally right in front of me. I knew it. Rick Runyon knew I would.

"Son of a bitch," Jeanie echoed my statement.

Chapter 20

THE TEMPERATURE TOPPED one hundred degrees the morning they put former Detective Rick Runyon in the ground. He had a sister who flew in from Florida. She fainted as the honor guard handed her his folded American flag. There was no one left to take it. The officers in full dress uniform caught her before she hit the ground. The funeral director got her into an air-conditioned car as they played taps.

Runyon had no other family. He had cops. They sat shoulder to solemn shoulder. Runyon's sister finally made her way back to the gravesite. Another woman came to stand beside her. She put an uncomfortable hand on the sister. The other woman had a high beehive of cotton candy hair dyed red. Runyon's sister collapsed in her arms, making the other woman look around nervously.

I stood away from the main crowd. Maybe I shouldn't have come at all. But no matter what else he was, Rick Runyon had served this town for thirty-eight years. It mattered that I pay my respects.

"Sounds like Father Ruiz didn't want to let them bury

him here," Miranda whispered beside me. "Can you believe that?"

"He's old school," I said. "Or so I've heard."

"Well," Miranda said. "Most of the congregation can't stand him anyway. He grandstands."

"They don't like him because he's not Polish or Irish," I said. "Though I suppose I'm not one to talk. I haven't been to mass regularly since ... well ... since after my mother's funeral."

She was buried here too, about a hundred yards to the west of us.

"That's the last time you were here, wasn't it?" Miranda asked.

I didn't like to think about it. I hated cemeteries. They meant nothing to me. I honored my mother by taking care of the children left behind. I could never see the point of putting flowers on a cold, gray stone. Her spirit wasn't here. It was in me. It was in my brothers and sister.

"No," I answered. "I haven't."

Miranda gently squeezed my arm. "It's okay," she said. "She probably wouldn't want you to."

"Tell that to my father," I said. I didn't want to remember that either. He had briefly kicked me out of the house when I was sixteen years old for refusing to come to my mother's gravesite with him on her birthday. It lasted a weekend. Then Matty let me in the next Monday morning so I could get him and Vangie ready for school. My father either forgot or decided not to care anymore. He never brought it up again.

As the clouds rolled in and the humidity rose, Miranda jolted beside me as the first crack of Rick Runyon's twenty-one gun salute rang out.

Runyon's sister wailed. She hadn't let go of the red-headed woman and it became obvious to me she had no idea who the woman even was. She kept trying to make eye contact with the officers standing around her, hoping someone would take Runyon's bereft sister off her hands.

Father Ruiz came to the red-headed woman's rescue and took Rick Runyon's sister in his arms. The other woman thanked him, then practically ran toward the cars, tottering on her high heels. Miranda gasped beside me. We thought the same thing at once. It looked like the lady was about to fall right into the open grave. Miranda did a quick sign of the cross. She got an unlikely savior in Eric Wray. He shot a hand out and grabbed the woman by the elbow just before she went fully over. She threw her arms around him and wept. Now it was his turn to look for rescue.

After that, the crowd at the gravesite started to disperse. I'd tried to go unnoticed. It didn't work. I felt the heat of the stares from every member of the Delphi P.D. in attendance. It burned through me hotter than the sun.

Except for one.

After he'd extricated himself from the red-headed woman, Eric shook hands with the chief and deputy chief. He caught my eye over their shoulders, gave a terse smile, then excused himself and headed straight for me.

"I'll go start the car," Miranda said. "Get the air going at least."

"Thanks," I said, handing her the keys. "I'll be there in a minute."

A muscle in Eric's jaw jumped as he clenched it and strode toward me. He put a firm hand on my elbow and led me away from Rick Runyon's freshly dug grave.

"What exactly are you doing here?" he asked.

"It mattered," I said. "That's all."

"To who?" he said, his voice an aggressive whisper.

"To me. And whether you believe me or not, I think it matters to Rick Runyon. I think he might have been a good man. Or tried to be. And this whole thing just makes me sad, Eric. I wanted to pay my respects."

"You have any idea how many feathers you've ruffled this time? Hell, half the guys on the force think you might as well have just pulled the trigger yourself."

"That's not fair," I said, matching his tone. "I'm trying to do my job. You know that. Up until a couple of weeks ago, it mattered to you to help me."

Eric gritted his teeth. A group of officers passed by us on the way to their vehicles. They stared hard at Eric.

"Eric, I've combed through Runyon's report. Something's wrong with it. There's a statement missing. The index doesn't match up. Runyon pulled an interview statement. I know it. I can't prove it yet, but I know it. It wasn't even hard to figure out. I think Runyon knew that. So he blew his head off when I started asking questions …"

"Jesus," Eric said, pulling me further from the crowd. "Lower your voice."

"I should start screaming from the rooftops. Runyon was hiding something. Something so bad he'd rather die than let it come to light. There's no other explanation that makes sense."

"I don't know that yet," he said. "You have to trust me to carry through with the investigation into his death."

"How the hell are you going to do that? You're in this with me, Eric. Everyone knows it."

"Dammit, Cass," Eric said. "Rick Runyon was a good man."

"What if Sean Allen Bridges is too?" I asked.

"It doesn't have to mean what you think it meant," Eric said. "Runyon was working twenty-hour days on the Menzer case. It was hot, just like this. Hell, I was fourteen years old and walked with that search party for maybe an hour or two at a time. I remember feeling like I was going to die from it myself. You have no idea what it would have been like for Rick. It lives in you. It sticks to you. He probably hadn't slept for three or four days in a row. So he misnumbered an index. That's all you have?"

I took a step back from him. "You're kidding me with this. Right?"

"It happens," he said. "He was human."

"Eric, this wasn't some dealer-on-dealer homicide or a run-of-the-mill robbery. This was Heather Menzer. It was national news. You're a good detective. Probably the best we have. Are you really going to stand there and tell me Runyon would have made a careless mistake like that?"

His nostrils flared. Eric opened his mouth and clamped it shut twice before he finally answered.

"Dammit," he muttered.

"Exactly."

"So why didn't Bridges's lawyer point that out? Dushane had access to the same stuff you do twenty-four years ago. By all accounts, he was a decent defense lawyer. All eyes were on him too. Why don't you ask him that question?"

"I can't. He died a decade ago. I paused a beat. "As for the rest, I just don't know. And I never will."

"Damn," Eric said.

"Eric, everyone who has anything cogent to say about this case is either dead, dying, or refusing to talk," I said.

He turned his back on me and paced a few steps. I could practically see steam coming from his ears.

"Eric," I said. "I'm sorry. But you can't stand there and tell me you didn't have instincts on this one."

"I made a promise to Todd Menzer," Eric said, whipping around. "Don't read too much into that. I sure as hell didn't intend to shit all over a good detective's reputation."

"That's not on you. Runyon's the one who pulled that

trigger. He knew how it would look. And I think he knew what I would find."

"Which is nothing. No judge will grant Bridges a new trial based on what you have right now. This is probably pointless."

"Eric," I said, coming toward him. "You're going to have to decide whether you're working with me or against me. I'm not your enemy. Two weeks ago, we were on the same page. I'm truly sorry about Runyon. He was your mentor. I get that. If this were different ... if it was Jeanie ..."

"Yes," Eric said. "That is exactly what this is like for a lot of people in the department. Rick Runyon helped teach me and a lot of others how to be a detective. Did you know he's the one who encouraged me to put in for the bureau in the first place?"

"I'm sorry," I said. "I can't imagine what this case did to him. And maybe whatever happened was an oversight or something that snowballed. Maybe we'll never know. But if there's even a sliver of a chance that an innocent man went to prison for this ..."

"Bridges isn't innocent," Eric said. "Don't kid yourself about that."

"He was a two-bit drug dealer. I have no delusions about his character. Only that's a far cry from murder and you of all people know the difference."

Eric's eyes glinted. I'd hit on something I hadn't meant to. He swallowed hard.

"What do you know?" I pressed on. "Was there something in that footlocker? If it's anything to do with the Menzer case, you know you have to tell me. You're still under a duty if it's exculpatory."

"It's an ongoing investigation," he said. "You know I can't share that yet."

"What can you share?"

Eric dropped his head. The first of the disbanded motorcade made its way out of the cemetery. There were still a dozen or so mourners scattered around.

Eric went back to whispering. "Cass, the footlocker was empty. I know you were hoping for some magic bullet. It's just not there. I'm not even supposed to tell you that. And ... Bridges isn't or wasn't the only one dying. Runyon had stage IV lung cancer. They'd suspended treatment. His docs didn't expect him to make it to the end of the summer."

"Crap," I said. "I thought it was something like that. I really am sorry. It just doesn't change the fact that he did what he did because I came to his front door."

"Maybe," he said. "I know what it looks like."

"You lost your mind, Wray?" The voice came from behind me. Eric moved fast. He grabbed me by the arm and pulled me behind him.

It took me a beat, but I recognized the man charging toward us as Mark Pruitt. Brian Billings's partner. The cop who had been dodging my calls for three weeks.

"Pruitt," Eric said. "Calm down. Not here."

"Oh, I think it needs to be right here!"

Pruitt raised a finger and jabbed it in my face as I moved out from behind Eric.

"Look," I said. "I'll leave. I just came to pay my respects. That's all."

"You don't get to do that. You think I don't know what you've been after? I know exactly how you work. You lose my number. You forget Rick Runyon's good name. You file so much as one motion, I'll end you."

Mark Pruitt's face turned a mottled shade of purple. His green eyes blazed against his bloodshot whites. His lips contorted as he stepped forward.

My anger rose. "Is that a threat, Detective?"

Eric stepped between us. "Enough," he said. "Goddammit, Mark, this is busting me up as much as it is you. More. Don't do this. Walk away."

"You kidding me?" Pruitt said, his attention on Eric now. "You think this gash is worth it?"

It happened so fast I barely had time to draw breath. Eric turned, and landed a blow across Pruitt's jaw. Pruitt staggered sideways, then charged forward.

He lunged at Eric and caught him around the waist. The two of them stumbled backward. Pruitt tried to get off a punch of his own but Eric had his arms around him. Pruitt snorted. Spit flew out of his mouth.

"Cass, go," Eric said. "Please."

"I'm not your enemy either, Pruitt," I said.

"Cass!" Eric shouted. "Get the hell out of here!"

I met his eyes. Behind Eric, the remaining mourners from the Delphi P.D. had seen everything. The deputy chief was heading straight for us.

I threw Eric one last look. I mouthed an "I'm sorry" then went to find Miranda.

Chapter 21

"You're sure that's all of them?" I asked Tori.

She set up new stacks of paperwork on the conference-room table. Jeanie brought in two separate card tables to hold the rest of the Menzer murder file. The complete trial transcripts had finally come in. Tori was already halfway through indexing those. So far, there was little room for optimism. No new stones to uncover. No earth-shattering revelations from the reams of witness testimony and lukewarm cross-examination from the late Lowell Dushane.

"Ineffective assistance of counsel?" Tori asked. She stood at the end of the conference table, chewing on the end of a pencil. "I mean ... time after time, he just sits there while the state gets everything in unopposed."

"You'd have to show a reasonable likelihood of a different outcome," Jeanie said. "Abuse of discretion. All I see here is harmless error, Tori. I'm sorry. But Wray was right. Runyon's suicide doesn't cut it. The missing witness statement, if there really was one, doesn't cut it."

"But why didn't Dushane pick up on that back then?"

Tori said. "It took us one afternoon combing through and cross-checking these reports."

I shrugged. "It's impossible to second guess. For all we know, Dushane *did* question Runyon about it."

"Not on the witness stand," Tori said. "And he made no note of it in his own file."

Two days ago, Jeanie had procured Lowell Dushane's own case file from his former law partners. It was a mess of coffee-stained, dog-eared pages. Whatever went on in Dushane's mind, very little of it made it into the file.

I stood at the board. We had taped 16X20 blow-ups of all the most damning physical evidence side by side.

"We still have no way to discount how Heather's blood made it in Sean's car. How his hair winds up in and on the fibers of her shirt. The prosecution's experts claimed close, intimate contact. I would have pushed them harder on that theory. But Dushane's failure to do it still doesn't get us a new trial. We'll be in front of Judge Castor with this. I know him. We don't have enough right now."

On the second board, Tori had taped the worst of the crime scene photos. Jeanie sat beneath the blow-up of Heather Menzer's shirt. It was open at the collar. The picture was of a high enough resolution I could still read the shirt size slightly obscured behind the sharpie marking with the initial of Heather's last name. She wore a medium.

"You two should go home for the day," I said.

"I want to help," Tori said. "I'll go insane if I stare at the four walls of my bedroom again tonight. Miranda's great. But she's been hovering a lot lately."

Jeanie caught my gaze. "Have you heard from the hospital?" she asked. "How's your father?"

"Stable," Tori said. "Thank God he responded to the IV antibiotics. They say it's a miracle, but he's past the current crisis. He's getting transferred back to Handlon tomorrow morning. I wanted to ask you about that. There's a chance I might get to see him before he's discharged. It's a small window but …"

"Go!" I said. "My God, Tori, take the day off. Go be with your dad if you can. Don't even think twice about that."

"I know," she said. "I mean, thank you. For all of this. It's not just the help you've given with my dad. I know it's turned the entire practice on its ear. You've backburnered so many other things for this case. I can't ever repay you, Cass."

"Family matters," I said. "You matter. I told you from the outset I couldn't make you any promises. I still can't. But we'll see this through at least until I'm satisfied about what was in Rick Runyon's full report. I just want you to prepare yourself that it might not be what you're hoping for."

Tori pressed her lips together in a grim smile. Jeanie kept her eyes locked with mine. She knew me well enough to know I was lying to Tori. At least a little bit. It was better if she kept her expectations low. For me, every instinct in my body told me Runyon was hiding something explosive. I just had no earthly clue how I'd find it now.

"You heard from Wray lately?" Jeanie asked, easing one bit of tension, while ratcheting up another. It had been almost a week since Rick Runyon's funeral. Eric had yet to return my latest round of calls.

"No," I said. "I have a feeling he's been instructed not to have anything to do with me for the short term."

"Did he really punch Mark Pruitt out?" Tori asked. Unfortunately, but not surprisingly, the graveside incident got talked about on social media. Of course, no one got the story exactly right. There was one version floating around that Eric and Pruitt actually tumbled end over end into Rick Runyon's open grave.

The truth was bad enough. If there was anyone in town

left who didn't know I was looking into the Menzer murder for Sean Bridges, they knew it now.

"That's probably for the best, at least for now," Jeanie said. "Though I gotta say, if Delphi's chief were smart, he'd get an outside agency to review Runyon's actions on this case. Eric's in a hell of a bad spot."

"He's the best detective they have," I said. "And despite all of his ... entanglements, he's still the person I trust the most to bring the truth to light. He might not like what he finds, but he won't protect Runyon if he really did something wrong back then."

The tilt of Jeanie's head said "are you sure about that?" I gave her a silent nod. Plus, I wanted to change that particular subject around Tori. The less she knew about my history with Eric Wray, the better.

"What about these new files?" Jeanie asked. "Give me a clue what you're looking for and maybe we can help you narrow it down."

"It's a rabbit hole. Probably a wild goose chase. Pick your futile metaphor. One pile is all Runyon's other reports in the couple of weeks leading up to the murder. One is Billings's. The last one is Pruitt's. I don't know. I just want to get a picture as to who they were talking to. Their movements."

"What are you hoping to find?" Tori asked.

"I honestly have no idea. It's just something worth following up on. Maybe one of them mentions talking to a witness Runyon didn't index. I don't know. I just want to know the movements of the investigating officers as if I made them myself."

"Worth a shot," Jeanie said. She picked up the three files Tori got in response to my latest FOIA request to the Delphi P.D.

"Pick a card, any card," she said, waving the files.

"I'll take Billings," I said.

Jeanie raised a brow. "Interesting choice. Give me Runyon's." She handed Pruitt's file to Tori.

I clutched Billings's file close to my chest. "I'm going to camp out in my office and turn on some mood music."

"Ugh," Jeanie said. "Not that Lilith Fair crap you like to listen to."

"Hey," I said. "Better than your crap. If I have to hear Steely Dan one more time …"

She was still bitching as I left the conference room and closed the door to my office. I bypassed my desk and went straight for the couch.

Brian Billings's report file was organized chronologically. I'd asked Tori to get his log for the two weeks before and after Sean Bridges's arrest. When I tabbed through the dates, I saw she'd cast an even wider net. I had Billings's log from the beginning of June all the way through Labor Day.

It was dry reading for the most part. Billings worked afternoons, punching in at two p.m. and out at ten. Guys his age with no family attachments coveted those shifts. They made a mint on overtime in the mornings if they were called into court to testify on any of the arrests they'd made.

Billings was no different. As a beat cop, he spent most of his time patrolling the neighborhoods to the north end of Finn Lake. Traffic stops. Crowd control at a few of the parades Delphi sponsored. Unfortunately, the gravamen of Brian Billings's reports detailed various domestic disturbances within the city limits.

I read until my eyes felt like they might fall out of their sockets. As a cop, Billings was methodical. His reports were neat and detailed. A pattern emerged to the way he liked to work. He let his then partner, Pruitt, take the lead on most of their interviews. Billings generally stepped in when the use of force was required. He'd had a relatively mundane summer except for a suicide call on Gansett Road. That was just two streets over. Duane Staley. He'd been one of my father's drinking buddies once upon a time.

Duane's daughter Jenny had been in my grade. We were friends. During the dinner hours of July 4th, her father had barricaded himself in Jenny's bedroom with a .45 pointed at his temple. Billings and Pruitt were first on scene.

I closed the file. Jenny never told me any of this. But I remembered that fall, she transferred schools. One day she was in my life, the next she was just gone.

It took me a moment to draw the strength to pick up the file again. I didn't want to know these things about my neighbors. I knew enough. It was one thing when someone I'd known since childhood walked into my office asking for help. This felt different. Voyeuristic, somehow.

We all had our issues here on the east side of the lake. West-enders regarded us as white trash. I felt a strange kinship to Brian Billings as I read through those files. I, too, had the kind of job where nobody comes to see you when things are going well. One of my law school professors likened the practice of law to the man who follows behind the animals in a circus parade, shoveling all the shit they leave behind. Beat cops are like that too.

I flipped to the next page in the file. Billings was one of the first responders to a backyard fireworks display that went wrong on the south end of the lake. I didn't recognize the family name.

I flipped the page. What I saw there settled against my chest with the weight of an anvil. On July 6th, Billings and Pruitt responded to a domestic disturbance at 241 Trumbull. My parents' address.

With shaking fingers, I read through his narrative. It was terse, to the point. The neighbors had called after hearing screaming from inside the house.

"Where was I?" I said aloud. It was a Wednesday night in

the middle of the summer. I was eleven years old. According to Billings's report, only two young children were present in the house. A female social worker was called to sit with them while Billings and Pruitt dealt with the adults in the house.

I knew the story. The drill. I'd lived it a hundred times growing up. My father would drink too much. My mother would try to stop him. He'd punch a wall. He'd pick a fight with one of the neighbors if he was home. Someone down at Mickey's if he was there. My father would pick fights with Joe. He chased my mother with a baseball bat a few times. He never struck her. He terrorized her though.

But what stared at me in black-and-white block letters didn't track. This time, they took my mother into custody. My father declined medical attention. My mother was advised of her rights then arrested for assault.

I didn't remember it. He had it wrong. My mother was never the aggressor. Why didn't my father tell them the truth? If she struck him, it would have been to get him off of her or my brother. Or one awful night ... me. I closed the file. It was a mistake. Dad was sober that summer. He was good.

July 6th. Two days before we would have had a fireworks show at Grandpa and Grandma Leary's house. The house I lived in now. God. I could still remember that celebration. My father danced with my mother on the lawn.

None of this made any sense. I took the page out of the main file and tucked it in my messenger bag. I don't know why I did it, but I didn't want Tori or Jeanie finding it. It was mine. My history. My story. My nightmare.

I kept searching. There was nothing else of interest except for one last incident. Brian Billings and Mark Pruitt responded to a motor vehicle accident. That alone wasn't significant. I almost passed it by. But it happened on Ford Street at the Wisner Road intersection. That was just one block from Heather Menzer's apartment building.

June 29th. Ten days before Heather went missing. Eleven o'clock at night. Pruitt and Billings were working overtime that night. They came upon a pick-up truck flipped into the ditch that ran along Wisner Road.

They weren't first on scene, but they arrived ahead of the ambulance. A passerby had already stopped to assist the driver who'd been thrown from the vehicle. He was alive. He was badly wounded.

My pulse thundered between my ears. I flipped the page back and forth. I reread the same sentence maybe six times.

"Cass?" Jeanie stood at the door. I'd lost track of time. She was bleary-eyed. The sun had long since set.

"Jeanie," I said, bolting off the couch. "Read this. Tell me I'm not losing my mind."

Jeanie took the report from me. I watched as her eyes darted back and forth. She brought her hand to her mouth.

"I'll be damned," she said. "Cass, it doesn't have to mean anything. This is Delphi."

"But he never mentioned it. Not when I talked to him. Not in his trial testimony. Not in Runyon's report. But dammit, Pruitt and Billings met Heather Menzer ten days before she disappeared. She was studying to be a paramedic. Three of her friends testified how she was always stopping to help. A Good Samaritan. Jeanie. She was on scene at an accident involving Billings and Pruitt ten days before she went missing and they never bothered to mention it. Why?"

Jeanie set the report down. "Cass ..."

"I need to call Todd Menzer. I need to see him again. Now."

Chapter 22

I FOUND Tori asleep in the conference room as I gathered my things to leave. She'd fallen face first in her own stack of papers.

For a moment, and it was just a glimpse, but she reminded me of Vangie. When my sister was eight or nine years old, long after our mother died, I would find her like this, snoring on top of her desk as she worked on spelling lists or some other grade school subject that gave her trouble, like timed math tests.

Tori had the same wheat-blonde hair that Vangie did before she started coloring it even lighter. She was thin-boned like my sister too.

I wondered who had been there for Tori when she was eight or nine years old and needing help with her homework. Bridges was out of the picture. Her mother came and went. She just had Sean's mother.

Tori took a hard breath and woke herself. A piece of paper stuck to her cheek as she lifted her head.

"What time is it?" she asked.

"Late. Early, I guess. I'm heading home for a few hours to catch some sleep. Then I'm heading out to Luna."

"Menzer's house?" she said. I regretted even mentioning it. I knew what she'd say.

"Yes," I said. I didn't want to tell her too much. I was protecting her the way Sean asked me to. Until I had something concrete on this case, there was no point getting her hopes up.

"Let me go with you. I just need forty-five minutes to go back to Miranda's, grab a shower and brush my teeth."

"It's not a good idea," I said. "Todd Menzer is open-minded about my role in all of this. But I'm not the daughter of the man who everyone thinks killed his sister. I don't want to push his good graces, if you know what I mean."

"But I might think of something. You need eyes in the back of your head."

They were all good points. But I still wasn't willing to risk upsetting Todd Menzer or his mother if she was there and lucid today. He'd agreed to meet with me in two hours.

"Did you find anything interesting in the Pruitt file?" I changed the subject.

Tori yawned. Not yet. I wasn't ready to draw her attention to the car accident on June 29th. I had no idea if Pruitt even included it in his dailies.

"No," she said. "I was in the middle of making a list of all the people he mentioned having interviewed as part of the canvassing on the Menzer case. They were mostly people from that frat party. I was looking for the substance of those interviews. I thought I'd cross-reference them with Runyon's report to see if there are any missing. That might give us a clue what Runyon or someone else redacted."

"That's a good thought," I said. "You won't likely find the substance of any interviews on the Menzer case in Pruitt's logs. Those would have been appended to the main file Runyon kept. In Billings's all I have are simple notations of witness names, dates, and a reference back to the main file. Definitely if you see anything other than that, let me know."

"You sure I can't talk you into letting me go with you to Todd's?"

"I'm sure," I said. "Not this time. Like I said, he's been gracious with me but I'm a few steps removed from the players in this case. You're not."

"But you already said he thinks my dad is innocent," she pleaded.

"No. I didn't say that. I said Todd's got questions that were never answered about how Heather died. That's not the same thing at all."

Tori rested her chin on her hand. She wasn't happy, but she trusted my judgment.

"Keep looking," I said. "Your thorough inspection of these reports is most likely going to be the thing that breaks this case if it can be broken. I'm just tying up a loose end."

"Okay," she said. "And Cass ... I know I've said it before, but thank you. You have no idea what this means to me. I've grown up my whole life having to hide who my family was. People wonder why I even came back to the Delphi area. That's why my grandma moved away from here when I was little. The truth was, I didn't feel like I had anywhere else to go. When you offered me a job and I realized you worked here, I knew it was fate."

I reached for Tori and smoothed a strand of hair from her eyes. It was a maternal gesture that came naturally to me. Tori let me.

"One way or another, it's going to be okay. And I know a little something about what it's like to have people judge you for your last name. You just have to ignore all that and live your truth." Tori nodded.

I grabbed my messenger bag. I had just enough time myself for a shower, change of clothes, and de-fuzzing of my teeth. Then I had to figure out a way to handle Todd Menzer again.

I picked up Billings's reports. I tore out the pages detailing my mother's arrest and stuffed them into one of the pockets of my bag. There had to be a logical explanation for it. I had to decide who else to let in about it. Not Matty or Vangie. I wasn't even sure I wanted to tell Joe. For now, I had to sit with it by myself.

When I got back home, I found Matty sleeping on my couch with Marbury tucked under his arm. Madison slept on the floor in front of them, keeping guard. She gave me a tail wag and a hand lick as I moved past them up the stairs. I tucked the pages from Billings's report about my parents under my mattress right next to where I kept my .38. There it would stay until I could figure out a way to solve that particular mystery. If I had the courage to try.

Chapter 23

TODD MENZER MET me at the end of his driveway, his expression grim.

"You mind walking up with me the rest of the way?" he asked. I found him a bit bleary-eyed with at least two days' worth of rough stubble framing his face.

"Not at all," I said. "Is everything okay?"

"She watched the news the day of Runyon's funeral," Todd said. "My ma. One of them had a clip from Heather's funeral too. Runyon had been there that day. He stood next to my mom at the gravesite. He was with us the whole way. For a while, she treated him like family. I don't know. When she saw the clip, it confused her. It was like watching Heather's funeral all over again. Took me a day to talk her down and get her to realize that was all in the past. Her doctor prescribed some sedatives and that's keeping her calm. I just don't want to risk her seeing a strange car coming up the drive. She relives that day when they came and told us they'd found Heather. I just don't know what's going to set her off."

"I can't imagine. Oh, Todd, I'm so sorry. I won't stay

long. We can even talk out here if you want. I just have a couple of questions," I said, slipping my bag from my shoulder. I brought one page of Brian Billings's notes. I wasn't even sure what Todd could tell me about them, but I felt a strong hunch he held an answer.

"Nah," Todd said. "It's too damn hot. I've been sweating my ass off at the plant. Let's just go in through the back. Mom's in the front of the house watching her soap operas. Sorry if it's morbid, but the quietest place to talk is Heather's room. Mom won't come back there."

I opened my mouth to protest but Todd was already walking into the house. I had to practically sprint to catch up with him.

He led me through the kitchen and down the long hallway. I caught a glimpse of Mrs. Menzer sitting in her floral-print rocking chair as the television blared. She was a round woman with frizzy gray hair. She wore a pink housecoat and had plump, shiny bare legs. Her face was puffy and deeply creased, but I could see a bit of the pretty woman she had once been. It was in the glint of her eyes as she smiled at the TV. It struck me for a moment how much she looked like her daughter. Had she lived, Heather Menzer would be something like forty-four years old. Older than me. Maybe even a grandmother by now.

"Come on," Todd whispered. "Before a commercial comes on."

I walked into Heather's bedroom, once again feeling like an intruder or memory thief. I brought Heather's diary back with me. I had made several copies of it and wanted to put it back in her desk where it belonged.

"So Runyon," Todd started. "The guys down at the plant say he shot himself in front of you when you started asking about Heather."

"More or less," I said. "The cops aren't quite sure the cause and effect. I guess he was terminal with lung cancer."

"Bullshit," Todd said. "Eric gave me that same song and dance too. He knew something. He was hiding something. You know, I thought the same thing back then too."

"About Runyon? What do you mean?"

"I don't know. It was just a feeling. I know you've probably gotten sick of me saying that. But Runyon was too familiar. He acted like he was part of this family. Ma latched on to him right away. She once said he was like the son she never had. I was standing right there. It's one of the things that drove a wedge between her and Dad."

"You think Runyon wasn't telling you everything?" I asked.

"I don't know. At the time, I wanted him to live and breathe Heather's murder. I wanted to make sure he did everything he could. Looking back, I just wonder if maybe he got too close to it. Or all the atta-boys he got for solving it went to his head. That's kind of when he and my mother had a falling out. It started being more about him wanting her for photo ops than remembering Heather. You know he tried to angle his way into upper command over Heather?"

"No," I said. "I didn't know that."

I sat on the bed beside Todd. My eyes went to the various awards Heather had on a shelf above her bed. 4-H. She raised chickens. Softball. Soccer. Later, she played for her school's first ever lacrosse team. They made it to states.

"I'll cut right to it, Todd," I said. "I came across an incident that happened a few nights before Heather went missing. I wanted to get your thoughts on it. Do you remember her talking about it?"

I handed him the one-page incident report in Billings's hand. He had detailed the car accident and he and Pruitt's brief interview with Heather at the scene.

I waited and watched as Todd's eyes flicked over the words. I left the bed and went to Heather's closet. It still struck me how neatly she kept her things.

"She did this a few times," Todd said after he finished. "I mean, even before she was an E.M.T. Once, we were riding bikes and she found some homeless guy on the side of the road. A drunk. He was having a seizure or something and Heather got to him. This was before cell phones and all. She rolled him to his side and stayed with him while she had me ride back into town and call an ambulance."

"But this truck accident on the 29th. Do you remember her talking about it? There was no reference to it in her diary."

Todd picked up the diary and leafed through it. He came to the month of July. He turned the pages back and forth.

"I guess she didn't," he said. "That's weird she didn't write about it. You think that means something?"

"Not necessarily." I wanted to keep some of my suspicions to myself for the same reason I was protecting Tori. The bigger conversation I needed to have was with Mark Pruitt. There was no testimony from him either about encountering Heather Menzer before she went missing.

"I'm still trying to figure out who this friend Em of hers was," I said. "I'd like to talk to her if that's still possible."

"Yeah, I don't know," he said. "You gotta remember. I was fifteen when she passed. She was almost five years older. I didn't know all of her friends. At the time, she was pretty much my bossy, bitchy older sister. We didn't get the chance to be close as adults."

"I know," I said. "I'm sorry."

I turned back to the closet. My heart clenched as my fingers landed on a blue satin dress with puffy sleeves.

"From her senior prom," Todd said. He pulled one of the pictures off her corkboard. Sure enough, a smiling

Heather stood in the arms of a tall, skinny boy wearing a tux with matching cummerbund.

I let the dress swing back into place.

"Mom hated that one cuz it was off her shoulder. She said it was too cha cha. Whatever that means. Now you see what these girls wear with their bellies showing. If I had a daughter, she'd be wearing a potato sack."

"They grow up on you," I smiled, thinking of Vangie. I was gone by the time she went to her senior prom but remembered Joe calling me, furious about what she planned to wear.

I pulled the next shirt out. My heart tripped a little. It was a Mickey's Bar & Grill shirt just like the one she wore the night she died. This one was clean and pressed. It was a strange juxtaposition to the photograph I now kept on the wall of its torn, blood-stained twin.

I ran my fingers down the stiff collar. "Starch," I said. "She actually used starch to iron her things?"

Todd laughed. "Yeah. She did it for my stuff too. I hated it."

The tag had popped up. I smoothed it down. For a moment, I forgot to breathe.

"Todd?" I asked. "Do you mind if I borrow this for a while?"

"What, her work shirt?"

"Yeah. I'll get it back to you."

Todd shrugged. "Hell, I don't care if you keep it at this point. I mean, what does it matter?"

"I guess it doesn't," I said.

"When Ma is a little more with it, I'll try and ask her about this accident on the Wisner. She might remember. She lives in that summer more than I do. Even more so lately."

"Thanks," I said. "I really appreciate it."

"Let me get you a bag for that," he said. "Just in case

Mom sees. She won't notice it's gone, but she'll notice you walking out with it if she catches us in the hall."

Todd reached further into the closet and pulled a plastic garment bag off a different dress, the kind you get when clothes come back from the cleaners. He wrapped it over the hanger and folded it over. I tucked it into my messenger bag.

It was nothing. Probably. But I knew my next stop would be Mickey's Bar & Grill.

Chapter 24

MICKEY'S BAR hadn't really changed an inch since it opened in the mid-fifties. Sure, there were big-screen TVs in the back room now. Mickey Jr. had finally installed point of sale computers behind the bar, but the menu and decor hadn't changed one bit.

Mickey Cox Sr. opened the place with the money he got from the G.I. Bill after serving in the Korean War. He then worked every day behind that bar until he finally dropped dead behind it one Fourth of July in 2009. Mickey Jr. and his brother Bo thought about selling, but the town wouldn't let them. Now they worked mostly in the office and left day-to-day management to their cousin, and main bartender, Scotty Teague.

"Do you ever sleep?" I asked Scotty as I walked up to the U-shaped bar. I swear, no matter what time of day I came here, Scotty was always back there. He gave me a wave with one hand while he poured a draft beer with the other. It was just past eight in the evening. A slow time after the dinner rush and before the second shifters got off work and filled every bar stool.

"Hey, Cass," he said. "You haven't been out here much."

"Busy summer," I said.

Scotty gave me a nod. "I heard." His eyes flicked to the left. I followed them. At the copper-top table in the corner, I recognized a group of Delphi's finest. Eric wasn't among them and they hadn't seen me yet. Hopefully, I could get in and out before one of them noticed.

"Is Mickey in the office?" I asked. "I called earlier this afternoon."

"Yep," Scotty said, sliding the frosted beer mug down the bar to one of the patrons. "He just went down to change out the mix on the Coke. Give him five and head on back."

"How long have you been working here now?" I asked.

Scotty considered the question. "Since I was twenty-one," he said. "Half my life."

Twenty-one years. So he wasn't working the summer Heather Menzer did. One of the waitresses came up to the bar beside me and put down a cocktail napkin. Just like Jeanie noticed, the girls here were still wearing the same polo-style shirts and jean shorts like they'd done in the mid-nineties. Only the knit looked different. I had the one of Heather's I'd taken from Todd's in my purse. It was a thicker cotton. Now they looked a bit thinner and probably much more comfortable.

"Do you want a table?" she asked. She was bright and pretty with a gap-toothed smile. The girl looked familiar. She was likely the daughter or maybe little sister of someone I went to high school with.

"I'm fine," I said. "I might just order a drink. Thank you though."

The waitress smiled back and went to her next table.

"He's up," Scotty said, gesturing toward the back of the room. Sure enough, Mickey Cox Jr. rounded the corner and gave me a wave as he headed down the back hallway.

"You want something to take back there?" Scotty asked.

"I'm good for now," I said.

I thanked him again and weaved through the crowd, taking the long way so I wouldn't walk right by the table of cops in the corner.

Mickey kept the office door open. I passed by the break-room and said hello to another waitress as she punched in and tied an apron around her waist.

This one I recognized as Lindsey Clausson. She gave me a nervous glance and I couldn't blame her. I had occasion to question her on a different murder case last year.

I stepped into Mickey Jr.'s office. It was dark and dingy with wood paneling, a cluttered desk, and pictures of Red Wings players.

"Hey, Cass," Mickey said as he rifled through the piles of paperwork on the desk. I hoped he had what I'd asked him for.

Mickey Cox Jr. was as wide as he was tall. He looked so much like his father, some of the older bar patrons didn't realize Mickey Sr. had died. Mickey wore thick, coke-bottle glasses perched on the end of his nose. He had beefy fingers that looked more like Play-Doh than filled with actual muscle and bone. His cheeks were bright red and I hoped he had a good cardiologist. The climb from downstairs had winded him.

"Good to see ya, Cass," he said. "What can I do you for?"

"Thanks for seeing me. As usual, what I'm here about won't make me the most popular attorney in town."

Mickey raised an unkempt brow. "Are there any popular attorneys in Delphi? I can't stand mine, come to think of it. Arrogant dipshit."

I laughed. "Well, it's real talent if you can pull off both."

"So it's true," Mickey said. "You're poking the bear on the Heather Menzer deal?"

"I am," I said. I waited for a beat to gauge Mickey's reaction. Would he get in my way? But Mickey just shrugged and leaned back in his leather chair.

"Do you remember her?" I asked.

"She was working here," Mickey said. "Everybody knows that. Pops was so broken up about what happened. Heather had worked for us for two summers. Good kid. Smart. Ma liked her too."

Mickey's mother, Irene Cox, had just passed away a couple of months ago.

"They gave her some money," Mickey said. "Not many people know this cuz Pops didn't want to brag and he also didn't want girls coming through this place expecting it. But he used to give some of the waitresses help. College money. Five hundred here or there."

"That's really sweet," I said.

"I've tried to do the same but my accountant wants me to set it up official. Some kind of scholarship fund. I'm working on that."

"That's really great, Mickey. I appreciate you taking time out of your schedule for this. I'm trying to figure out everyone Heather would have worked with that summer and I guess the summer before. Were you able to find those records I called you about?"

Mickey leaned back and pulled a file under a bigger stack of files. It was coffee-stained and dog-eared.

"Supposed to get all this crap on the computer," he said. "Ma up until she passed was working on that. Can you believe it? Eighty-five and she was teaching herself how to scan documents and save 'em on a hard drive."

"That's amazing. They broke the mold after her, didn't they?"

Mickey had a faraway look. He smiled and snapped back to the present. He handed me the worn file.

"These were easier to find than I figured. Ma kept them separated from the others. It's 'cause you weren't the first person who ever asked for those. I had to dig for the ones from the year before but the year Heather worked here, the cops were already all over them. Ma actually testified in the trial."

"Right," I said. "I've seen the transcripts. She's how they established when Heather was last seen alive. She clocked out after eleven. Was that unusual, do you know? I mean, the bar has always closed at two."

"Nah," he said. "I looked. The Menzer girl was under twenty-one. So she couldn't bartend. Pops would always send the younger girls home first and keep the older ones on to close. We thin out after eleven so he'd cut down on payroll. The older waitresses could do double duty behind the bar. The younger ones couldn't. I still do it that way."

"Makes sense," I said. I flipped open the file. It contained old, cardboard time cards. A red sticky note taped to one in particular drew my eye. It was a placeholder. The other cards were all originals but this one was a photocopy. It was Heather's card from the night she went missing. The original was part of the police file I'd seen in the Safety Building basement a few weeks ago with Eric.

"We had six girls on staff that summer," Mickey said. "That's actually pretty light. We're lucky though. We don't get turnover like some other bars and restaurants do."

Mickey had made a list of all the girls working as waitresses That Awful Summer. I flipped to the back of the file.

"You never worked here though?" he asked.

"I did not," I said. "It was uh ... not the best place for me to be. This was my dad's hangout back in the day."

"Right," Mickey said. "I suppose that woulda been

tough. Joe Sr. was a mean-ass drunk. I hope you don't mind me saying that. I betcha my pops had him thrown outta here a hundred times over the years. He banned him once or twice but he could never stick to it."

"That sounds about right. My father was a charmer when he wanted to be."

"You know whatever happened to him?"

I leafed through the employment records on each of the girls. Hopefully, Mickey wouldn't mind letting me make copies of all of this before I left.

"My father's been AWOL for a few years," I said. "Last I heard he maybe made his way down to Florida with some woman or another. Like I said, he is a charmer when he wants to be. I honestly haven't talked to him in maybe six or seven years."

"Huh," Mickey said. "That's a shame. I'd give just about anything to sit and have one more beer with my pops."

I smiled. "Apples and oranges, Mickey."

He grew silent, regarding me for a moment. "Maybe. Maybe not."

I looked again at the documents in front of me. I skimmed them once and found something puzzling. I checked again. "I only see five W-2s going out. You listed six girls as working here that summer."

Mickey leaned forward and looked at the file upside down. "At the time they only would have been getting three bucks an hour or whatever minimum wage was for tipped employees. They'd need to work pretty much a full summer to meet the threshold for a W-2. We probably let one of them go or she quit. Probably that first thing. Nobody ever quits unless it's at the end of the summer and they leave for school. They make too much damn money."

There was a knock on the office door. Scotty stood there.

"Hey," he said. "Sorry to interrupt. That new girl, Lacey, she needs a shirt."

Mickey swiveled in his chair and leaned over. He picked up a wrapped plastic bag containing a red Mickey's Bar shirt.

"She's a small?" he asked.

"Yeah," Scotty answered.

Mickey took a sharpie from a mug on his desk and wrote an "L" on the tag, then handed the shirt to Scotty. Scotty grinned and excused himself.

On a hunch, I pulled Heather's shirt out of my bag.

"Classic style," I said, waving the shirt.

"That Heather's?" he asked, his eyes growing wide.

"It is," I answered.

"Man," he said. "It looks almost brand new. These ones we get now, made in some Southeast Asian sweatshop or somewhere. That was Bo's idea to save money. I told him it's not saving him if I have to replace the things after the girls wash them a dozen times or so."

He reached forward and felt the hem of Heather's shirt. "You mind?"

I handed the thing to him. Mickey looked at the label on the inside of the shirt.

"See that," he said. "Made in the U.S.A. Man. I wish that company was still in business."

He ran his finger over the collar tag. "Ha. That's Ma's writing. She always made her capital Hs with that middle line slanted like that. And she wrote in all caps all the time. It's the little things like that you forget. She was a note writer. I'm still finding sticky notes with instructions from her every-where. Don't tell Bo, but it's saved my ass more than once. I swear, every damn thing I do around here was the way she taught me. I should have appreciated her more when she was here."

"Isn't that always the way?" I said. "Look, I really appreciate all of this. And you don't mind if make copies?"

"Go ahead," he said. "I gotta go take some paperwork to the new girl to sign. Help yourself to the copier. Just come out into the bar when you're done."

"Thank you, Mickey. For all of this."

Mickey heaved himself out of his chair, scooted around his desk, and left me to his copy machine.

It took me about ten minutes to make all the copies I needed. I put the old file on Mickey's chair where he would find it and showed myself out of his office.

The crowd was loosening up a bit as Scotty poured the drinks. I went the long way around the bar again, hoping to make a quiet exit.

I wasn't that lucky this time.

Two steps before the door, I came face to face with Mark Pruitt and two other off-duty cops.

I squared my shoulder and adjusted my bag. "Detective Pruitt," I said. "Your face is healing nicely."

I suppose I should have been more diplomatic. It's just I tend not to feel charitable to men who call me a gash.

"The hell you doing here?" he asked.

"I live here," I said.

"No," he said. "You're working. I know the look."

"Great. You're not. So I'll just let you get back to your night off."

He was drunk. His eyes were slightly unfocused as he looked me up and down.

"You murdered that man," he said.

"I what? And who? Runyon?"

"Mark." One of Pruitt's companions put a hand on his arm and tried to pull him away.

"I know you're the one behind it. You're leading Wray around by the sac."

"All right," I said. "That's about all I need to hear. I don't have anything to say to you tonight, Pruitt. You need to go home and sleep it off."

I turned back to the bar. "Scotty? You might want to cut this one off."

Scotty eyed me and saved a stony glare for Pruitt. He made a subtle gesture with his chin. Two of the bouncers edged closer.

"I'll end you, you got me?"

"And that's the second time you've threatened me in front of witnesses, Pruitt. Not too smart."

"Pruitt, enough, let's just go back to the table." Pruitt might not be getting it, but his two companions were. They were younger guys. Mid-twenties. I wouldn't be surprised if Pruitt was supervising them at work. Terrific.

"Scumbag defense lawyer bottom feeder," he said. "You think a word or two from me can't do you damage? You'll be lucky to still get court appointments."

"Go sit down," I said, getting in his face. It was like I could feel my Leary DNA flaring.

"You think that scumbag Bridges is innocent? I know you. I know your type. You'll take some bullshit and twist it. You'll throw Runyon under the bus. Well, I won't let it happen. You feel me?"

"Oh, I feel you," I said.

"Will you just go?" Pruitt's companion said. "He's drunk. We'll handle it."

"You learning from him?" I asked. "Is that the deal? How long have you been on? Two years? Five? Just make detective? Do yourself a favor and use your own heads."

"Fuck you!" Pruitt said. He swayed backward. I think he might have been trying to lunge at me. I held my ground. Pruitt's two companions grabbed him. The bouncers got closer.

"We got it!" one of Pruitt's friends said. The two of them moved as a unit and pulled Pruitt away from me. He was still swearing as they got him back to the copper-top table.

"You okay?" Scotty said. He'd come out from behind the bar.

"I'm okay," I said.

"Sorry about that." Scotty looked back at Pruitt's table.

"I can take care of myself," I said.

"Yeah," Scotty said. "I know. It's just ... that guy. He's trouble. Just watch out for him. And maybe don't be here when he is."

"Free country, Scotty," I said. "Make sure you tell him not to be here when I am."

Scotty nodded.

As I went for the exit, I knew I had to figure out a way to get Mark Pruitt under a subpoena. He knew something he wasn't telling me. I felt it in my bones.

Chapter 25

THREE DAYS LATER, the temperature reached the highest ever recorded in Michigan. That mid-nineties summer was no longer the most awful. This one was worse.

I got to the office before dawn. Miranda, of course, was already there. She wasn't alone. I found her at the back door trying to get rid of a man I recognized as a *Detroit Free Press* reporter. His name was Ned Valente and he worked their crime beat.

"We don't comment on existing cases or clients," Miranda said.

"So you can at least confirm you have an existing case and client in Sean Allen Bridges."

"No comment," I said, brushing past him. I got between Miranda and Valente.

"Look," he said. "I'm posting my story online as soon as I get back to my car. Unless you have something to add."

"How do I know what to add if I haven't seen the story?" I asked.

"You've ruffled more than a few feathers," he said. "The implication is former Detective Rick Runyon may have been involved in a cover-up on the Heather Menzer murder. That's big news. It's stirring up a lot of emotions around town."

"You can post what you want," I said. "I really have no comment."

I put a hand on Miranda's back and turned mine on Ned Valente. I hoped like hell he left the parking lot before Jeanie showed up. She was liable to try and run him over.

I didn't fault the guy. He was trying to do his job just like I was. The irony was, Mark Pruitt was making that more difficult for everyone. He was so concerned about Runyon's posthumous reputation but every time he made a scene, he got people speculating even more.

"Tori's not coming in today," Miranda said. "She's finagled a visit with her dad."

"I'm glad he's feeling up to it. That's good news. I wish I had more to give him."

I carried the stack of copies of Mickey's employment records. It took me all of yesterday and the day before to make sense of them. I hoped to finish cross-referencing them with the police interviews. So far, I'd reached a big, giant dead-end.

I had Heather's work shirt neatly folded on top of the pile. Thankfully, Valente hadn't seen it or if he did, he didn't know what he was looking at.

"I moved most of your stuff down here," Miranda said. "The window units aren't cutting it upstairs. The only hope any of us have of not sweating through our clothes today is if we stay on the ground floor and pray."

"I get that," I said. We walked into a wall of heat as it was. The building was old. I had to upgrade the electrical before I could do something about the lack of central air.

True to her word, Miranda had basically recreated everything from the conference room down in Jeanie's office.

"You should have let someone help you with this," I said. She had it all set up except for the whiteboards.

"Tori helped me with it last night before she left."

"Good," I said. "I'm going to need to see the dailies from Billings and Pruitt again." I stood with my hands on my hips, surveying the stacks of paper and files.

Miranda weaved through them and picked up two piles. She handed them to me with an unceremonious thud.

"Use Jeanie's desk," she said. "She's not coming in until after lunch. She's got a custody hearing at ten. Your schedule is clear for the day. Castor's office called to postpone your settlement conference on the Becker case. I'm no psychic, but I have a feeling they're going to make another offer by the end of the week."

"Good," I said. I felt a little guilty. The Bridges case had taken up almost all of my energy lately.

Miranda rattled off a few other cases of mine she'd moved around and put out fires for. I forgot what I paid her. I had to figure out a way to double it.

I spent the morning checking off names and re-reading witness statements. Between Runyon's footwork and Bridges's original lawyer, I could find no obvious gaps in the narrative. The missing witness statement was still firmly missing.

I almost didn't hear the door open. I wouldn't have even looked up if my stomach hadn't growled at precisely the same moment.

Eric Wray stood in the hallway. Miranda cleared her throat. "You got a minute for an old friend?"

I put my pen down and folded my hands. "You sure this is wise for your career?" I asked.

Eric thanked Miranda and stepped inside. She quietly closed the door.

"Just a professional courtesy," he said. "I wanted to tell

you in person that the investigation into Runyon's death is officially closed."

I pushed my chair back. "Am I going to like the *official* findings?"

"Suicide," he said.

"Obviously. That's not all of it though, I suspect. Let me guess, you're really here to tell me the department has decided not to reopen the Menzer murder case in light of recent events."

Eric dropped his head. He hadn't moved away from the doorway.

"Was this your call?" I asked.

He raised his eyes and met mine.

"No," I said. "Don't answer that. I'm not sure I want to know."

"Cass ..."

I meant to leave it there. Eric and I truly were at crossed purposes. I'm not sure what I had to gain recovering this ground. Only, with each breath I took, my anger rose.

I came out from behind the desk. Eric moved deeper into the room. We met in front of Jeanie's coffee table. The worst of Heather Menzer's crime scene photos were spread out on top of it.

"Say it," I said. "I want to hear it."

"It's not enough, okay?" he yelled. He curled his fists at his sides. Tearing a hand through his hair, he walked past me and plopped down on Jeanie's leather couch. His eyes fell to the crime scene photos.

"It's not enough," he said more quietly. "I wish to hell I could tell you something different. I wish I could tell that to Todd. But all this? It can't erase the truth. Your client lied to Runyon. Her blood was in his damn car. I know you had high hopes for that footlocker. There was nothing there,

Cass. Vacation pictures. His dead wife's wedding ring. That was all. "

The air went out of the room. The lights flickered, grew brighter, then dimmed. There was a great whooshing sound and then silence as the power went out.

"Great," he said. "Probably overloaded the grid with all the air conditioners on blast."

It had only been three seconds and I could already feel the heat rising.

"Then it's going to be a busy day for you. Don't let me keep you."

He looked up at me. "Are we okay?"

I looked at him. Really looked at him. Eric had the bright-blue eyes that stood in contrast to his dark brows. The lines had deepened around his eyes. He probably hadn't slept. I couldn't help that a part of me felt guilty about that. He'd been through a lot in the last year and much of it was the direct result of things I'd done.

"Eric," I said coming around to sit beside him. "I don't know what you want me to say."

"I want you to stop looking at me like that. I'm trying to do my job."

"And I'm trying to do mine. You cannot sit there and tell me every instinct you have wasn't tripped by what happened with Runyon. Something doesn't add up. You're trying to do your job but you're also trying to be a friend to Todd Menzer. I know this case haunts you. You said yourself it's the reason you became a cop in the first place."

"So what's your working theory then?" he asked. "Dammit, Cass, if you have something. Anything. Give it to me. I swear to God I'll turn over every rock I have to."

"You sure about that?" I said. "I know it wasn't your call not to reopen the case. It came from the chief or someone close to him. I know the department's gotten a black eye in the last year and a half on some high-profile cases. And I know me being involved in this one probably has everyone's radar blipping on top of that."

"You're not wrong."

"I ran into Pruitt at Mickey's the other night. It didn't go well."

Eric let out a breath that made his nostrils flare. "You really are a magnet for trouble. What happened?"

"What do you think?"

Eric stiffened. "Did he threaten you again?" His voice went dark and toneless. He clenched his fist so hard his knuckles turned white.

"What kind of cop is he?" I asked. "I mean, before all of this. Eric, his actions ... his defense of Runyon. It just seems out of proportion to the situation, somehow."

"Don't cross-examine me," he said. "Tell me what you're thinking. Straight out."

"You're the detective," I said. "What's that old saying about how the simplest explanation is usually the right one? If I was getting close to something, if Rick Runyon was scared, it's because he didn't want to stick around to answer for this."

Eric shook his head. "I knew Rick. I'm telling you. He was a good man."

"And I've known other good men who do dark things when pushed to it."

Eric's eyes flashed. Once upon a time, he'd been pushed. I was the only other soul on the planet who knew how far.

"You think this was him?"

He picked up one of the crime scene photos. It was a blow-up of Heather lying on her stomach in the mud. Her head was turned to the side, her mouth gaped open as if she'd died mid-scream. One of her arms was crooked over

her head. Twigs and wet leaves stuck to it. There was
bruising on her forearm. A red welt around her wrist.

Eric held the picture up. He turned it, ran his fingers over
it. My eyes zeroed in on her wrist. My heart went still. I tilted
my head to the side.

Eric waved the picture. "He made a mistake. That's as
best I can figure. I don't even know what it was. I can't
find it."

"Eric," I said, my voice dropping low.

"Dozens, hundreds of killers are behind bars because of
this man. Whatever he did. Whatever he thought he messed
up ..."

"Eric!" I said, slowly rising to my feet.

He turned on me. "Are you listening to me?"

I lifted my hand. "Let me see that."

Eric's eyes narrowed. He looked at the picture then back
at me.

My hand was shaking when he placed the picture in it. I
went to Jeanie's desk and shoved her stapler, candy dish, and
some loose paperclips out of the way. The light was best
here. A ray of sun fell across the desk, illuminating the
airborne dust like glitter.

I'd missed it before. I hadn't been looking for it. This
picture just blended in with so many others and all the
exhibits from the file. But now, the red-and-blue mark
around Heather Menzer's wrist caught my attention. I'd seen
that same mark before.

I turned to Eric. I took two strides toward him and slid
my hand across his waist. His breath caught. His eyes darted
over my face.

"Cass?"

I found what I was looking for. Folded in his jacket
pocket, I felt the hard, circular outline. Eric put his hands up
as I slowly pulled his handcuffs out.

I went back to the picture. I laid my arm beside it, mimicking the position of Heather's crooked arm. Blown up like it was, her arm was nearly the same size as mine.

I loosened the handcuffs and turned one on its side so the hard edge hit the desk. I placed it over the marks on Heather's wrist in the photo.

Eric was at my shoulder. I felt him go rigid beside me. "Cass …"

"Sean had marks like that on his wrists when I saw him the other day," I said. "They cuffed him to his hospital bed. The guard got angry when I asked if he'd loosen them."

"Cass, you can't," Eric started.

I turned to him, my mind racing. "Her driver's license wasn't in her wallet, Eric. Todd's been asking himself for twenty-four years why the hell she would have gotten out of that car in the middle of the night. Her *driver's license*. It wasn't in her wallet because she took it out. She was *asked* to take it out!"

Eric took his handcuffs back from me. He looked at the things as if they'd gone radioactive. He looked down at the crime scene photo. He placed the cuffs over the image of Heather's wound.

Now that we'd both seen it side by side, there was no denying the impression in Heather's flesh and the cuffs made a perfect match.

Chapter 26

"WELL, SHIT ON A STICK," Jeanie said. She stood in her office almost exactly where Eric had been when I slapped his cuffs beside the crime scene photo.

He stayed speechless, all color draining from his face. I could see the conflict swirling inside him like a tornado. There was still an innocent dead girl in the ground. And now, I knew to the marrow of my bones, an innocent man rotted behind bars because of it.

"What's Wray going to do with this?" Jeanie asked.

"They'll crucify him. He knows it."

"You think it was Runyon himself who did this?" she asked.

"No," I said. "Ugh. I don't know. He has an alibi for the night Heather disappeared. He was in Alabama for some FBI task force training. I already looked into it. He didn't get back to town for three days after."

"A cop." Tori sat on the couch looking just as white as Eric had. He left hours ago with a promise to do something. Only I worried his hands were tied. No matter what else happened, there was still strong physical evidence linking her father to the crime.

"A cop or someone posing as a cop," Jeanie said.

"I don't think it was a poser," I said. "I mean, I would have, except for Runyon. He took himself out because he was afraid of what I might find. I know it. If it wasn't him, he was trying to protect somebody close to him."

"Who though?" Tori asked. "They framed him, didn't they? That's how that blood got in Dad's car."

"Maybe," I said. I didn't want to go too far down that path. "But if they did, it would have had to involve more people than just Rick Runyon. He would have been rarely, if ever, alone with Heather's body or your father's car."

"Plus, how the hell would he have had access to strands of Bridges's hair? And you saw the report. Some of those strands were actually embedded in the fibers of her shirt."

"Close intimate contact," Tori said. "I know the hair transfer expert's testimony by heart."

"And it bothers me that Pruitt, Billings, and Runyon made no mention of the encounter Pruitt and Billings had with Heather at this traffic accident a few nights before."

"You think it was one of them?" Tori asked.

"Pruitt and Billings? I only know they're the first two I'd like to try and rule out."

Tori excused herself. A few minutes later, she came back holding the file I'd given her with Mark Pruitt's daily reports the summer of Heather's murder.

"July 9th, Pruitt was on duty," Tori said, flipping to the detailed index she made. "He worked recall. A double shift. That was the weekend of the Polish Festival downtown. He was on until six a.m."

"Heather punches out of work at 11:23. Where's Pruitt then? Do we have that?"

Tori thumbed through the pages. "Traffic stop on

Milburn Road. D.U.I. arrest. That's at 10:08. He clocks his next thing at 12:47. Domestic disturbance at 2152 Clancy."

"So he's got an hour and a half window," Jeanie said.

"But Clancy and Milburn are on the same side of town. Heather's car was found at just about the dead opposite end of town."

"Difficult," I said. "Not impossible. And Pruitt's working alone that night?"

"Uh ... he called for backup on the Clancy deal. But other than that, yes. He was assigned to afternoons so he normally would get off at ten. So he's picking up the night shift during the time Heather's last seen. Billings is off duty."

"What are you thinking?" Jeanie asked.

I rolled a pencil in my hand. "I'm thinking I want to establish where the hell Billings was that night as well. And I want to make Mark Pruitt sit down for an interview."

Jeanie leaned over and grabbed a pink Post-it Note. She wrote down a number and handed it to me.

"Call Tom Bryce," she said. "He's another detective with Delphi. Works in internal affairs. Tori, do another F.O.I.A. request on all three of them. Billings, Runyon, Pruitt. Let's have a look at whether any of them got themselves in any departmental trouble over the years."

"Good thinking," I said, reaching over to take the note from her. Tori was already on her feet and running back to her office.

Chapter 27

Tom Bryce agreed to meet with me two days later at a coffee shop in Tecumseh. He was a hell of a lot younger than I would have figured. Maybe my age, mid-thirties with thick brown hair that he brushed back. He wore an impeccably tailored navy-blue suit with a yellow tie.

"I.A.?" I asked. "At your age? You must not be looking to make too many friends in the department."

Bryce laughed. "I'd say I'm looking to make about as many friends as you are doing what you do."

"Fair enough."

Bryce reached into a worn leather briefcase and pulled out three red file folders. He slid them across the table to me as we gave the barista our orders. He went with black coffee. I went with a caramel latte.

I did a quick scan of the files. Runyon's was the thinnest. That surprised me and I said so.

"You didn't know Rick," Bryce said. "I mean ... other than ..."

"Other than the day we met, no," I said.

"Good cop. Truly. The thing is, if you're in this long

enough, eventually you're gonna have a complaint filed against you. It comes with the territory."

"Wow," I said. "I don't suppose there are too many regular cops who take that kind of view of your department."

Bryce blew over his mug before he took a sip. "Oh, I'm the Antichrist. I get that. Runyon though. He was about as clean as they come. He got named in a civil rights claim twenty or so years ago. Nothing came of it. It's all in his file."

"What about Billings and Pruitt?" I asked, flipping open the files.

"Pruitt's a hardass. You'll understand I can't comment on open files."

I flipped to the back of Pruitt's file. Sure enough, he was in the middle of an investigation over the events at Rick Runyon's funeral.

"You were actually on my list of people to interview," Bryce said.

"Eric Wray's being investigated too, isn't he?" I said.

Bryce took another sip of coffee. "You filed requests for these three, not Wray."

It was as close to an affirmation as he'd give me.

"You wanna tell me what went on out there?" Bryce asked.

"It was nothing," I said. I had no love for Mark Pruitt, but I hated having any part of trouble for Eric. "It was an emotional day."

"Did Pruitt threaten you?"

"Like I said, rough day for all of us. Despite what you may have heard, I never had it out for Rick Runyon either. And unless I'm under a subpoena, I'd rather be kept out of whatever you have going on."

Bryce narrowed his eyes.

"Tell me about Brian Billings," I said.

"Way before my time," he answered. "I brought you what we have. Billings only worked for Delphi for just shy of three years."

"Pretty thick file for such a short time," I said. From my cursory review, I saw that he'd had two brutality claims filed against him. One was dismissed. The second had a notation of a satisfactory disposition.

"What does that mean?" I asked, flipping the document over so Bryce could see what I referenced.

"Case was settled to my office and the union's satisfaction."

"He was fired over it," I said. "You're telling me Brian Billings was forced out?"

"I'm not telling you that at all. I'm telling you the matter was resolved."

I sat back in my chair. "He was hired in Chelsea after he left Delphi. You were never contacted by them?"

"Not me personally. If our office had any other communication with an outside agency, it would have been noted."

"So Brian Billings quits or gets fired during an open misconduct investigation two years after Heather Menzer's murder. And you can't tell me anything more specific than that?"

I scanned the documents as quickly as I could. In both misconduct cases, Billings had been accused of using excessive force with the alleged perpetrator of a domestic violence call. In the more recent incident, the victim's nose had been broken when Billings pushed him into a wall.

The file included pictures of the complaining witness. I couldn't help it, I kind of sided with Billings. He'd been in the middle of arresting this guy for shoving his pregnant wife down a flight of stairs.

Pruitt's file, however, made my pulse trip. He'd had a personal protection order filed against him by an ex-wife.

There were stalking allegations. She claimed he tied her up and threatened to shoot her when she broke things off. It chilled me to the bone. I made a note to have Jeanie get this woman on the phone by the end of the day.

"Thank you for this," I said. "I really appreciate it."

"Just doing my job," Bryce said. He threw a twenty on the table, waving off my offer to pay. "Just let me know if there's anything else I can do for you."

Against my better judgment, I looked up at him as he rose and said something I hoped wouldn't do more damage than good.

"As good a cop you think Rick Runyon was? Eric Wray's even better. If you're looking for me or anyone else to vouch for his character, consider this a full-throated endorsement of the man."

Bryce gave me a lop-sided smile. "It was good meeting you, Cass." He offered me his hand to shake.

As he walked out, I flipped open Mark Pruitt's file once more. My stomach churned as I saw the grainy reprints of his ex-wife's bruised face.

Chapter 28

CHELSEA, Michigan is a quaint little town just a little northwest of Ann Arbor. A little more upscale than Delphi, it has
a tucked-away jewel in the Purple Rose Theatre. Like
Delphi, nothing bad ever happens there. At least, it's not
supposed to. Until it does.

I expected to get asses and elbows from the Chelsea
Police. Brian Billings hadn't worked here in something like
fifteen years, but for better or worse, he was still one of
their own.

I met the records clerk in his office during the lunch hour.
Twelve fifteen and the temperature hit 103. I had everyone
from my office working from home today. The power came
back on, but the A/C blew. It would be at least a week before
I could get someone out to deal with it.

"I've heard of you," the clerk said. He was an old-timer.
His hair was salt-and-pepper gray and he wore it combed to
the side. His mustache though was still jet black.

I reached across the desk and shook his hand. "I really
appreciate you seeing me on such short notice, Officer
Daniels."

"Not much going on today," he said. "You caught me at a good time. Though I could have saved you the trip. I could have sent everything you want in a PDF."

"I'm aware of that. I was actually hoping I could ask you a few questions face to face as well," I said.

He handed me a thin envelope. I'd asked for copies of any formal complaints filed against Officer Brian Billings during his tenure with Chelsea.

"You made some waves last year," he said. "That coach down in Delphi. Serious son of a bitch, that one. I got a niece who got tangled up with him. Course, I didn't know it at the time. If I had, I can tell you right now ... I just would have needed five minutes alone with that bastard and he never would have been able to hurt another girl."

Daniels's eyes went cold and dark. I believed him. He wasn't the first person to say those exact words to me about Delphi's disgraced basketball coach.

"I'm so sorry to hear that," I said. "If your niece needs help, there are resources. The school district has actually set up a support group ..."

"She's okay," Daniels said. "Lives in London at the moment. Can you believe that? She got the hell out of Delphi and works as a photographer."

"That's impressive," I said. "You must be very proud."

"My little sister's kid. Shocked the hell out of me. Nobody gets out of that crap town of yours. No offense."

I smiled. "None taken. But you're wrong. One or two have managed to get out. And some of them even decide to come back."

I don't know why I felt so defensive. He wasn't wrong. Delphi was somewhat of a crap town. But it was *my* crap town.

"I won't waste much of your time. I was just hoping you could tell me a few things about the subject of my request.

Former officer Billings. How long was he with the department?"

"I didn't remember," Daniels said. "I looked over those records you asked for though. I was a beat cop here for most of my career. Never interested in command. You don't know how many times people have asked me why I didn't go for detective. It wasn't because I couldn't, let me tell you. I just always liked the one on one with the people here better. I threw out my back though. Two surgeries and it's still pathetic. So I took this desk job. It's not glamorous. But it's quiet."

"I'm sure," I said. Officer Daniels liked to talk about himself. If I could just get him to talk about Brian Billings.

"Did you know Brian Billings personally?"

"Oh sure. I know everybody. Told ya. I like the one on ones. He trained with an ex-partner of mine. Ed Mamet. He's dead now. Poor bastard had a heart attack the week before he was set to retire."

"That's awful," I said, keeping a friendly smile in place.

"Anyway, Billings. Know-it-all. Didn't like taking directions. Whoever the hell trained him in Delphi taught him bad habits. He was too rough. Didn't know how to de-escalate things. Hotshot."

I opened the envelope and slid the thin stack of papers out of it. There were two complaints. Both alleged police brutality. Both ended in a no cause finding.

"I wouldn't read much into those," Daniels said. "You stay a cop long enough …"

"He wasn't though," I said. "A cop. Not for long, I mean. He came here after only two years with Delphi. He was out the door here, what, four years later? So six total years as a cop. That's a drop in the bucket."

"It's not for everybody," Daniels said. "It's frustrating seeing the same people doing the same stupid things. Never learning. It eats at you. Every academy cadet you ever meet will give you the same answer when you ask them why they want to be a cop. They want to make a difference. They want to help people. You don't ever end up doing much of that."

"Sure," I said. "It's never big things. It's the little ones that make a difference."

"Yeah. But try telling that to some of these young guys. Man, they think they have all the answers."

I put the envelope in my bag. "I suppose that's the way of youth."

Daniels snorted. "You're just a kid yourself."

As Daniels talked, I skimmed the personnel file as quickly as I could. It detailed Billings's hire date, his shift assignments, his pay tier, and the two brutality complaints filed. I saw only one written reprimand relating to a high-speed chase resulting in a non-fatal bystander injury. Billings was cited for excessive speed.

Daniels read upside down. "That was for show," he said. "We were catching heat after a kid got killed two counties over. Like that had anything to do with us. Chief and the mayor just wanted to make sure everybody thinks we take that seriously. Which we do."

"Of course," I said. "It shows Billings resigning just shy of five years on. He went into the private sector after that. But I see a notation where someone in personnel with the Detroit Police Department checked his references and requested this file. They didn't hire him or he chose not to pursue it?"

Daniels shrugged. "You'd have to talk to D.P.D. about that. Probably for the best though. That kid never would have made it in a big city like Detroit. He barely made it here."

"Why do you say that? I mean, why specifically? You just

said the excessive speed issue was just for show. He was exonerated in the brutality claims. I mean, other than being a know-it-all, what were you worried about with Billings?"

Daniels looked past my shoulder. We were basically alone. It was the lunch hour in the office. There was a desk sergeant out front, but the cubicles outside Daniels's office were basically empty.

"Billings wanted to be a cop because he liked 'em on TV. That's about all I can tell you. He had bad instincts or no instincts at all. Guy burned his way through something like eight partners in four years."

I looked back at the file. His partners weren't listed, but his multiple shift changes were.

"They were moving him around a lot."

Daniels pursed his lips and nodded. "Is what I'm saying."

"Was he dangerous?"

"Like I said. The kid was a hotshot. Gung ho. Didn't like following his training. Even in a little town like this, that can get you hurt. It can get you dead."

If true, it was disturbing. But it shed no real light on whether Billings knew more about what really happened to Heather Menzer.

"But you don't know why he left," I said. "Why he chose to quit."

"Listen," Daniels said. "There's resigning, then there's resigning."

He sat back and folded his hands as if he'd just delivered the clearest statement in the world. I waited for him to elaborate. He didn't.

"Officer Daniels, help me out. What does that mean?"

"A guy can be strongly encouraged to pursue a different career path."

"Is that what happened with Brian Billings?"

Daniels flipped his palms up and shrugged. It was infuriating. The man liked the attention my questions brought him. He didn't seem inclined to be more specific. If he was, then I might stop asking.

"Well," I said. "I appreciate what candor you've been willing to give me." I buckled my messenger bag and started to go.

"Wait," he said. Just as I suspected, Daniels wasn't yet ready to give up having me as his audience.

He reached into his desk drawer and thumbed through some paperwork. He produced a business card and wrote something on the back of it. He slid it across the table.

The card had the Chelsea Police logo on one side. He'd written a phone number and the name LeAnn Morris on the back.

"Talk to LeAnn," he said. "She was one of our civilian secretaries for ages. She worked just outside this office at that desk there."

"And you think she'd know something about Billings I'd be interested in?"

"Honey," Daniels said. "They were engaged. They lived together for a while when he worked here. Let's just say it didn't end on good terms. LeAnn still lives in Chelsea. She married another cop but they got divorced."

"Thank you," I said, pocketing the card. "You've been more helpful than you know."

I shook Daniels's hand and headed out of the office. I sat in my car for a few minutes, letting the engine run so the air conditioning would kick on. Then I dialed the number on the card.

LeAnn Morris answered on the first ring. Her hello was backed with a resigned sigh and I knew Daniels had called her the second I turned my back on him. LeAnn already knew why I was calling.

"Hi, there," I said. "My name is Cass Leary and I ..."

"I know who you are," she said, confirming my suspicion. "And yes. I'll talk to you. It's about time somebody started asking the right questions."

"Thank you," I said. "Ms. Morris, I can be over …"

"Not today," she said. "I need to square a couple of things away when we talk. And not here. Not in Chelsea. There's this vegan place in downtown Ann Arbor. Me and my girlfriends like to go there for lunch sometimes. I'll be there Friday at one."

"Perfect," I said. "You can text me the address."

Then LeAnn Morris hung up on me before I could so much as thank her.

Chapter 29

THE DAY before my meeting with LeAnn Morris, Tori came in with the last bunch of records we'd requested on Billings, Pruitt, and Runyon. I wanted to widen my net and see their daily reports in the few weeks leading up to and the day Heather Menzer's body was found.

Tori sat beside me with a red pen in hand. "I want to try and find any and every encounter they might have had with your father or Heather Menzer during that time frame."

Tori was methodical; working with fevered precision she wrote down her list of names and cross-checked them all with every other data point we had. The trial witness lists, Runyon's case file on the Menzer murder, Heather's diary. When she finished with those, I'd have her start on Mickey's employment record in a day or two.

"I never realized how much crap went on in Delphi," she said. "I recognize about half these people as parents of classmates or neighbors or people I've worked with."

"Small-town life," I said. "There are no real secrets here." I checked myself. "Except maybe this big one."

"I knew my dad wasn't an angel," she said. "And I'm not

naive. He's been honest with me about how he made his money back in those days. He was a drug dealer. I know that. But I also know he wasn't a murderer. He's changed."

"I hope so," I said. "And I think he has to."

For the first time in weeks, a breeze blew in through the conference-room window, rifling the papers on the table. Tori was quick, leaning over the table to keep them from flying loose. It was short lived though. The breeze died down almost as soon as it started. The air conditioner was working again, but as we approached mid-August, I feared we wouldn't see cooler temperatures for a few more weeks.

We worked quietly together. Miranda popped in to bring us some real lemonade she'd made just last night. It was heaven going down and I slid the glass over my forehead.

"Any progress?" she asked.

"Nothing big yet," I said.

"It bothers me that Dad's original lawyer never pursued any of this as hard as we are."

"Lowell Dushane was a good lawyer once upon a time," Miranda said. "He overextended himself toward the end. It kills me to think he might have missed something that would have changed the outcome for your dad. But I do know Lowell would be the first to tell you to do whatever you had to to make it right. Even if it means throwing him under the bus."

"It would have been convenient to just think it was Lowell Dushane doing a poor job of it. It's just looking more and more like there were bigger, darker forces at play."

I hadn't yet told Tori about my planned meeting with Brian Billings's former girlfriend. Until I had something solid to grab on to, I refused to get her hopes up. It was me trying to protect her, but also what Sean wanted. We'd had a phone interview just last night. He sounded surprisingly upbeat and heartier than I'd heard him in a while. That was the good news. The bad was the why of it. I suspected he'd declined any more chemo.

Miranda refilled our lemonades, then left to answer the phones. Jeanie wasn't coming in for another hour after a motion hearing she was handling for me.

"Leary," Tori said, picking up a sheet from one of the Pruitt files.

"What?"

"No," she said turning the page toward me. The print was too small to read from across the table. "Pruitt and Billings responded to an accident involving someone you're related to, I think. June 1st. Ten a.m."

"Let me guess," I said. "O.U.I.L.?"

Tori looked back at the paper. "Er ... yeah."

"My father was no saint either. They did eventually take his license away. He got it back after a while."

Tori's eyes narrowed. "Oh. I'm sorry. But, Cass, this isn't your father, I don't think. It says Lynn Leary."

"She was in the car?" I asked.

Tori's color turned a little green like she was embarrassed. "Mmm ... no. Sorry. This is none of my business."

She put the paper down. I reached over and picked it up.

"A little early for Dad to be out of the house," I said, more to myself than Tori. When I flipped the page over and read Officer Pruitt's report, it took a moment for my brain to register what I was seeing.

Not Joseph Leary. Lynn Leary was arrested for driving under the influence that morning. It made no sense. My mother never drank. I read the notes again and again. She had to be covering for my dad. Maybe she lied and said she was driving. It was like her to have taken the hit to keep him out of trouble.

But there was no mention of my dad. He wasn't in the car. She'd hit a telephone pole on MacGregor Lane just two miles from the middle school. Joe and I would have been in class that day. It was a Tuesday. According to the report, my mother hadn't been alone.

No. This had to be a mistake. She couldn't. She wouldn't.

Before I knew what I was doing, I was on my feet.

"Cass?"

I held a hand up. "I need to go handle something. You okay to keep going without me?"

"Sure," Tori said. I tucked the police report into my bag and left to find my brother.

Chapter 30

I FOUND Joe in the water. He was off today on account of the excessive heat. He'd taken a job painting one of the new houses going up on the west side of the lake. It paid obscenely well, but the weather made it slow going.

He sat in the shallow water on one of my white plastic chairs with Marbury sleeping on his lap. Madison was walking along the beach watching the minnows.

"Tons of perch," he said. "Next year ought to be fantastic fishing."

I kicked my shoes off and sat on the edge of the dock, dipping my toes in the water.

"Marby loves this," he said. "He's a fish himself."

"Marby?"

Joe smiled. "Seems more suitable than Marb ... Mardbury ... what was it?"

"Marbury," I said. "But I like Marby too." I had the excerpt from Pruitt's old report in my hand. I unfolded it.

Joe's face grew serious to match mine.

"What's that?"

"Joe," I said. "I need to tell you something. I debated keeping it to myself. I'm still not sure how to process it …"

"Cass," he said. "What the hell. Just tell me."

I waded through the water and handed him the report. I carefully lifted Marbury out of his arms so he could read it. The puppy gave a wide yawn, his pink tongue curling, then he settled against my chest and snored.

Joe's eyes darted over the words.

"It's Mom," I said. "I was doing some research on one of the cops involved in the Menzer murder. It's a long story. But this happened the same summer a few weeks earlier. I have to do a little more digging, but it says they found a bottle of Percocet in her car. She was zoned out on it. Driving. Joe, Matty and Vangie were with her. I mean, they would have been only one and what, three years old. There's something else. About a month after this, I found an arrest report. I've debated coming to you with it. But they arrested Mom for assault."

I watched my brother's face, waiting for the color to drain. Waiting for the brick to hit him in the chest like it had me. My father was the drunk. My mother never even drank the wine at church on Sundays. She was steady. Solid. Sober. This made no sense. My father, in all those years, on any of his worst days, had never gotten behind the wheel with one of us in the car.

But Joe's face didn't go white. His jaw tightened and he met my eyes. My brother. The closest person to me in the world. He could practically read my thoughts with a single glance. It was the same for me with him. A second brick hit me in the chest.

"You knew about this," I said.

Joe curled the paper into a ball. "What does it matter now? She's dead."

I sat down hard on the dock, gently putting the puppy

down beside me. He took a staggering step, then curled up, ready to fall back into a deep sleep. Madison came and sat on the other side of him, ever the protective mama.

"Dad was sober that summer," I whispered.

Joe's face betrayed nothing. After a beat, I realized I was wrong. It betrayed everything.

"This is why he was sober that summer?"

"It wasn't easy being married to him," Joe said. "Can you blame her for losing her own shit a little?"

"A little? Joe, she wrapped the car around a telephone pole. They took her to the hospital. I remember that part. She had stitches over her eyebrow. She said she walked into a door and I remember all the looks people would give her. They thought Dad hit her."

"He did hit her sometimes," Joe said.

"Matty and Vangie were in that car!" I yelled, rising.

Joe got up with me. He scooped up the puppy and the two of us walked back to the house.

A blast of cool air hit me. It should have soothed me, but I felt like nothing could.

My mother. My angel. She swallowed too many pills and almost killed my brother and sister. Or herself.

"She slipped up," Joe said. "That's all. She wasn't seriously hurt. The kids weren't hurt at all."

"Stop," I said. "Just stop. None of that is the point. You don't get it. That summer ... everyone talks about how terrible it was. I don't remember it that way. I never have. Dad was ... good. And you're telling me it's because Mom wasn't and you *knew* that?"

This was Joe. This was me and Joe. When we lost my mother, we had protected my brother and sister together. We never kept secrets. Not about our family.

"She got help after that," Joe said. "Dad, for all his faults ... he was worried. Scared to death actually."

"Scared enough to quit drinking for a couple of months," I said.

"Yes."

"Do they know? Matty and Vangie?"

"No!" Joe shouted. "And there's no reason for them too. There was no reason for you to know."

"That's not up to you! She was my mother too. You don't get to have this ... piece of her ... that I don't."

"I was home when they brought her back," he said. "You weren't. You were at some friend's house studying. But I was there. Cass, she made me swear. She wanted me to protect you."

"You don't protect me!" I said, hating that I couldn't keep from shouting. Hating that my memories of that summer had just turned to ash, consumed by the fire of lies.

"She did get better," Joe said. "She got it under control. She was good. She was everything."

I couldn't breathe. I felt like I had a tank sitting on my chest. The room spun.

"Joe ..." I quietly said. "Her accident ... *their* accident. Was she ..."

No. I couldn't hear it. Didn't want to know it.

"No," he said. "She wasn't high when she died. I told you. I promise. She was good. What happened with that first accident, it was a one-time deal. The other accident that took her from us wasn't her fault. I promise."

I searched his face, trying to read the lie. I saw none. I only saw my brother's pain just like I had the day they told us my mother was never coming home.

"I swear to you," he said. "And you know I never lie."

Except he had. For twenty-four years, he'd lied to me. He didn't want it to matter, but it did.

Chapter 31

On Friday morning, LeAnn Morris didn't show. I waited at the vegan place shop on Ann and Ashley for over an hour past our meeting time. I called her twice and left messages. On my third attempt, I got a pre-recorded message that her number had been disconnected.

"Son of a … she blocked me!"

"Would you like a refresh?" The waitress stood at the end of the table smiling. She was polite, of course, but I'd been taking up one of her tables at the busiest time of the morning and had ordered nothing but a three-dollar coffee with cream.

I put a ten-dollar bill on the table. "Thanks. I'm good. You can keep the change."

So, I'd driven an hour into Ann Arbor for nothing. Worse than nothing. This wasn't just some miscommunication. Something had spooked LeAnn Morris. Or someone had gotten to her and now she didn't want to talk.

I slid behind the wheel and gave the call command for Jeanie's number.

"Hey, kiddo," she answered. "How'd it go?"

"It didn't. LeAnn Morris appears to have gone to ground. She never showed. I've been ghosted."

"Damn," Jeanie said. "Why do you think?"

"Who knows. But I don't like it. Officer Daniels was awfully chatty when we met. Chelsea's a small town. Who the hell knows who else he told about my visit."

"Well," Jeanie said. "At least we know you're barking up the right tree. You think it's worth paying another visit to Billings?"

"He's on my list. In the meantime, I want to chase down a lead on Mark Pruitt. Tori got me an address on his ex in Saline. I'm only about fifteen minutes away so I thought I'd see if she'll talk to me."

"You mean the one who got the P.P.O. on him?" Jeanie asked.

"Yeah. It was quite a few years ago, but who knows. Pruitt and Billings were tight back in the day. It's worth a conversation. And it'll make me feel less pissed about driving out here for no reason."

"Good plan," Jeanie said. "I'll see you when you get back."

"Jeanie," I said. "There's something else I'd like to talk to you about today. I found some things in Billings's daily reports from that summer."

Jeanie got quiet. I heard her let out a hard sigh. It made my heart sink. She knew what I was talking about. Had she been one more person who'd lied to me about my own mother?

"I'll be here," she said, her tone going flat. "I'll be here all afternoon."

"Thanks," I said, as I slowed the car and made my exit. It was the longest of shots whether I'd even find Deena Pruitt home in the middle of the day. Tori did my homework for me. The woman worked as a bartender at one of the local

V.F.W. halls. They didn't open until four o'clock and it was just past noon now.

My GPS took me right to her front door. She lived on a tree-lined street in a two-story brick house. A clean, quiet neighborhood with kids riding bikes on the sidewalk and the whir of lawnmowers coming from all directions.

I parked two houses down in the street and walked up to Deena Pruitt's front door. I needn't have worried if anyone was home. I heard laughter and splashing coming from the backyard. I rang the doorbell.

A woman came from the back, wrapping a towel around her waist. She called out, "Lance, you watch your brother for a sec. Don't take your eyes off him. I think my FedEx came."

As she stepped into the light, Deena saw I wasn't FedEx. Her eyes flickered but she kept her smile in place. She was a pretty woman, with bleach-blonde hair slicked back into a wet ponytail. She wore a pink-and-yellow-striped bathing suit with a SpongeBob towel wrapped around her waist.

"Yes?" she said brightly.

"Hello. Mrs. Pruitt?"

Her face fell. "It's Mrs. Levi."

"Oh, of course. My apologies. Look, I have no smooth way to make this segue. So forgive my clumsiness. It's not my style to come unannounced. But my name is Cass Leary. I'm an attorney from …"

"Shit." Deena Levi put a hand to her forehead. "I didn't … you can't."

I put a hand up. "I'm not here for anything involving you and your family. Your current family. My client is in prison. For murder. I believe he's been wrongfully convicted and I just want to ask you a few questions about Officer Pruitt, your ex. I can see I've caught you at a bad time …"

Deena looked over her shoulder. I expected her to slam the door in my face. She didn't. Instead, she called out to

Lance again and secured a promise that he'd handle things in the pool area for a few more minutes.

Then Deena stepped out to the porch with me and shut her front door.

"What's he done?" she asked in a whisper.

"I don't know," I said. "Maybe nothing. I'm investigating the Heather Menzer murder."

Deena's eyes widened. "They caught the guy. Sean Allen Bridges? You're his lawyer?"

"Yes," I said.

Deena whistled. "Yeah. I don't have anything to do with that."

"Your husband was working on the case. He was a patrolman."

"I know what he was," she said, her tone turned to acid. "You think he had something to do with any of it?"

"Well, he was heavily involved with that investigation. He worked under a Detective Rick Runyon."

Deena looked over her shoulder. "He's dead. I read it online."

"He is," I said. "And I'm afraid I was there when it happened. I have reason to believe there was more to that investigation than met the eye. Do you remember that time? Do you remember Mark talking about it?"

"I can't help you," Deena said.

"Mrs. Levi, you should know. Detective Runyon killed himself about two minutes after I started asking questions about the Menzer case. I have reason to believe there was a cover-up during the murder investigation. Someone knows something. Your husband, Brian Billings, and Runyon were the main people working on that case. I'm asking for your help. Not to free Sean Bridges. But to make sure Heather Menzer's chance at justice wasn't stolen from her."

"I said I can't help you," she said. "You don't know Mark. If he even knew I was talking to you …"

"He threatened me," I said. "More than once. I know he's a volatile man. You were with him when he was on the Menzer case. If there's …"

"There isn't," she said. "Mark is a … well … he's a lot of things. He's not a good man, Ms. Leary. But I am done with all of that. I haven't had contact with my ex in over ten years. I'm keeping it that way. I don't even want to hear or speak his name anymore. I want to forget it."

"Mrs. Levi, I'm not trying to put you in a position that would be harmful to you or your new family. I swear it. I'm just asking you if, at the time of the Menzer murder, That Awful Summer and beyond, did he ever do anything, ever say anything that would lead you to believe there was something else going on? Something that would make Rick Runyon blow his head off rather than face it coming out?"

She tilted her head, regarding me with a quizzical eye. "I'm sorry," she said. "The truth is, if I did know something, and it was the kind of thing that would make trouble for Mark, I'd let you know. I wish Mark was the one who ate his gun. I really do. I remember Rick as a nice guy. He tried to help me when … when he realized how not a nice guy Mark is. But no. There's nothing I can tell you about that Menzer case. Mark … he was a shitty husband, but he's actually a great cop. You have to trust me when I tell you it's not easy for me to say nice things about that man."

"Mom!" Lance or one of the other boys called from the back of the house.

"I have to go," she said. "I'm sorry. I hope you find what you're looking for. But if someone told you Mark did something wrong in that case, I don't believe it."

She turned and shut the screen door as I thanked her for her time.

I'd wasted mine. Again. The bitch of it was, I believed Deena Levi. At least, I believed she believed in Pruitt as far as his police work went. If there was some big secret about what he did on the Menzer case, she didn't know it.

I found it odd that she was so protective of Runyon, just like Mark had been. She'd just admitted he intervened in whatever domestic drama Pruitt and Deena had. It couldn't have made Pruitt happy. And yet, he was ready to take me down to keep Runyon's reputation from sinking any further. There was a reason for it. I could smell it. Mark Pruitt might just be the key to cracking this whole thing open.

Chapter 32

IT WAS a smooth drive back to Delphi and I welcomed the
calm monotony. As she promised, Jeanie was waiting for me
in her office when I got there. It was late. Miranda and Tori
had already gone home for the day. My stomach growled
and I realized other than the coffee, I hadn't had anything
all day.

"You look like shit," Jeanie said.

I smiled. "I feel like it."

"Get anywhere?"

"Nowhere." I gave her the highlights of my conversation
with Pruitt's ex.

"Hmm," she said. "So Billings's ex goes mysteriously
AWOL. Pruitt's ex, despite serving as his punching bag for
the majority of their marriage, extols his virtues as an ace
cop."

"That's about the size of it," I said.

"And Rick Runyon takes whatever ate at him about it all
to the grave."

"Right again," I said.

"Damn."

"Jeanie … I don't want to talk about the Menzer case for a minute. I want to talk about the time my mother wrapped her car around a telephone pole. The accident Pruitt and Billings logged in their reports that June."

Jeanie leaned back and put her hands behind her head.

"Percocet," I said. "She had a non-therapeutic dose in her system. She was high as a kite, Jeanie. And my baby brother and sister were in the car with her."

"I'm sorry," she said.

"For what? That she did it? For not telling me?"

"It wasn't my place to tell you. It was my job to protect Vangie and Matty's privacy."

My heart turned to lead. "You were …"

"That's how I met your family, Cass. You were what, twelve? Eleven? The court appointed me Vangie and Matty's guardian ad litem. Child protective services got involved."

I sat down slowly. "God. That's why my father was suddenly sober. They did a home study as a condition of her sentencing. Is that it?"

"Like I said, I'm sorry."

"But why now? After all this time, why didn't you see fit to let me know?"

Jeanie shrugged. "To what end? Your mother's been dead for over twenty years, Cass. You know I moved heaven and earth to keep you all out of the foster system after she died."

"Jeanie," I said. "Please tell me the truth. Did she relapse? Is that what happened in her second accident?"

Jeanie's eyes went up to the ceiling. She took a beat then focused back on me. "I don't know. That's the truth. I don't think anyone does."

"There would have been an autopsy though."

"That only your father would have access to as her next of kin. Just let it go, Cass. It's a million years ago now. Your mother's gone. Your father, for all intents and purposes ... he's gone too."

I dropped my head. "I know. I know all of that. It's just ... I wanted to believe there was this one thing that wasn't wrong with me. That my mother ... if she'd lived ... we could have ..."

"What? Lived like Ozzie and Harriet? Come on. Just let it go. So your mother wasn't as saintly as you thought she was. No one's is. And maybe your dad, at least for one moment, wasn't the bastard you thought he was."

I wanted to be angry. I was. I wanted to rail and scream and smash Jeanie's crystal paperweight against the wall. I hated that she and Joe had kept this from me all these years. But she was right about one thing, it did no good. There was no one left to blame.

My cell phone rang, startling me back to the present. Eric Wray's number came up.

"Great," I sighed. We hadn't left things on the best terms. I was emotionally and physically spent for the day. I almost let it go to voicemail. Only I didn't think I'd be much fresher in the morning.

"Hey, Eric," I said.

"Cass," he answered, sounding a little breathless and a whole lot serious. "There's ... where are you?"

I sat straighter in my chair. "I'm in my office."

"Good," he said. "Stay there. Promise me."

"What? Why?"

"Just stay there. Do not try to drive ..."

"Eric!"

"I'm sending a patrol car for you. You're going to wait for it, okay?"

It felt like my chest had caved in. Jeanie saw the look on my face and rose from her chair.

"Cass," he said. "Your house is on fire."

I heard the words. They were simple words. But the meaning took a moment to become clear.

My house was on fire.

"How bad?" I asked.

"Just stay there," he said. "My guy will be there any second."

He said other things. I don't remember them. I just remember the wailing siren drawing closer and the flashing red lights hitting Jeanie's stunned face through the window.

Chapter 33

GREAT-GRANDPA LEARY BOUGHT the land on Finn Lake one hundred and two years ago. He emigrated from Ireland in 1910 at the age of fifteen with ten dollars in his pocket and fierce determination. He'd proudly served in World War I as an infantryman as the legend went and earned a Bronze Star when he saved four men from his unit by carrying them out of harm's way. All while suffering a shrapnel hit to the head that left him blind in his right eye.

He came home alive though. He bought the lake property for fifty dollars and built a home here, even though it took ten years to do it.

His foresight and work ethic kept the Learys afloat during the Great Depression when so many others in Delphi lost their homes.

Grandpa Leary, his son, added on to the house after World War II. He raised four sons and a daughter here, including my own father.

Grandpa was proud but poor. He tried to live out the ideals his father taught him and instill them in his own sons.

He didn't succeed all the way, at least when it came to my dad. But the lake house stood as a reminder of those who came before us. Though my father and uncles did their level best to destroy the family name, the house meant something. It showed us you could come from nothing but still make something that would last.

Great-Grandpa Leary died here at the age of eighty, more than ten years before I was born. I never knew him. But I felt him. Here. In this little house on Finn Lake that brought me so much joy.

Now it was gone.

Eric parked five houses down on the street side. He yelled after me as I leaped from the back seat before he even put the car in park.

Black smoke curled up high above the treeline. You could see it no matter where you were on the lake. Even in the dark, a few people had fired up their boats and jet skis to take a look.

"Cass!"

Eric called after me. His voice sounded so distant. So harsh. I don't remember crossing the street. I don't remember trying to run into the house. He told me later that I had. If Eric hadn't been so quick, maybe I would have succeeded in breaching the back porch as the orange flames shot out of the windows and warped the wooden beams.

Eric had his hands around my waist. He lifted me off the ground and pulled me back behind the barricades.

They called in three pumper trucks. Some idiot had parked in front of the fire hydrant across the street and they'd had to break through his car window to get the hoses hooked up.

I watched in horror as my bedroom window blew out. The big, crooked oak tree on the edge of the property went up. I'd first climbed it when I was five years old. Grandpa had built a treehouse up there. Eventually the wood rotted and we had to tear it down.

I think half of Delphi came out to see the Leary house burn that evening. Later, they'd say it was a lucky thing.

Lucky.

Lucky that the house was situated on a small peninsula. If my house was tightly packed next to my neighbors—like every other house on Finn Lake—two or three more houses would have burned.

Lucky we hadn't had rain in almost two weeks. The fire seemed to tear through the house in seconds, eating it from the inside out.

I saw a shadow in the flames. The smoke played tricks on me. But I swear I could almost see Great-Grandpa's figure, pointing toward the sky.

Joe was at my side. I sank to my knees, watching my house ... our house ... die.

For a moment, I thought they'd spare the shed. Joe and Matty built it for me when the roof caved in on the old one. Then the fire shifted and an ember ignited the roof of the new structure.

"They can't put it out," I whispered.

"No," Eric said. I'm not sure if I meant it as a question. "They're just trying to contain it, keep it from turning the whole east end of the lake into an inferno."

There was yelling. Out in the water, someone got too close in a jet ski. One of the firemen shouted for him to stop. He'd come all the way up to the dock. When Joe realized what was happening, he broke through the line and ran out there. He untied the pontoon boat and shoved it away from the dock.

"He's out of his mind!" Eric yelled. He still had a firm

grip on my arm. But I'd come into myself. I knew there was nothing I could do but watch.

My neighbors grabbed the mooring line and pulled my new boat to safety. It was something at least.

Matty stood beside me, still as a statue. My heart turned to ash at the same rate as the house when I saw him crying.

"What happened?" I'd collected myself enough to turn to Eric. "How?"

He shook his head. "No way to tell that now. I'm just glad you weren't home. You're safe."

He wouldn't let go of me. It was almost as if he needed to touch me to convince himself that I was, indeed, safe. It comforted me. I wanted to fall apart. One look at my brothers and I knew I couldn't.

"We should go," Eric said. "I can take your statement later. There's nothing else we can do here. I'm just ... thank God you weren't in there."

As I watched the house burn, it felt like my entire family was on fire. Matty's pain was palpable. His face lost all color. The whites of his eyes turned red.

I knew what he felt. This house. This place. For as long as any of us could remember, it represented peace. An escape from the volatile chaos of our father's house. We could come here and feel loved and protected by our grandparents. When they died, he'd been angry with me for a time because they left it to me, not him. I'd left home. For ten years, I was out. Then I came back and took away the one place that ever felt like home to him.

Except I hadn't. It took us some time to get close again. But now Matty knew the lake house was his home as much as it was mine.

As I watched it burn, I became aware of a million pairs of eyes watching me. The neighbors stood on their lawns pointing, mouths agape. Firefighters worked in heavy gear to keep the blaze contained so it wouldn't touch them. So I would be the only one to lose anything that day.

Then, slowly, I felt the others. Several patrol crews had come in mostly for crowd control. I did not feel sympathy in their gazes. I felt contempt.

I knew what they thought. Maybe I deserved this. I was stirring trouble for one of their own. As far as they knew, my actions had led directly to the loss of one of the most beloved members of the Delphi Police Department. I realized the contempt-filled stares weren't meant just for me. Eric still had his arm around me.

Another unmarked cruiser pulled up behind Eric's. My heart turned black when Detective Pruitt emerged.

I pulled away from Eric.

"Cass …"

"I'm okay," I said. "You don't need to save me."

He tilted his head to the side. Then he saw Pruitt approach. Eric made a stopping gesture with his hand then left me to go talk to Pruitt outside my earshot.

"Cass," Joe said. "How the hell did this happen?"

"I have no idea."

"Those assholes look happy about it," Matty said, picking up on the hostility some of the cops were showing.

I felt ice creeping up my spine despite the blast of heat from the fire and the oppressive temperature we'd all been living in for weeks now.

"Cass?" Joe saw my face. He knew me so well.

I had been about to say it was an accident. It had to be. Across the street, Mark Pruitt jerked his arm away from Eric's.

I lost it. Rage overtook me. I stormed across the street leaving Matty and Joe in my wake.

"Was this you?" I pointed a finger at Pruitt. "I swear to God if …"

"If what?" Pruitt said, his voice dripping with vitriol.

Once again, Eric tried to get between us. It was usually my brothers I had to contain when the cops were around. Now I felt a rage so strong I could barely breathe.

This was him. Pruitt. Or one of the other cops. It was a warning. The Leary house on Finn Lake had been here for generations. It didn't just burn down. It couldn't have.

"I'm not going to stop," I said. "Know that. If it takes me twenty years or the rest of my life, I'm going to find out what really happened to that girl. I don't care who it hurts."

"Cass," Eric said through tight lips. Joe had a hold of me. He started pulling me back. It only made me more furious. I wanted to scratch Pruitt's eyes out. I knew who he was. I knew what he was capable of. I'd seen what just the mention of him had done to Deena Levi. He'd hurt one woman. He might have killed Heather Menzer.

"Did she tell you off?" I asked. "Is that what pissed you off? You were some big-man cop. Heather turned you down?"

I was losing it. It was like I was two people. There was the rational, methodical lawyer tucked back in a cold corner of my brain. Then there was the hellcat Leary my father raised.

"Go to hell, you crazy bitch!" Pruitt said. The fire in his eyes matched the blaze behind me.

"You don't like when women say no to you, do you?" I said. "Big man with a badge. Only Heather had the good sense to see you for what you were."

"Cass!" This time, it was Matty getting between Pruitt and me.

I wanted him angry. I wanted him to slip up and say something. I was fooling myself though. He was an asshole, but he wasn't stupid. A smug smile came over his face and he folded his arms as Matty and Joe finally dragged me away from him.

"Calm the hell down," Joe said. Over his shoulder, I saw three people standing there recording my tirade on their cell phones. Matty spread his arms wide and threatened them to step back. Four uniformed cops joined him and told the video people to go on home.

It was too late though. No doubt the scene would find its way on to social media within a few minutes.

A loud boom went straight through my heart. The back of the house caved in on itself sending flames belching toward the sky.

The kitchen. Grandma Leary's kitchen disappeared.

Then it hit me so hard I doubled over. "Cass?" Joe said.

All reason left me. Panic set in.

"The kitchen!" I screamed.

Eric came running. More cell phones came out.

Matty held me back. "Cass, pull it together."

"No," I said. They didn't understand. "The kitchen. Oh God. Marby and Madison. I had them crated there. Marby can't be loose in the house yet."

At least, that's what I meant to say. I'm not sure if I got it out. Eric looked confused. So did Matty. Horror came into Joe's eyes as he was the only one who knew what I was talking about.

"Oh God," he said, covering his mouth as if he were going to throw up.

I turned to Eric. "The dogs," I said. "Eric, the dogs were in the kitchen."

He dropped his head. More black smoke billowed out from the crater where my kitchen used to be.

It was gone. Obliterated.

I sank to my knees.

"Aunt Cass!" a tiny voice screamed. I looked to my right. Vangie and Jessa came walking around the curve in the road. Jessa carried Marbury in her arms. Maddie walked briskly at my sister's heels.

I covered my face and cried out with relief.

Chapter 34

"You hanging in there, kiddo?" Jeanie asked. She and
Miranda stood outside the conference room door. With the
air conditioning back in commission, we'd moved all the
Bridges/Menzer stuff back up here. Tori had spent a
painstaking afternoon reassembling the whiteboards and
organizing the files again. I held a stack of colored file folders
in my arms that I'd brought in from my office. It contained
all the employment records from Mickey's. He'd sent a few
new ones over at my request.

"I'm okay," I said. "Homeless, but okay."

"You know I've got a perfectly good guest bedroom," she
said.

"I know. Thanks." For the time being, I'd set up camp on
Vangie's couch. Her rental house was just down the road
from mine on the lake. But it was just a two bedroom. Still, it
was the Leary way to take care of our own. It made Jessa feel
better too. She'd scarcely put Marbury down since she and
Vangie walked up on my burning house. Her therapist said it
was good for her to keep the dogs close by for now.

It was good for me too. Losing my house was bad

enough. If anything had happened to those scruffy mutts, I didn't think I'd be upright at the moment.

"Any word from the fire investigator as to what caused it?" she asked.

"They're staying pretty tight-lipped for now. Morbid as it is, Eric told me the dogs are the thing that has them suspicious."

"Come again?"

"Apparently, it's a hallmark of insurance fraud. If the pets just happen to be away when the house goes up, the adjusters get suspicious."

Jeanie rolled her eyes. "Good Lord. They think you set your own house on fire?"

"They're ruling it out."

"What do you think?" she asked.

"I try not to. It makes me sicker when I do."

"I've noticed." Miranda joined us. "Honey, you aren't eating. It's doing you no good."

"I'm fine," I said. I'd said that maybe a thousand times in the last few days. I said it to Eric. To my brothers. Vangie was the only one who hadn't asked. She'd been through enough trauma in her own life to understand not to.

"Thanks for looking out for me," I said. "I'll grab a bagel on the way to court."

"Well that's a spot of good news anyway," Jeanie said. "Nancy mentioned you've got your final settlement conference on the Becker case."

It didn't surprise me one bit that Nancy Olsen, the deputy court clerk, knew as much about my case as I did.

"Lou Harvey finally came around with a decent offer last week. I think his family finally talked some sense into him. The trial wouldn't be good for him."

"Dirty old man," Miranda said. "Good for someone."

"You, my dear, are in the minority for thinking that.

Never mind the Bridges case, half the town hates me for exposing Santa Claus for the lech he is."

"They hate Livvie Becker more," Jeanie said. "Unfortunately."

"Well, it'll be a good payday. We could use it. We're cash poor ever since …"

Miranda stopped herself. We all heard footsteps coming up the stairs. Tori was heading into her office. I knew she'd paid a visit to her father yesterday afternoon. Whatever happened, it had taken enough out of her that she'd asked for the morning off. It was the first time she'd done that in the months she'd been working for me.

"Well, there's nothing to be done but get back to work," Jeanie said.

I clutched the files to my chest. I don't know why it hit me at that exact moment, but rage bubbled up inside of me.

Jeanie had been walking toward me, her arms outstretched to take some of the files out of my hands.

"Cass?" she asked, stopping short.

"He's going to win," I said through gritted teeth.

"Who?"

I shook my head. "Pruitt. Runyon. Whichever one of them is responsible for what happened to Heather Menzer."

"Hey, we're far from done yet," Jeanie said.

I met her eyes and lowered my voice. "It won't matter. Sean Bridges probably won't survive the summer," I said.

"Stop," Jeanie said. "You can't think like that. You don't know. Look at me? Don't forget, I've lived past a death sentence myself. That man's got something to hold on to. He loves his daughter."

It all felt like quicksand under my feet. Every time I thought I'd made progress on this case, I hit another roadblock. No matter what else happened, the physical evidence against Bridges could not be explained away.

"Even if I find some new witness the cops missed, it won't be enough to overcome my burden of proof."

"You can't talk like that," Miranda said. There was a hard edge to her voice. "Not where that girl can hear you. She needs to believe we've done every last damn thing we can while her father still draws breath."

Miranda was angry. Her cheeks got red. She wagged a finger at me. The woman had gone full-on Mama Bear over Tori.

"I'm not giving up. I'm just saying …"

"Don't," she said. "Don't ever just say it. Tori has tortured herself over this. She cries herself to sleep at night. I'm worried about her. She has nobody else. No family. We're it."

"I know," I said.

"Do you? Do you really?"

"Miranda, I am doing everything I can. But it's time Tori started to accept it might not be enough. I'm good at what I do, but I can't perform miracles."

"You have to!" Miranda practically yelled it. I'd never seen her like this. I knew it was more than just Tori's predicament driving it. She was worried about me as well.

"Let's all just take a break," Jeanie said. "It's been a rough week."

"We don't have the luxury of a break," Miranda said. "You're right, Cass, that man isn't going to be around much longer. I just want to give her something to hang on to."

"I know," I said. "Believe me. I know. I've just been a little preoccupied the last couple of days."

I hadn't meant for my voice to take such a hard edge, but Miranda's behavior was so out of character for her.

Tears immediately sprang to her eyes.

"I'm sorry," she whispered. "Oh dear. I'm so sorry. It's

just. I've been so worried about you and so worried about Tori. I want to do something. Anything!"

She came to me. I let her take a couple of the files from my arms. She let out a snort that turned into a sobbing hiccup. Two of the files fell to the floor, scattering papers everywhere.

"Oh ... I can't ... I'm not."

I put the rest of the folders on the table and took Miranda Sulier in my arms so she could cry on my shoulder. She was a tough woman. Strong and smart. She was Jeanie's generation, nearing seventy years old. I'd basically forced her out of retirement to come work for me. She had been a friend of my mother's. I had yet to broach the subject of my mother's O.U.I.L. arrest and drug issues. Something made me hold back. I didn't think I could handle another person I loved keeping a secret that big from me.

"If you'd been home ... if you ..."

"I wasn't," I said, realizing what made her snap. "Miranda. I'm okay. Really. No one got hurt. It's all okay. It's just a house."

It was and it wasn't. Miranda Sulier, of all people, knew that.

She collected herself and gently pulled away from me. Jeanie handed her a tissue. Miranda sounded like a strangled goose as she blew her nose.

"I've got some fresh lemonade in the fridge," she said. She was such a mom. I loved her for it.

Tori came to the doorway. She had a smile on her face as she caught my eye over Miranda's shoulder.

"Oh, honey," Miranda said. She pulled Tori into her next hug. Finally, she collected herself and headed down to the kitchen.

"She's been like that all day," Tori said.

"She said you're the one who's been like that," Jeanie said.

Tori knelt down and started picking up the loose papers from the floor. She cleared a space on the table and began to organize them, making them face the right way.

"It's okay. It's just ... Cass, do you think what happened was deliberate? Your house? Did it have something to do with the work you're doing for my dad? Because if it is ... I'd understand if ..."

"No," I said coming forward. I put a hand on Tori's shoulder. "No. We'll find out soon enough what caused the fire. There's no point agonizing over the what-ifs until then. Like I said to Miranda, nobody got hurt. That's what matters."

"Right," she said. Tori took a seat at the table. She had all the papers assembled. I sat across from her and grabbed a stack.

It was pointless, really. I'd gotten nowhere with Mickey's records. I was no closer to finding the missing witness from Runyon's report. I had nothing to go on with Pruitt other than him being an asshole.

We sorted the papers anyway. It gave us something to do. And it made me understand why Miranda needed to make lemonade. She brought it in and I realized she had a point. The stuff was delicious. I had a second glass.

Jeanie excused herself to head across the street for a domestic motion. Tori and I worked for an hour. I was just about to tell her to head on home for the day when she froze reading one of the documents.

"Cass, why do you have my mother's time card?"

"Her what?"

Tori flipped the page over so I could read it. It was one of the records from Mickey's. Tori had been focusing on

Pruitt's reports. I hadn't had a chance to show her any of these documents yet.

"Where?" I asked, reading the page. It was for the last week of May, six weeks before Heather went missing.

"Tori, that's Rosemary Williams. She was one of the waitresses Mickey had working that summer."

"Rosemary Williams," she said. "That's my mom."

It didn't register. "Your mom was Mary Stockton."

"Right. Her name was Rosemary Williams though. Remember I told you she didn't have much to do with her real dad's family? George Stockton legally adopted her when he could. After she turned eighteen and didn't need her real dad to sign off on it."

"So why does that say Williams?"

Tori shrugged. "I don't know. I mean, I don't know when all the paperwork went through. I never had occasion to look it up. I thought it was before I was born but maybe it was after. I was always Stockton. She didn't want me to have Steve Williams's name."

I looked through more of the records. My heart caught. Rosemary Williams and Heather Menzer overlapped at Mickey's all the way through early June that year. Then Rosemary ... Mary dropped off the schedule. There was no W-2 for her. Mickey said she hadn't worked long enough to meet the threshold.

"Cass?" Tori's color drained. The implications of what she'd told me sank through her.

Rosemary Williams was Mary Stockton. Mary Stockton was Sean Bridges's girlfriend. And none of this showed up in the police report anywhere.

"You're sure that's your mom?" I asked.

"Yes," she said. "How many Rosemary Williams's do you think lived in Delphi that long ago? Plus, that's her social security number. I filled out the probate paperwork when she died. There was a small life insurance policy she never named a beneficiary for. Like ten grand. Just enough to bury her."

"Of course," I said. I tried to put on a light smile.

Tori was too close to it. She couldn't see it. For my part, I could almost feel the sands shifting beneath me. I needed to place a call to Handlon prison. Today.

Chapter 35

SEAN ALLEN BRIDGES was not doing well. He was wheelchair bound when they brought him into our meeting room. It had only been a couple of weeks since I last saw him, but he looked like he'd lost another twenty pounds and aged another ten years. But he was hanging on still. Despite the cancer ravaging his body, he was clear-eyed and ready to talk. I hoped he was also ready to listen.

"You sure you're up for this?" The correction officer assigned to Sean was a young, strapping African-American man with arms the size of tree trunks.

"No other time," Bridges said.

I gave the guard a quick nod and he left us alone.

"Not long," Bridges said to me. "I'll sleep the rest of the day after ten minutes of this."

"That's fine," I said. "I have some questions I need answers to."

"Where's Tori?" he asked.

"She's back at the office doing some things for me. She'll be here to see you next week."

Bridges's hands trembled as he held them in his lap. His wrists looked like sticks. Even though he stopped chemo early last month, he'd lost all the hair on his arms and it grew in wild, wispy patches on his head.

I slid my messenger bag closer. While Bridges watched, I carefully set out the documents I wanted him to look at. First, there was Rosemary Williams's time card. Then, an excerpt from Heather's diary.

Bridges tilted his head, but with the dim light in the meeting room, I wasn't sure if he could clearly read what I brought.

"I'm going to ask you a few things," I said. "When I first agreed to look into your case you made me a promise. Do you remember that?"

Bridges narrowed his eyes. His fingers kept twitching. "They don't let me smoke in here," he said. "You know, that's one of the worst things. It makes me feel better. I don't care that it's what probably got me into this predicament in the first place."

"Sean," I said, sliding the time card closer to him. "I need you to tell me what that says."

He leaned down and squinted. "Mickey's Bar. Never really liked it there. Do they still serve that shitty, watered-down draft beer?"

"Actually, yes."

"Then maybe I'm not missing much being in here."

"Sean, Rosemary Williams. You know who that is, don't you?"

Sean sat a little straighter. His breathing had grown more shallow since they wheeled him in. Not that I doubted his word, but he really would need to sleep the rest of the day after this.

"Rosemary Williams," I said again. "Tori figured it out. She worked at Mickey's the summer of Heather Menzer's murder. Sean, Rosemary is Mary."

He nodded. "She hated that name. Said it reminded her of an old lady. I always thought it was a pretty name."

"She knew Heather. Mary and Heather worked together. They were friends. You should have told me that."

He chewed his bottom lip. His gaze turned to ice.

"I saw your police interrogation. I studied it. I almost know it by heart. You were never asked about it. You never volunteered it."

"Never a good idea to volunteer anything to the cops; isn't that the advice you give clients, Cass?"

I slapped my hand to the table, covering the time card. "Heather knew Mary!"

I picked up the diary entry and slid it under Sean's nose. "Em. For weeks I've been trying to figure out who she's referring to. Em. I was looking for an Emily or an Emma. But that's not it, is it? It's 'M' for Mary. She's talking about her friend Mary. Mary Stockton. Your girlfriend. Tori's mother. You didn't think that was relevant to point out?"

"How the hell am I supposed to know who she's talking about?" he asked.

I shook my head. "That doesn't work. Not with me. The last few weeks of Heather's life, she's agonizing about her friend Mary. She's worried about the guy she's dating. She's talking about you! You've been lying to me all along."

He went still as stone. The tremor in his hands ceased.

"What was she afraid of?" I asked. I tapped the diary page again. "What did Heather see?"

He slid the page back toward me. "Hell if I know."

Fresh rage simmered under my skin. Sean Allen Bridges was cold, calculating. He sat across from me, his eyes narrowed to slits, his shoulders back. Even in his emaciated state, I could see the tough fighter he'd become. He'd spent twenty-four years in prison. He knew how to survive. Only he didn't know how to lie. That as much as anything else is what got him here in the first place.

"She tried to get in between you," I said. "Is that it? Maybe Heather started getting through to Mary."

He shook his head.

"The other girls you sold pills to, they weren't strangers. It was Mary, wasn't it? She's how you made contact with Heather. All that stuff you said about thinking Heather might have just been in some group of sorority girls. That was all bullshit. You knew damn well who she was."

"I. Didn't. Know. Her."

"No. But you knew of her. She was in your circle through Mary. Mary's the one who turned Heather on to the speed you were selling. What was it? She was an overachiever, her brother said. Things started piling up. She had trouble at home. Doing well in school was her only way out. She got desperate. Mary offered her a way out. Through you. Through the meds you could get."

His eyes flickered. I was good at reading people, but Sean Bridges went blank on me. Was it rage? Fear? I couldn't tell. Whatever it was, something boiled within him. But he kept it contained.

"I didn't know Heather Menzer. I wasn't lying about any of that. I never sold to her direct. I never had her in my car. I never talked to her. I didn't kill her."

Was he lying then? Was he lying now?

"But you knew Mary worked with her," I said. "You never told me. You never told the cops."

His face became a mask. He was hiding something.

"There's nothing to tell."

It was too much. I had waited for Bridges to snap. Instead, I did. I grabbed the copy of the diary page and crushed it.

"Do you have any idea what this case has cost me?"

He stared at me, still blank-faced.

"I've ignored pretty much my entire caseload. I've lost business from everyone in town who thinks I'm trying to exonerate the Antichrist. Every law enforcement officer in Delphi won't even look at me. And ... they burned down my house."

I didn't yet know the truth about that last part. At that moment, it felt true though.

A second passed. Then another. Bridges leaned forward, folding his hands together as if he meant to say a prayer. "I never asked you to take this case."

"I didn't do it for you!" I yelled. "I did it for your daughter. She's good. She's smart. She's loyal. She believes there's justice in the world. She believes in you. No matter what else happens, she deserves the truth. You owe that to her."

His lip twitched. Something got through to him. His eyes reddened and glassed over. He stopped short of shedding a tear.

"She deserves protection. She deserves a better life than I could ever give her. She has that with you. So, I'm grateful. It's all the peace I need as I leave this earth headed straight for hell."

"Did you kill that girl?" I shouted.

He looked away.

I came here looking for answers. Once again, I knew I would leave with so many more questions.

Sean lied about Mary Stockton's connection to Heather Menzer. He'd kept that secret for a quarter of a century, even from his and Mary's own daughter. Why?

And there were so many other clues that didn't add up. The marks on Heather's wrists were made by handcuffs. There could be no question in my mind. I knew deep down that Detective Rick Runyon's death wasn't just a matter of me being in the wrong place at the wrong time. There was something about this case that ate at him. My digging threatened to expose it. But what?

"No more lies," I said. "There's no point to it anymore."

He took a breath. "That's what I've been trying to get her to understand. There's no point to it. There's no happy ending for me. I'm going to serve my sentence no matter what."

"It matters to Tori. She believes in you. Give her the truth, no matter how hard it is to hear. It will do her no good to wrap herself in pretty lies for the rest of her life. She needs to know you are ... who you *really* are."

For an instant, I didn't know if I was talking about Tori or myself. I felt raw. Exposed. Was it really better for me that I knew the truth about my own mother?

"Sean," I said. "I know what it's like to believe one thing about your parent only to find out the truth is something different. It's not better that way. It just ... it makes you question who you are."

He sat back. Those cold eyes raked over me. Even in his ravaged body, I could still see a hint of the handsome charmer he used to be. He had a tilt to his head and a light in his eyes. He'd used that charm on Mary Stockton. Maybe he'd used it on Heather Menzer.

"You're a smart woman, Cass," he said. "And I think you're a great lawyer. I knew who you were before you ever made your way in here. I asked around when Tori told me you offered her a job. I was the one who convinced her to take it. Did she tell you that?"

"She didn't," I said.

"She's happy working for you. And she'll learn how to be like you. That's good for her. You be her role model. I was never cut out for the job."

"Sean, she needs the truth from you. Give her that. Give her at least that."

He looked above me toward the tiny window near the ceiling. It had started to rain. Thank God. It had started to rain.

"They say we're finally going to get a break in the heat. For a day or two anyway," he said.

"Sean."

He lifted his hand and made a circular gesture with his finger. Beyond the door, there was movement. He had summoned the guard.

"Sean," I said again.

"Go home, Cass. Go take care of your other clients. Tell Tori you did everything you could."

"I don't accept that."

He leaned forward. "Who do you think I really owe the truth to? Tori ... or you?"

I grabbed his wrist. "Both."

"Stop digging," he said. "There's nowhere else to go with this."

"Did you kill that girl?" I asked, my voice rising to almost a shout.

Sean took another breath. His lungs were ravaged and he started to cough. He pushed back out of my grasp and away from the table.

I rose, gathering my messenger bag and the loose pieces of paper still left on the table. I kept my gaze locked with Sean's. The door started to open.

"Tell me," I said. "No matter what. You know it goes no further. You know I can't even tell Tori if you don't want me to. Yes or no. Did you kill that girl?"

He tilted his head in that charmer's way he had.

The guard walked in. He put his hands on the back handles of Sean's wheelchair. Just as he was about to turn him toward the door, Sean looked back at me.

"No," he said. Just that one simple word.

The guard wheeled him into the hallway. The door shut behind them with a clang that rang hollow inside my heart.

I believed him. I may have been out of my mind. But I was fairly sure I still believed him.

Chapter 36

I DIDN'T HAVE to keep anything from Tori. She pieced it together herself.

"He's been lying," she said. I sat at my desk. Jeanie took the chair across from mine. Tori stood in the doorway. I'd just finished filling Jeanie in on the gist of my meeting with Sean Bridges. She hadn't yet had a chance to give me her take on it but I could guess. While I still had a gut feeling about Sean's innocence, Jeanie wouldn't. It was Occam's razor. The simplest solution to a problem is generally the correct one.

The physical evidence tied him to the murder. His layers of lies sank him with the police. And now, a motive emerged. Heather didn't think he was a good fit for Mary. She tried to break them up. Maybe she'd even threatened to turn him in for the drugs he sold. There was no way to tell.

"Why didn't my mother ever tell me she worked with Heather?" Tori asked. "I don't understand that."

"I don't know," I said. "How often did she really talk to you about the murder at all?"

Tori ran a hand over her brow. Her blouse stuck to her

with sweat. The eighty-degree respite we had the day before was gone. The hundred-degree heat came back with a vengeance.

"Never. She never talked about it. It was my grandma who finally told me why my dad was in prison."

"Do you think she knew about the connection between your mother and Heather?" Jeanie asked.

Tori shrugged. "I don't think so. You saw that scrapbook she kept. She used to drive the cops crazy calling every few months with different theories she had on the case. She went to a psychic once. A Louise Lathrop she read about in the paper on another case. The lady was a total kook, but she told Grandma Dad didn't do it."

Jeanie and I passed a look. I knew Louise. You could usually find her lurking around the courthouse during murder trials. Every other year, she'd get herself banned from the building.

"Grandma and Louise actually got to be friends for a while. Then Louise actually told her she believed Heather was still alive. That's when Grandma figured out she'd been stringing her along."

"How much did Louise squeeze her for along the way?" Jeanie asked.

"I don't know. A few hundred bucks here and there. Anyway, I can guarantee if my grandma knew my mom was friends with Heather, she would have run with that. She would have hounded her relentlessly, looking for some clue the cops might have overlooked."

"And that's probably why your mom never mentioned it," I said. "And it makes absolutely no sense to me that the cops missed it. Your mother was never called as a witness. She's nowhere on any witness list. She's a solid connection between your father and Heather Menzer."

Tori crossed her arms. "It still doesn't explain Runyon's

actions. It doesn't explain the cuff marks on Heather's wrists. And I swear, my dad never owned a gun."

"How do you know that?" Jeanie asked. "Tori ... listen, I want to make this work out for you. You haven't deserved the hell this has put you through. You're a victim of this murder too. Just in a different way. But at some point, we're going to have to find an endpoint to this. I wanted to find some new evidence too."

"This is new evidence," she said.

"It is," I answered. "But if anything, it weighs on the side of your father's guilt."

"Do you believe he did this?" she asked me. "Tell me the truth."

She squared off in the doorway; her eyes bored into mine. I felt Jeanie staring at me too.

More than anything, I wanted to tell Tori what I really felt. I still had the same questions she did. But I also knew it might be crueler to keep her hopes alive. In the end, I couldn't exactly lie.

"Tori, I'm not sure. That's the best answer I can give you."

"Are you giving up?" she asked, her voice breaking.

"No one's giving up," Jeanie said. "We just ..."

"No," Tori said. "Cass, I need to hear it from you. Are you giving up?"

"No," I said. "I am not."

"Because this still doesn't make sense." Tori walked across the room. She entered the conference room from the adjoining door. She came back holding an excerpt from Runyon's file. It was the list of supplement reports.

"We still don't have the missing witness statement."

"Well," Jeanie said. "That's the kicker, isn't it? Runyon's no longer here to question. Mark Pruitt's not talking."

"So talk to Brian Billings again," she said. "Please!"

Jeanie pursed her lips. The movement was slight, but she shrugged. The gesture said "why not?"

"I will," I said. "At least, I'll try. But you have to prepare yourself, Tori."

"Cass, I've been preparing myself my whole life. I'm not naive. I know how long a shot this is. I know that even if someone stepped forward and confessed to the whole thing, it's probably too late to help my dad. But I'll know. The rest of the world will know that Sean Allen Bridges didn't do this thing. The truth has to be enough."

I forced a smile. Her words echoed.

The truth has to be enough.

I hoped to God she was right.

Chapter 37

FOR THREE SOLID DAYS, Brian Billings wouldn't take my calls. I drove down to the office of the private security company where he worked. After getting asses and elbows from the office manager there, she let it spill that Billings no longer worked for them. I got no further details as to why and a burly security guard stepped in to show me off the premises.

I sat in my car at the nearest McDonald's and weighed my options. They were few. I had Jeanie go online and find an address for Billings.

"It's not far," she said. "He lives in Erie, just over the state line."

"Eerie?" I said. "Fan-damn-tastic."

"Erie like the lake. Not eerie as in spooky, Cass."

"Still fan-damn-tastic." I pulled the address she sent me up on the satellite map on my phone. It was straight-up farm country with an expanse of corn fields on either side of the house.

"You sure this is right?" I asked. "The place looks way too nice for a guy who can't seem to hold down a job these days."

"It's right," she said. "It's where he's paying his property taxes, anyway."

"Thanks," I said. "I'll come up with a game plan."

"You going to head over there now?" she asked.

My stomach growled. It was just after five o'clock and I hadn't eaten all day. The smell of golden fries was both appealing and depressing.

"I'm going to grab a bite, then take a drive," I said. "Just keep Tori occupied. I want to do this interview solo."

"Got it. She's staying busy organizing files. I think she's going to visit her dad again in the morning."

I wasn't sure how I felt about that. At this point, I didn't know what good it did for either of them. I just hoped I could bring back some answers that made sense.

"Any other calls I should know about?"

Jeanie sighed. "Your insurance adjuster called. Said he couldn't reach you on your cell."

"I turned it off when I was driving," I said. "Hopefully it's to tell me they have a check waiting for me. The investigation has gone on way too long."

"Eric Wray called twice," she said. "It sounded official. He wouldn't clue me in, but I have a hunch they're closing the file on Rick Runyon's death. Not that we were counting on it, but there's going to be no more help from the Delphi P.D."

"Wonderful," I said.

"For what it's worth," Jeanie said. "Eric sounded miserable about it."

"Well, he should," I said. "He's one of the main people who turned me on to this case."

"Cut him some slack," she said. "In his own way, he's trying to do the right thing. And he's got a soft spot when it comes to you."

My throat ran a little dry. "Don't start," I said. "I don't need a matchmaker in my life, Jeanie."

She laughed. "Did you miss a day? You know me better than that. I just know a good man when I see one."

"And you also know a married man when you see one," I said.

She snorted. "Wendy was cheating on him for years. She was fixing to leave him and clean him out. Besides all of that, she's gone now for all intents and purposes. I have my sources at the nursing home. So he's barely married."

"That's like saying someone's barely pregnant. It doesn't work that way."

"He's married only on a technicality. Like I said, his marriage to Wendy was over years ago. Then she went and had her accident. She's never coming out of that coma, Cass."

"For someone who claims they don't matchmake, you're working pretty hard in the opposite direction. Besides, I'm not interested in romance right now. You of all people can acknowledge my taste in men has caused me epic complications."

Jeanie went silent for a moment, then laughed. "That's an understatement."

"Thanks," I said.

"You're over that one though, right?" she asked. I knew by *that one* she meant Killian Thorne, my ex-fiancé. His shadier business dealings had nearly cost me my life more than once. It hurt. But I felt like I'd finally started to get him out of my system over the last few months.

"Goodbye, Jeanie," I said.

"You're changing the subject," she said.

I had more points to make on that score but didn't get the chance. Another call cut in. I was about to let it go to voicemail but the number caught my eye. I recognized it as LeAnn Morris's.

"Jeanie," I said. "I'll call you back in a few."

I hung up and switched the call over.

"Hello?"

I was met with silence on the other end. Then a woman cleared her throat.

"Ms. Morris?" I said, figuring I might as well force the issue so she'd know I knew it was her.

"How did …"

"I'm sorry we couldn't connect the other day. I was hoping to reschedule. I really would like to talk to you."

LeAnn sighed. "That's not … we don't need to meet. I just wanted to call so you knew that. I don't know why I agreed to the other day. I don't have much to say."

"I don't believe that," I said. In the back of my mind, I knew it might be better to take a gentler approach. I was just so damn tired of getting nowhere on this case. If the woman had something to say, I needed to hear it. Now.

"I just have some questions about Brian Billings. I know you dated him when he worked for Chelsea. I spoke to an Officer Daniels who said you'd be the one to talk to. You know I'm looking into his time in Delphi. I also know Daniels probably called you and told you exactly what I'm after."

"Brian's time in Delphi was before we met."

"I know that. And you also know he worked on the Heather Menzer murder case. Did he ever talk about it?"

"No," she said. "And I never asked."

"Fair enough. LeAnn, you've worked around cops your whole life. If we can just cut right to it. What kind of cop was Brian?"

She cleared her throat. "Average."

I was surprised she answered so bluntly. "Do you know why he left Chelsea?"

"Brian had a tough time getting along with more seasoned cops. He didn't take direction very well."

"A know-it-all. You know, that's how he described one of the cops he worked on the Menzer case with. Detective Rick Runyon. Did Brian ever mention working with him?"

"He didn't have to," she said. "I knew Rick."

She stunned me into silence for a moment. "How?"

"Chelsea and Delphi are tiny towns. I worked as a civilian clerk for years. Every once in a while we'd get calls from Delphi or Tecumseh or wherever. It's a small world and it's an even smaller law enforcement world."

"Of course," I said.

"Why did Brian leave Chelsea? If you know."

She let out another exasperated sigh. "Brian never played well with others. He was one of those guys who always had some line of bullshit about the next big thing he had on the horizon. He was going to be hired in as a detective in Detroit."

"That never happened though," I said.

"Of course it didn't. His line of bullshit finally ran out on him, I guess."

"Did he ever tell you why he left Delphi for Chelsea? I understand he would have had to take a pay cut to do that."

"I don't know," she said. "He never had anything good to say about Delphi, so I assume it was similar to what happened in Chelsea. He was on to what he thought was the next big thing."

"Except Chelsea was a step down, then," I said.

"I don't know."

"Did he ever talk to you about Rick Runyon?"

"Sometimes," she said. "He didn't like him. He thought Runyon was overrated as a detective. Runyon's not the supercop everyone thinks he is. I remember Brian saying that once or twice."

"Was he specific about why he thought that?"

"No," she said.

"Do you know whether Runyon and Billings stayed in contact after he left Delphi?"

"Not that I know of."

"Was there anyone else he did keep in contact with from the department in Delphi?" I asked.

"Runyon wrote a reference for him," LeAnn said. "That's one of the reasons Brian got hired in at Chelsea. Runyon went to bat for him."

"That's interesting," I said. "And yet you're saying Billings didn't seem to appreciate him for that."

"Brian acted like it was the least he could do."

"I don't want to put words in your mouth, but I'm getting the impression maybe Brian thought Runyon was taking credit for things Brian was involved in?"

"Yes," LeAnn said. "That's it exactly. Brian acted like the whole town of Delphi was lucky to be standing since he left. I imagine he feels that way about Chelsea too. And look, Brian was a sweet guy. He treated me okay. I don't have the best track record with guys and I'm a sucker for cops. As they go, Brian was decent. He didn't drink too much. He didn't go silent on me. But in the end, that was one of our problems. I could never get him to focus on anything other than himself. And he … you know … this is nobody's business … but he wasn't faithful. I didn't hear about that until after we broke up though."

"I see," I said. I made a note. Maybe I could get LeAnn to name some names. "Other than Runyon, did he talk about or stay in contact with anyone else from Delphi?"

She paused. "He had a partner, Pruitt. They talked."

"They were friends?"

"Not friends. No. Brian ... look, I shouldn't be telling you this. It's none of my business."

"But you are telling me. You called me. LeAnn, I know there was a reason you wanted to meet. I need you to tell me what that was."

"I read about you," she said. "You're not very popular in Delphi, are you?"

"It's easy to make enemies in my line of work. That's true," I said.

"I read there was some kind of dust-up at Rick Runyon's funeral. And I knew who was at the center of it. It was Detective Pruitt."

"It was," I said. My heart started beating a little faster.

"That guy," she said. "He's an asshole. I told you, Brian's a bullshitter and apparently a cheat. But Mark Pruitt ... that man is just plain mean. I've looked into his eyes. It's dark there. Listen, I think Brian knew something about him. You need to ask him. I tried. Brian got pretty angry with me. It was the beginning of the end for us."

"What makes you think that?" I asked.

"I think Mark Pruitt gave Brian money to keep quiet about something. It happened maybe ten years ago. We had a barbecue at my house. Brian was living with me at the time. He and Pruitt were still chummy. I have no idea if they still are. Anyway, I saw the two of them talking in the back-yard. Pruitt handed Brian an envelope. A thick one. He stuffed it in his back pocket. Later, after the guys had a few beers, I looked in the laundry. There was two grand in that envelope."

"Did you ask Brian about it?" I asked.

"I tried. He got so angry. He put his fist through a wall and told me to stay out of it."

"Did Brian ever get violent with you?" I asked.

"No. Not at all. He was pretty even keeled. I'd never seen

him lose his temper except that one time. I mean, he liked to talk shit about people. But he wouldn't hurt a fly. Pruitt though ... you might want to talk to his ex."

"I have," I said.

"Right. Well, that's all I can tell you. Brian doesn't know I called. I'd like to keep it that way."

"Do you still talk to him?"

"Every once in a while. A lot less, lately. I've been dating someone. It's serious. Brian's happy for me."

"LeAnn, I really appreciate you talking to me. I may have follow-up questions."

"I really don't have any more to tell you. I need to go now. I'm late for work. I've been bartending. It's way better money than I ever made in Chelsea. No benefits though," she said.

"I understand. Thank you. I really mean that."

"No problem," she said. She hung up, leaving me staring at my phone screen for a moment.

And now, I had a much more urgent reason to talk to Brian Billings again.

Chapter 38

Brian Billings lived in a two-story white house with red shutters. It was set back from the road and bordered by corn fields. He had neighbors on either side but they were each about a quarter mile down the road. One lived in a double-wide trailer and a lawn adorned with statues of the Virgin Mary. His next closest neighbor lived in a huge, Victorian-era farmhouse that looked like it had undergone an extensive remodel. The place was gorgeous, with a huge wrap-around porch and massive newly painted red barn behind it. I guessed the original owners of that house probably owned all the surrounding farmland way back when.

I parked my car across the street a little ways down. I can't say why I didn't just drive up to the house. It occurred to me LeAnn Morris or someone else might have clued him in I was coming. I figured a sneak attack might give him less time to dodge my visit like he had my calls. I got a friendly wave from an old lady sitting on her porch sipping lemonade. I waved back.

It was just after dinnertime and the tangy smell of barbecue lingered in the air. A chorus of locusts rose.

Heading into late August, they heralded the impending end of summer. With the heat still hovering in the triple digits, the cooler fall temperatures seemed impossible. They would come though. Likely overnight.

I left my messenger bag in the car and took just a single notepad. I knew Brian Billings was home. I'd seen movement through the window as I approached the house. I never even got to the front door. As I walked up the drive, he came around from the back, shielding his eyes from the setting sun. He froze for a second, then recognized me. Instinct told me I was right not to have given him time to prepare for my visit.

"Mrs. Leary?" he called out. I resisted the urge to correct him.

"Officer Billings," I said. He wasn't that anymore, but I figured he'd like it.

"Nice night," he said. "Supposed to rain after midnight. We could use it."

"I'm sorry to just barge in on you like this. I was hoping to catch you at work. Do you mind talking to me for a couple of minutes? I have some follow-up questions on the Menzer case."

He nodded. "I figured you might."

He was wearing a pair of ratty cargo shorts and a Jim Beam tee shirt. On his feet, he wore tan flip-flops.

"Want a drink?" he asked. "I've got maybe one cold Bud left." He was drinking one himself. He raised the can to his lips.

"Thanks, no. Wouldn't want to take your last beer."

He tilted the can toward me as if to say cheers. Then he downed the last of it and tossed the can into a blue plastic bin tucked beside the porch.

He gestured toward two wooden rockers on the porch. We sat.

"You really have a bug up your ass about this case, huh?"

"I just have a lot of unanswered questions. Right now, you're the only one on the investigation team that's been willing to talk to me."

Billings smiled. "Runyon talked to you. You've sure pissed a lot of people off with that one."

"I'm sorry for what happened to him," I said. "And it's never been my intention to cause trouble for him or anyone else. I'm just trying to get to the truth."

"We already got to the truth. Your guy ... he's in prison for it. How's the golden boy doing these days?"

"He's not well," I said. I debated revealing anything about Sean's condition. In the moment, it seemed like the right thing to do.

"He's dying, Brian. Pancreatic cancer."

Billings nodded. "I figured it was something like that the last time you came out."

"There were some things," I said, "about Runyon's reporting that don't add up. Do you have any idea why he would have taken his own life?"

"Nope. Been a long time. A looong time. I did my job."

"I know that. But like I said. So far you're the only one who's been willing to talk to me. Mark Pruitt has refused so far."

Billings smiled. "I hear he's done more than refuse. That's Mark for you. Mr. Top Cop. He's got them all snowed."

"How so?"

"Pruitt's the kind of guy who likes to take credit for other people's work. You know? The Menzer case was a feather in Runyon's cap. Mark didn't like that. It was his idea to question Bridges. I already told you that."

"You did."

I had a copied excerpt from Runyon's report folded in my notebook. I took it out and handed it to Brian.

"Do you see that? Second paragraph? Runyon talks about a supplemental report from a witness. Attachment fifty-nine. I checked his index and all the supplemental interviews. One is missing. It's not a mistake, in my opinion. I think something was left out."

Billings scanned the page. He scratched his chin. "Huh." He handed the page back to me. "That'd be a question for Rick," he said. The coldness in his tone shocked even me.

"I think it was an interview that either you or Pruitt took."

I pulled out the other copied page I brought. It was Rosemary Williams's time card at Mickey's. Billings glanced at it.

"There were statements taken and recorded from every other employee who worked with Heather Menzer," I said. "Except for her. Rosemary Williams's statement is missing from the report."

Billings shrugged.

"Do you remember talking to those employees?"

"Sure," he said. "We talked to a lot of people."

"But not Rosemary?"

"Maybe," he said, surprising me.

"She was actually let go or quit a few weeks before Heather went missing. Would that have been significant to you or to Runyon?"

"Maybe," he said. "We were looking for anybody who was in Heather's life. And you're asking me to try to remember bullshit details from something that happened twenty-four years ago. How many things do you remember about what happened twenty-four years ago?"

He looked hard at me. Maybe I was just sensitive, but the comment seemed pointed.

"I understand that. But like I've said. You're the only one talking. And you might be right. Maybe the truth really did come out. But I want to understand what Rick Runyon was afraid of. I want to know why a few simple questions about a twenty-four-year-old case caused him to go into a back bedroom and blow his head off. I think Mark Pruitt knows. I think maybe you know he knows. If Pruitt and Runyon did something, don't you want that to come to light? You keep calling Bridges the golden boy. That's not true though. I think Runyon and later Pruitt got a lot of the glory over his arrest. I've never seen your name mentioned in any of the press surrounding the case. But you were just as integral to it as they were. Maybe more."

The corner of Billings's mouth curled up in a smile. LeAnn Morris had him pegged just right. Of course it would eat at him that Pruitt got promoted to detective while Brian Billings, for whatever reason, got shown the door in Delphi. I'd hit the right note. I was sure of it.

"Was it you who took Rosemary's statement?" I said. "She said something exculpatory. Didn't she? Is that why Pruitt and Runyon told you to bury it?"

"I didn't bury anything," he said.

"But you talked to her?"

He reached into his pocket and pulled out a vape pen. "You care?" he asked.

"Of course not."

He started puffing. "I think they're going to come out and say this shit is even worse for you than cigarettes. Isn't that a bitch?"

"What did Rosemary Williams tell you and Pruitt?" I asked. "Now's your chance, Brian. If the wrong guy went down for killing that girl, you can make it right. Right here. Right now. Enough people know I've been asking questions. If I got this far, somebody else will too. This is all going to come out. There's no stopping it. It'll be your name all over the internet. Runyon can't tank your career this time. "

It was a gamble, that last bit. He stopped puffing.

"Pruitt paid you to keep quiet," I said. "I already know that. And I know that someone put cuffs on that girl before she was shot. That never came out. I don't think that was an accident either. I think Runyon misdirected the investigation on that point too. Somehow. Tell me what you know, Brian. There's nothing more they can do to you. You can sell your story now. You could be on every news show in the country."

He had a glint in his eye. I could swear he envisioned it.

"Runyon knew," I said. "It was Pruitt, wasn't it? I know about his history. His ex got a restraining order against him. He's violent. He's dangerous. I've seen it in him. I can't prove it yet, but I'm pretty sure he set my house on fire to keep me from digging into this anymore. Runyon knew it too. Pruitt had something on him. If you know what it was, it's time for it to come out. Sean Allen Bridges is going to die in prison no matter what happens. There's no one left who knows the truth. I think you own this story now, Brian. I can help you get it out. Blow the whistle. You'll be able to write your own ticket. I swear it."

Billings took another puff on his pen. His hand trembled. I swear I could almost see him salivate. He was so close to telling me something. I could feel it.

Finally, he turned to me. My pulse roared in my ears.

Say it, Brian. Just say it.

"Sorry," he said. "You got the wrong guy. Too bad Rick didn't want to stick around to talk anymore."

"Brian ..."

He pointed to the page from Runyon's report. "Mary ain't worth the trouble."

"You talked to her," I said. "Back then."

Billings looked skyward. The sun had set. The motion lights on his porch had come on and every insect around flocked to them. I slapped my arm as the first of an army of mosquitoes found me.

"I'm done talking," he said.

"Brian ..."

He rose to his feet. "If she wasn't in the report, it's because Runyon didn't think she needed to be there. Unreliable maybe. Who knows. But I've got nothing more to say."

He left me there and walked into his house. A mosquito took a chunk out of my neck.

My pulse still thundered inside of me. It was something, just under the surface. It niggled at me as I made my way down Billings's driveway and headed back to the road.

Mary. He called her Mary. Not Rosemary. It was such a tiny little detail. It probably meant nothing. Except instinct me it did.

I popped the locks on my car and reached for the door. A shadowy reflection appeared in the window behind me. I opened my mouth to scream, but a hand clamped over it, pulling me backward into the darkness.

Chapter 39

I WHIRLED AROUND, ready to fight. I took two steps back.

"Cass!" Eric's voice cut through the rising panic. He had a hand on my arm and pulled me down so we both squatted behind my car.

"For God's sake!" I said.

"Quiet," he whispered. "Keep your voice down."

He stood in the ditch beside my car. I slid down so I sat on the burm beside him.

"What the hell are you doing?" I said.

It was full dark now. There was just a porch light on from the farmhouse behind us. Earlier, the little old lady had sat there sipping her lemonade.

"I came here to talk to Billings," he said. "You wouldn't return my calls."

I looked over my shoulder. Billings's house was quiet now. I could just see the flicker of a television set through the front window.

"I just did," I said. "And why are we whispering?"

"I didn't want him to know I was coming," he said.

"What do you want to talk to him about?" I asked. Eric

and I hadn't shared information in weeks. I debated telling him about the Rosemary Williams/Mary Stockton connection. "You told Jeanie the investigation is closed."

"There's just some ... some things I wanted to follow up with him on. What did *you* want to talk to him about?"

We sat there staring at each other in silence for a moment. If anyone drove down this old country road, God knows what they would have thought seeing us crouched behind my car. It occurred to me Eric's car was nowhere in sight.

"How the hell did you get here?" I asked.

I could barely make out his features in the shadows. But I swore I could feel his exasperated gaze.

Then it hit me. "Eric, you're not here to question him. You're doing surveillance. And you're doing it off book. Admit it. Let me guess; if anyone from the department found out, they'd hand you your ass."

He blinked.

I put a hand on his arm. "Tell me what's going on!"

"First, you tell me what you talked to him about."

Again, a stalemate.

After another beat, Eric made an irritated grunt. "Dammit, Cass. Whether you want to believe me or not, we're on the same side. I want the same answers you want. At some point you're going to have to trust me."

"It's not you I don't trust," I said. "Every instinct I have tells me somebody in your department covered something up. Something big enough that Rick Runyon didn't want to live with it."

He smashed a fist into the dirt.

"You show me yours, I'll show you mine," I said. "That's the best deal you're going to get from me."

He paused. I could almost hear his heart beating. Then ... finally.

"Someone came to see me last week," he said. "Do you remember that woman at Runyon's funeral? With the big red hair and the makeup?"

I did remember. She'd been crying but hanging back from the rest of the crowd. At first I thought she was Runyon's sister, until his real sister nearly fell into his open grave. Runyon's sister had latched on to her and it seemed as though the other woman was uncomfortable about it.

"Yes," I said.

"Her name is Geri Purcell. Geraldine. Turns out she was a pros a million years ago."

"A hooker?"

"Yes."

"Eric …"

"She knew Runyon. They had a long-standing relationship, apparently. It had been a few years since she'd seen him. But for a while, it was a regular thing."

"And she was involved with him during the Menzer murder," I said. I felt like my lungs were filling up with sand. Even with the sun down, the oppressive heat choked at me. I knew where this was going.

"She blackmailed him," I said. "I was in his bedroom, Eric. He practically had a shrine to his late wife. You said there was more of it in that footlocker."

"It wasn't her blackmailing him," he said. "She was torn up about it. I think she actually might have loved the guy."

"Someone found out," I said. Pieces slammed into place. "No. Not someone."

"Billings popped her coming out of a hotel room earlier the same year Heather went missing. She'd been with Rick. At first, she told me she thought Runyon set her up. That wasn't it though. It was just Billings. She's sure Runyon didn't know a thing about it."

"So Billings held it over Runyon?" I asked.

"First he held it over Geri. She couldn't afford another collar. She'd started using pretty heavily then and she kept it from Rick. Later, he helped her get clean. I think he might have really cared for her. But at that time, she wasn't anywhere close to quitting. Billings held her over a barrel and set Runyon up for the next time."

"Pictures?" I asked.

"And video. Yeah."

"Good lord," I said. "Was Pruitt in on it?"

Eric blinked. "She didn't say that."

"Eric, Brian Billings's ex was a civilian clerk when he worked for Chelsea. She told me she caught wind of Pruitt giving Billings some kind of payoff."

Eric scratched his chin. "I don't know what that would have been about. Geri never had any dealings with Pruitt that she told me about. I asked her over and over."

My head spun. Billings had pictures and videos of Rick Runyon and a hooker. Did Pruitt know? I took a breath.

"Eric, I came to talk to Brian today because I think I might have found the witness whose statement was left out of Runyon's report."

"I'm listening," Eric said.

"A Rosemary Williams worked at Mickey's the same summer as Heather Menzer. Rosemary Williams and Mary Stockton are the same person. She went through an adoption and name change with her stepdad sometime in that era. Tori made the connection. It was under my nose the entire time. It was under everyone's nose except nobody bothered to comb through those records until we did. It wasn't even hard to find once we had all the pieces assembled, Eric. Once we knew what to look for. The stupid thing is, I might have walked away, given it all up as a dead end, until Rick Runyon blew his head off. I might never have taken it farther."

"It's a small town, Cass. Who knows …"

"Eric, listen to what I'm saying. Mary Stockton was dating Sean Bridges that summer. I think Mary Stockton was the 'Em' Heather mentioned in her diary. The one whose boyfriend she didn't approve of. It was Mary who brought Bridges and Heather in the same circle. He didn't kill her, but he supplied her with some off-book Ritalin. He was telling the truth about that. And for some reason, Billings, Runyon, Pruitt … they kept Mary's statement out of the official report. Now why would Runyon do that?"

The whites of Eric's eyes disappeared as he closed them and let out a sigh. "Son of a bitch."

"Exactly. I think Mary Stockton told them something that would have exonerated Sean Bridges. I don't know. Bridges clammed up on me when I brought all of this to him. But I don't think he was trying to protect himself. I think maybe he was trying to protect Mary … or rather, Tori from finding out her own mother sold him out. I'm just not sure."

Eric's attention went to something behind me. He popped up from the ditch like a meerkat. I turned to see what caught his eye.

"Shit," he whispered. "The hell's he doing?"

A motion light came on in Brian Billings's backyard. From across the street we could hear him singing *Sweet Home Alabama* out of key. Even at this distance, I could see he carried a red gas can in his hands. He walked to a rusted metal fire pit in the center of his yard.

"Damn fool's going to blow himself up!" Eric said.

Billings flicked a lighter and ignited whatever kindling he had in the pit. Then, while Eric and I watched in horror, he poured gasoline on it. The flames shot up and let off a boom. Billings laughed as he covered his face and jumped back.

"What an idiot," Eric said.

Billings disappeared from view for a moment. Then he returned carrying a cardboard box. Eric pulled a pair of binoculars from his jacket. He'd come prepared and I wondered how long he'd really been watching Billings.

"What is it?" I asked.

"He's got some papers. I don't know. Photos, I think."

"Eric," I said, my pulse skipping. My interview with Billings replayed in my head as if it were on tape. I thought I'd been so clever. Instead, I'd done nothing more than tip him off.

Eric pulled the binoculars away from his face. His jaw dropped.

"Stay here," he said.

I grabbed the binoculars from his hands and looked myself.

It was hard to make out. If it weren't for the light of the fire and the motion-operated porch light, I wouldn't have seen. I did see it though.

Brian Billings had a gun in his hand. Even from here, I could see it was a Glock.

"You don't think …"

"Stay here!" Eric said through gritted teeth. He drew his own weapon from the holster at his side. He pointed it down as he came out from behind my car. He looked both ways then disappeared back into the shadows as he made his way toward Brian Billings's backyard.

Chapter 40

Eric moved like a wraith across Billings's front lawn. He took a position on the side of the house, crouching low. Billings seemed to have no idea he was there. He kept right on singing as he threw more items from his box onto the fire.

The initial blast had settled and the flames crackled inside the fire pit. I could just make out through the binoculars some of the things he threw in. It looked like polaroids. Maybe a few newspapers. Nothing terribly out of the ordinary. He kept the gun he'd pulled out in the waistband of his cargo shorts.

Eric moved in closer, taking cover behind the hedges on the east side of the house.

There was a glint of metal as Billings drew another item out of the box. I squinted through the binoculars. Billings moved and I had to readjust my focus. I took slow, cautious steps and got out of the ditch. I stayed tucked behind my car but rested my arms on the trunk.

Billings set the box down and moved closer to the fire. He tossed the metal item between his hands. I tried to follow its trajectory but any body movement I made took Billings out of focus. I tried to hold my breath.

Then I saw what he was holding. Bile churned inside of me. My heart dropped to my knees.

He was holding a pair of handcuffs. He stepped closer to the fire and raised his arm to throw them in.

"Freeze!"

Eric must have seen what I did. He held his weapon in a ready position, trained at the center of Brian Billings's back.

Billings froze. Then he squared his shoulders.

"Don't move," I heard Eric say. He took a few cautious steps toward Brian. "Put your hands up where I can see them."

Billings started to turn. I couldn't hold the binoculars steady anymore. They dropped to the ground.

A bang. A pop. Something set off a tiny explosion in the bonfire. It was just a split second, but it was enough. The second bang was a gunshot.

Lights went on in the house behind me. The old lady opened her front door.

"What's going on out there?"

"Stay back!" I called out.

I heard another gunshot. Someone cried out.

I grabbed my phone from my back pocket and dialed 911.

"Please state the location of your emergency."

"My name is Cass Leary. I'm at 425 Palmer in Erie. There have been shots fired. Detective Eric Wray from the Delphi P.D. is in pursuit of a suspect. Brian Billings. He's armed."

"Has anyone been hurt?" the dispatcher asked.

I felt around for the binoculars, blood racing.

"I don't know. I don't know."

I could hear the dispatcher speaking to someone else,

relaying the information I provided. I could only hear bits and pieces.

"Possible officer-involved shooting. Suspect is armed."

"Ma'am," she said as I found the binoculars and raised them to my eyes. My hands shook too much. I couldn't see a damn thing.

"Ma'am, we have crews on the way. Tell me where you are in relation to the shots. Have you been hurt?"

"No. I'm across the street …"

Another shot rang out. I crouched lower behind the car.

"I hear shots fired," the dispatcher yelled to someone on her end.

I dropped the phone and grabbed the binoculars with both hands.

BIllings had moved away from the fire. I scanned the yard. From my vantage point, I saw Eric pinned down on the side of the house.

Billings had the advantage. He knew the terrain. I saw him on the side of the shed on the northeast side of the yard. He had his gun drawn and trained on Eric.

Eric saw it too. He moved. At that moment, the yard was pitched into darkness as the porch light went off.

Another shot rang out.

Eric was a sitting duck.

I did the only thing I could think to do. I reached in through the car door and lay on the horn.

I heard the last shot ring out over the blare of the horn.

———

I THINK every member of the Monroe County Sheriff's Department and surrounding law enforcement showed up that night. I would have stayed pinned down in the ditch if I hadn't heard Eric's voice call out.

I went on auto-pilot. I ran toward the sound of his voice as Brian Billing's motion sensor went off and flooded the backyard with light again.

Eric's shot hit Billings in the shoulder. His gun flew out of his hand and rested by the side of the shed. Eric had him pinned down on his stomach.

"You have the right to remain silent," Eric said, breathless.

Billings squealed as Eric cuffed him. He kicked Billings's gun out of reach, careful not to touch it.

The fire drew me like a beacon. Slowly, I walked toward it.

"Cass," Eric called out. "Don't touch anything."

"I know," I said. But I couldn't look away. I had to see. I had to know.

Billings had dropped his pair of cuffs just outside the fire. I squatted down to get a closer look. The fire danced beside me, reflecting in the metal.

I tilted my head to the side. The cuffs were used and worn. Even with my untrained eyes, I could see a defect on one of them. Like a chunk was taken out. I wondered what could make that mark. With cold horror, I knew. The ballistics experts would verify it all. But I knew. A bullet had made that mark in the cuffs.

I looked across the yard. The sheriffs' vehicles seemed to all arrive at once. Brian Billings's yard lit up with flashing red lights.

"Cass!" Eric called out.

He didn't have to tell me. I knew. I rose slowly and put my hands on top of my head. It would take them all a moment to sort everything out.

I saw. I knew. Brian Billings lay on his stomach, his shoulder likely screaming in agony. But his eyes. I knew I would never forget his eyes.

He was laughing at us. At all of us. And ten feet away his Glock lay on the ground. There was a clip still in the box beside the fire. I knew in my soul that the rounds would be a perfect match for the bullets found in Heather Menzer's body.

Chapter 41

FLAMES LICKED at the edges of the grainy polaroids Brian
Billings threw in the bonfire. I saved the ones I could as the
deputy sheriffs descended on the property. Eric shouted
directions as Billings writhed on the ground.

Eric clipped him in the shoulder, his firing arm.

"Step back ma'am," one of the deputies told me. "We'll
take it from here."

I did as he asked. He blasted the fire with an extinguisher.
The photos Billings hadn't yet burned scattered over the
ground.

Most were of a much younger Rick Runyon and a
cotton-candy-haired redhead I recognized as Geri, from the
funeral. Their positions were compromising, to say the least.
It was odd though, I felt no disgust. I felt sorry for Rick
Runyon. Somewhere, deep in my heart, I wondered if he
truly knew what Brian Billings was capable of.

But I did. A stack of photos lay in a charred clump; the
images they portrayed were lost beyond hope. At least to my
eye. Maybe some specialists could retrieve part of them. I

hoped so. But a single picture survived and it was all I needed to see.

It ripped my heart to shreds.

It was Heather. She knelt in the woods near a pile of leaves. Her hair stuck to her forehead and cheeks from sweat and tears. Her hands were cuffed behind her.

I looked away. That photo would haunt me until the day I died.

Anger rose inside of me. I walked toward Eric and away from the smoldering fire pit.

Billings was on his feet. An ambulance had just arrived.

"I know my rights," Billings spat as Eric shoved him forward.

"Eric," I said. "He's not worth it."

Eric's jaw jumped as he clenched his teeth. He jerked his chin. Two more deputies came forward and Eric handed Billings off to them.

"I want a lawyer," Billings said. He stared straight at me. "I want what you promised. TV interviews. A book deal. I'll tell it all."

I walked up to him. I heard Eric shout a warning. I choked on the rage I felt.

I stared into the face of evil. I should have seen it before. I knew now his was the last face Heather Menzer saw on this earth. My stomach churned.

"You're the only lawyer good enough to get me what I need," Billings said. "It'll make you a millionaire too."

I curled my fist to my side, letting my nails dig into my flesh.

"Shut your mouth, Brian," I said. "That's the only piece of advice you'll get from me."

"I know who you are," he said. "I know what you've done. You'll be famous. This is the last time I'll offer."

"Cass," Eric said behind me. He had a hand on my arm.

I shook with fury. I wanted to claw Brian Billings's face off. For Sean. For Tori. For Todd Menzer. For Heather, because she never got the chance to do it.

Eric held me back just as I lunged at Billings. I fought him like some crazed wildcat.

"Just once!" I yelled, my darker nature taking hold.

Billings's eyes went wide. Then he laughed.

The medical crew got a hold of him. I had one last shot to make my mark.

"Cass," Eric said. "You're right. He's not worth it."

He wasn't. But I couldn't just let him go. I did the only thing I could. Just before the crew pulled Brian out of reach, I reared back and spat in his face.

THREE HOURS LATER, I sat in the passenger seat of Eric's car. He climbed in beside me. It was so late it was early now. Well past midnight and moving toward dawn.

"Are you all right?" I said, turning to Eric. My heart finally felt like it had settled back where it belonged. Now that the adrenaline rush wore off, I felt more tired than I'd ever been.

They questioned Brian Billings for hours. Now that he'd been caught, he couldn't seem to shut up. He asked for a lawyer three times, then talked anyway.

I was the one who called the Delphi prosecutor's office. I gave them a heads-up to make sure they got Billings to waive his rights in writing and on tape if he insisted on rambling like he did at the bonfire.

"You were right about the traffic stop," Eric said. He'd driven me away from the station. In my drowsy stupor, I hadn't even asked him where we were going.

"I was?"

"Yes," Eric said. "Pruitt and Billings came upon a car accident a couple of weeks before Heather went missing. That's when Billings first saw her. He said he asked her out after that. He's telling a story that she was playing hard to get."

"I think I'm going to be sick again," I said.

"Put your head between your knees."

I did.

A moment later, I sat up and turned to Eric.

"Did he admit to killing her?" I asked.

"Pretty much. He's claiming she asked for it all. This guy ... he's a psychopath. The shrinks are going to go apeshit profiling him. Inferiority complex on top of a superiority complex. Heather didn't pay attention to him. He used his authority to make her. And he's loving it all now. Cass, he's lapping it up right now because all eyes are on him. He gets to be the most interesting guy in the room. It's all about him."

"Christ."

"They recovered this from the box beside the fire pit," Eric said. He pulled out his phone and swiped it open. The air went out of me again as I grabbed it to bring it closer.

"Heather's driver's license," I whispered.

"The gun, the cuffs, he kept it all as a souvenir. You got too close to it, Cass. He knew when you came to his house today that you were putting it all together. That's why he went out there to try and burn this. After all this time."

"He waited for her after she got off work," I said, still staring at the picture of Heather's driver's license. It had been the one thing missing from her wallet.

"Apparently."

"She knew he was a cop. She'd met him before. He pulled her over?"

"Looks that way," Eric said. "Of course his story is she

set the whole thing up. That she had this cop fantasy he was playing out for her."

I put my head between my legs again.

"Right," I said. "Her fantasy include taking fourteen rounds?"

"Yeah," Eric said, his voice turning bitter. "He's having a bit of trouble selling that part of the story. There's more though. Other assaults over the years we think he might have been involved in."

I buried my face in my hands. "You need to talk to LeAnn Morris again. She said he cheated on her with a bunch of other women."

"We will," he said.

"Where's Pruitt in all of this?" I asked.

Eric let out a breath. "He's still being interviewed. I don't want to be naive and say I know the guy. I thought I knew Rick Runyon. So far, he's saying he had no idea Billings killed Heather. But he knew about the pictures Billings had of Geri and Rick. It sounds like over the years, Rick confided that part of it in Pruitt. Either that or Pruitt pieced it together himself. Runyon kept on seeing Geri for years. It was eating at him. Pruitt thought it was just because of the infidelity. So Pruitt went to see Billings to try and get him to turn over whatever he had on Rick."

"He tried to pay him off," I said. "That's what LeAnn Morris witnessed."

Eric nodded. "If Pruitt's telling the truth, yes. I think he is at this point. But we'll get to the bottom of it. No matter what, Mark is probably going to get forced into early retirement at a minimum over this one."

"I just don't understand," I said. "I mean, Runyon. He falsified that report, right?"

"Pruitt says Mary Stockton ... Williams ... whatever name she was going by left a message for him. He remembers

Billings volunteering to take the interview since it was his day off or something. He's pretty sure the interview took place, but he doesn't know what she said. Then, when all the physical evidence came back tying Bridges to Heather, it never occurred to him to follow up on it and obviously Runyon didn't push for it."

I rested my head on the seat back. "She's the connection," I said. "Eric, Mary Stockton was the physical connection between Sean Bridges and Heather Menzer."

"What do you mean?" he asked.

I could barely breathe as the adrenaline coursed through my blood again.

"What time is it?" I asked.

"What? It's like three o'clock in the morning," Eric answered.

"The bar closes at two. He'll still be there. My brothers joke he's part vampire." I grabbed my phone out of my purse and fumbled for a number.

Mickey Cox Jr. answered on the third ring.

"Mickey," I said, breathless. I hit the button to put him on speaker.

"Hello?"

"Mickey, it's Cass Leary. You're still in your office?"

"Of course."

"Mickey, how many shirts do the waitresses get issued?"

"What?"

"Mickey," I raised my voice. "I'm sorry this is coming from out of the blue. It's important though. How many bar shirts do you give the waitresses when they get hired?"

"Just one. If they want a second one they have to pay for it. Most of them don't. Cass, what's this about?"

Even Eric looked confused.

"The tags," I said. "Remember you looked at Heather's shirt with the H on it? You told me you recognized your mom's handwriting. Mickey, think hard. Is it always their first initial you write on them ... that she wrote on them?"

"Cass, are you okay?"

"Mickey, it's important. I'll fill you in on everything later."

"Okay," he said. "Uh ... yeah. We write the first letter of their first name on the tags when we hand them out."

"Thanks," I said. "Sorry to bother you. I'll talk to you later." I hung up on Mickey.

"Eric," I said. "Todd's mother kept Heather's room like a shrine. You've seen it. You've been in it. A few weeks ago, I went back. Heather had her shirt from Mickey's hanging in the closet. It had an H written on the label for her name."

I pulled up my phone. I'd cataloged the evidence from the property room. I pulled up the picture of the shirt Heather Menzer was found in. I zoomed in.

Eric leaned in close and looked. "What am I supposed to see?"

"That's an M written on that label," I said. "Not an H. An M. I just ... I just assumed Mickey's mom wrote M for Menzer. But she didn't. She wrote M for Mary. Mary had quit or got fired a few weeks earlier. She didn't need her shirt. What if Heather borrowed this one from Mary, her friend? Her friend who was sleeping with Sean Bridges. Or maybe they just got them mixed up. All I know is Rosemary, Mary, was the only other girl working in that time frame whose name started with an M. The shirt in Heather's closet had an H written on the label."

Eric ran a hand over his face. "Holy God," he said, getting to the same place I had. "Sean's hairs were on Mary's shirt. Heather was wearing Mary's shirt."

"I'd bet money on it. Keep Brian talking," I said. "But I bet that's exactly what Mary called Pruitt and Billings about."

"And exactly why Billings pressured Runyon to keep Mary's statement out of the report."

Eric punched his steering wheel, setting off the horn. Lights came on in the neighboring houses. I'd been so cooked, I hadn't really paid attention to where he drove me.

I did now. We were parked in the street right outside his house.

"Come on," he said. "You're sleeping at my place tonight."

I blinked hard.

Eric gave me his patented lopsided grin. "In my spare room."

He held the door for me like a gentleman. I realized I was too damn tired to put up a fight and stepped out of the car.

Eric lived in one of the newer neighborhoods on the west side of the lake. I knew it had been his wife Wendy's dream house with a big backyard, swimming pool, and room enough for kids to play.

They never had any of that and the specter of Wendy Wray hovered over me as I stepped into the foyer.

"Come on," he said. "You can sleep in the guest bedroom. I just figured you wouldn't want to answer a lot of questions from Vangie or your brothers tonight."

My shoulders sagged. It felt as if he'd lifted a physical weight from my back.

"Thanks," I said.

Eric stood in the foyer. The moon shone through the long window next to the front door, casting him with a blue glow.

I was bone tired. My brain was fried. But my heart still skipped as Eric looked at me with that glint in his eye.

I took a step toward him and put a light hand on his cheek. It was rough with stubble and the lines near his eyes seemed more prominent. He was just as exhausted as I was.

"You know," I said. "For a minute there, I thought you up and got shot again."

"For a minute there, I thought I did too."

Eric rolled his shoulder. Less than a year ago, the man had taken a bullet meant for me. I squeezed my eyes shut past the memory of him lying there in his own blood. Then, I thought for sure he was dead.

"I'm glad you didn't," I said.

He put a hand up and covered mine where I touched his face. His skin felt so warm. There was a spark between us. We both knew it. And yet, standing in Wendy's house, with the frenzy of the day still crackling through me, I slowly pulled my hand away.

"Me too," he said.

We stood there, staring at each other. Almost suspended in time.

"Come on." Eric broke the spell. "I'll show you where the guest room is."

He brushed past me and I followed him down the hall. I paused for a moment as I passed a gilded portrait on the hallway table. It was Eric and Wendy on their wedding day looking blissfully happy and full of love.

Chapter 42

THE TUESDAY AFTER LABOR DAY, all the kids in Delphi went
back to school. They considered postponing it as the temperature still hovered in the triple digits. Instead, the school
board compromised and decided to make the first week half
days so the kids would make it home before the worst of the
heat kicked in.

I stood in Judge Felix Castor's empty jury room, waiting
for my client.

I rose to my feet as four deputy sheriffs wheeled Sean
Allen Bridges in. He had an IV in one arm and an oxygen
tank rolling behind him. His skin was gray and hung from his
bones. Death clung to him, but his eyes stayed fierce and
clear as he looked at me.

There were no chains or shackles this time. Sean's cancer
kept him bound enough. The deputies brought him to the
table then left us alone to stand guard outside.

"Place still smells like piss and paper," he said, erupting
into a dry cough that I thought might finish him.

I reached for the paper cup filled with water and handed

it to him. Sean took it gratefully. His fingers trembled as he brought it to his lips.

"The state withdrew their objection to my motion for a new trial," I said. "Brian Billings signed a full confession. His lawyer is trying to argue for a lesser charge and a reduced sentence."

Sean wiped his mouth and set the cup on the table. "How?"

"It's a Hail Mary," I said. "Ballistics came back. The bullets found in Heather's body came from Billings's gun. It was the service weapon registered to him by the Delphi P.D. He bought it from them when he moved on. It's sickening. He worked with the murder weapon as his side arm for two years. Hid it in plain sight all that time. And Heather's DNA was on the cuffs. He was issued new ones a few months after the murder and nobody thought anything of it. Why would they? One of the shots he took at Heather actually struck them. And ... they think he may be involved in some other unsolved rapes and assaults. He's holding that as leverage, trying to get consideration on his sentencing. And ... he likes the attention. It's sick."

Sean nodded. "That poor kid. Heather."

"Sean," I said. "Nobody will admit it, but I think the higher command at Delphi P.D. is still trying to cover this all up. Rick Runyon's role in this hasn't been made public. I mean ... not his full role."

Sean kept my gaze. His mind was crystal clear.

"Does she know?" he asked.

I paused for a moment. It was in me to ask him what he meant. But I knew.

"You're putting me in a very difficult position. Tori's smart. When the facts started coming in, she figured out about as quickly as I did that Heather might have been wearing Mary's shirt. That's how your hair got on her. But the rumors around town are that the evidence against you was planted. We know it wasn't.

"The blood though. What they found in your car. The media hasn't picked up the Mary Stockton connection. And I didn't even need it for today's motion. The strength of the physical evidence at Billings's house coupled with his confession is all that's in the public record right now. The cops aren't talking about it either. It makes them look bad. It's better for them if this was just one rogue psychopath former cop. If it gets out it went beyond Billings ... all hell's going to break loose."

"No shit," he said.

"I have a theory," I said. "I mean, I racked my brain for days trying to figure it out. I came up with a million complicated scenarios. I mean, Billings could have figured out a way to plant the blood evidence. It was just dumb luck for you that those hairs were found."

"Wrong place, wrong time, wrong girl," he said.

"Then I started thinking maybe it was simpler than I was trying to make it. And you really never knew, did you?"

He shook his head.

"You let Mary drive your car sometimes, didn't you?" I asked.

He stayed stoic, staring at his nails.

"That's it, isn't it? Mary would drive your car sometimes. She carpooled," I said. "It's all over Heather's diary that her dad took her car keys away from her when they fought. She would have needed a ride to work. The experts never really established how old the blood was definitively. Your lawyer, Dushane, he was in over his head on all of this. There's no evidence that he ever talked to Mary himself. He failed you miserably on top of everything else. He took everything Runyon fed the prosecutor at face value."

Sean finally met my eyes. I saw the glisten of a tear in his.

A broken man sat before me and it had nothing to do with the cancer.

"Mary drove a shitty Chevy. The thing was always breaking down. So yeah. She drove mine sometimes when she had to work late that summer at Mickey's. I didn't want her breaking down in the middle of the night after the bar closed. You never knew what kind of creeps were out there then."

There was irony in his tone.

"So Heather was probably in your car when Mary drove her. I can't prove it. With everything else we got with Billings, I won't have to. But it seems likely Heather could have cut her finger or something before she got in that car, who knows. If I took another crack at it, I'm pretty sure I could get another expert to say so. There were really only a few drops of blood found in that car. Dushane should have gone after that too. I wish he were still alive so I could tell him off."

Sean said nothing.

"Sean," I said. "Did she ever tell you she tried to go to the cops for you?"

He shook his head. "For almost twenty-five years I thought I'd been framed. Nobody would listen. Until Tori. And now you."

"You weren't though. Wrong place. Wrong time. Wrong girl."

He let out a bitter laugh.

"Mary tried to tell Runyon about it. She knew Heather was wearing her shirt. She knew Heather had been in your car. But Billings got there first. He blackmailed Runyon to pull the statement. He's admitted to all of that. Mary tried to tell them the truth. She tried to help you. But then Mary clammed up about it all. She let everything unfold against you."

Sean slowly closed his eyes. "I saw it coming. She tried to hide it from me. But Mary was already moving on to the harder stuff back then. A guy I knew from the street tried to warn me."

"She'd been arrested for possession," I said. "About a week after Heather's murder. The charges were dropped. Runyon made that happen too. I asked around."

He curled his fist and pounded the table.

"Sean, Mary sold you out. She tried to tell the cops the truth. They leaned on her. They used her addiction against her."

"It's my fault!" he yelled. "God. Maybe if Mary never would have met me, she could have stayed away from the stuff. She kept hounding me for more and more."

"She was sick," I said. "She was already too far gone."

"You can never tell her," he said. "Tori. You said the media doesn't have Mary's part in this. They just have Billings's confession and the evidence you found. Let everyone keep thinking the evidence was planted and it was all on the cops. Nobody ever has to know what Mary did or didn't do. It'll do nothing but hurt Tori more."

"Sean," I said. "It's the truth. This whole thing has been about giving Tori the truth and setting you free. She isn't stupid. She'll put two and two together just like I did."

"No," he said. "I told you. What happened to Mary was my fault. She never would have gone on to harder shit if I hadn't gotten her hooked on the small stuff. I brought that element into her life. And she had my kid. She tried to turn her life around. Whatever Tori pieces together, I don't want it coming from me. Tell her something else. Tell her anything."

"But because of her, you never got the same chance to turn your life around. Your chance to be Tori's father and help raise her was stolen from you. Mary could have prevented that."

"It doesn't matter now," he said. "We're both dead. Tori isn't. Let her have the good parts of us to remember."

"Sean ..."

"Don't you get it?" he said. "I'm right where I was always going to be. I didn't kill that girl. But I wasn't a good man. It wasn't just Mary who was moving on to the harder stuff. I had plans in place. I was moving up the food chain. I could taste it. I was making my mark. If they hadn't set me up for this ... I would have eventually gotten popped for something else. I wasn't going to stop. I liked it too much and I was arrogant enough to think I was untouchable. No matter what, Cass, I was always going to spend my life behind bars."

I dropped my shoulders. "But you can't know that. Tori made you different. You know that."

"No," he said. "I know who I am. Or who I was. Yeah. That kid made me a better man. But I think it wouldn't have happened in time. I can't change that. I can't be the father she should have had. But I can at least give her the mother she thinks she had. I won't take that from her. Mary's dead."

I sat back hard. There was a soft knock on the door. One of the deputies poked his head in.

"Judge is going to take the bench in five."

"Thank you," I said. Over his shoulder, I could see Tori waiting in the hall with a beaming smile on her face. She blinked back tears.

The door softly closed and I met Sean's eyes.

"I can't promise this won't get leaked. Tori may find out what her mother did anyway despite our best efforts."

Sean pursed his lips and shook his head. "I doubt it. The cops have too big a reason to keep it out. It hurts them more than it hurts me. You watch. Nobody but us will ever know they bought Mary off. They'll spin it that it was all Billings.

They'll let people just assume he planted evidence. And they'll keep Runyon out of it. I'll bet my life on it."

His lips curved into a wry smile at his dark joke.

I hated this. Every part of it. But Sean Bridges was my client and he'd asked me to keep his secret. I had no choice.

The door opened again and the deputies came to wheel Sean into the courtroom. Through the jury room, they could do it without facing the gauntlet of press in the hallway.

They would come after. With my motion unopposed, Sean Allen Bridges would leave this courtroom a free man. Tori would get her father back for however long he had.

I squared my shoulders and stepped into the courtroom. It was time to give Sean Bridges and Heather Menzer their justice in whatever way I could.

Chapter 43

SEAN ALLEN BRIDGES died just over two weeks later in the comfort of his daughter's arms. It was on the first day of fall.

I would like to say he found peace. In a way, he did. But nothing could ever restore what had been stolen from him and from Tori. We could all spend the rest of our lives thinking about all the if onlys.

Tori didn't break. Sean worried what his incarceration cost her. I only saw a strong, empathetic woman with a sense of justice that would drive her the rest of her life. I felt lucky to be a part of that.

On the first day of October, we gathered to say goodbye to Sean one last time. He wanted no funeral, no memorials. So Tori arranged for a simple graveside service at St. Cecelia's cemetery.

Tori was able to give her grandmother the last thing she asked for before she died as well. Sean was buried in the plot right next to hers under the shade of a pear tree overlooking a reflecting pond. We brought some greens to feed the ducks floating by.

We formed a small, respectable group of mourners. I

managed to keep the service a secret. We had been fielding media inquiries ever since Sean's last day in court. Vultures began to circle.

I made Sean two promises before he died. One, that I'd keep Mary Stockton's role in his conviction a secret from their daughter as long as I could. Two, that I would protect her from those circling vultures. So far, I'd kept them both.

"Goodbye, Dad," Tori whispered. She laid a wreath of lilies on the ground. Miranda took her hand.

"We'll meet you back at the house," she said. "I made some sandwiches and things."

I nodded at her. Jeanie stood beside me. Eric came to pay his respects. I knew that was a risk for him. The Delphi police were under national scrutiny now for the Heather Menzer cover-up.

Todd Menzer came as well. He laid his own bouquet of flowers. He turned to me and pulled me into an embrace.

"Thank you," he said. "My mom doesn't really know what's going on, but the other day out of the blue, she smiled and said Heather came to her in a dream. She said she seemed happy. I know it's kooky and probably doesn't mean anything. But I kinda like to think that was my sister telling her she's at peace now. Thanks to you."

"Thanks to all of us," I said. "You'll come to Miranda's with us, right?"

He smiled. "I'll stop by. I don't come here very often. But I think I'm going to check in on Heather."

He gestured with his chin toward the northwest end of the cemetery. Heather was buried here too as it was the only Catholic cemetery in the township. Most of the long-lost Learys, including my own mother, were also here just over the hill.

"Good idea," I said. "We'll see you later."

Todd walked back up the hill leaving me alone with Eric

and Jeanie. A soon as we heard Todd's car door shut, Jeanie turned to me.

"Do you think she knows?" Jeanie asked. She took a few steps down the hill. There was another plot a bit to the east of us. The headstone was small and flat. Jeanie knelt down and brushed some cut grass away from it. Mary Stockton was here as well.

"I think maybe Mary found some peace today too," I said. "I know Sean forgave her. If anything, he blamed himself more than Mary."

"It might come out anyway," Eric said. "The attorney general is going to look into the whole department. I could get fired for even saying this, but Tori has a case on her father's behalf."

"I'm aware," I said, smiling. We'd talked about it. Tori told me if anything came of it, she planned to donate the lion's share of any settlement she received to the Innocence Project and other organizations that provided access to justice for those who couldn't afford it.

Eric rose. "I should head back."

"Will we see you at Miranda's?" Jeanie asked.

Eric looked skyward. "Best not. I'm not popular right now at work. The wagons are circling and everyone's watching close to see where everyone's loyalties lie. You know where mine do. But it's best if I keep a low profile for the time being."

"Good plan," I said. I walked down to him.

"I'll see you around," he said.

"What about Pruitt?" I asked. "Can you tell me at least that much?"

Eric gave me a grim nod. "He's taking early retirement. I know it's a small consolation, but I believe that he had no idea about Billings and Heather Menzer. He thought he was protecting Rick from Billings's little blackmail scheme. Geri

Purcell is singing like a bird now. She claims Rick once told her someday somebody was going to knock on his door and start asking questions about the biggest case of his career. She says he told her it would be the end of him."

"Whew," I said. His words made my heart trip a little faster.

"Don't blame yourself …"

"I don't," I said. "Not for a second. I blame Billings. And I blame Runyon. I don't even blame Mary Stockton. I think Sean had it right. She got caught up in something she couldn't control. And in her own way, I think she tried to do the right thing for Tori."

Eric nodded. Jeanie had come down to join us.

"She raised an amazing kid in spite of all her faults and all the cards stacked against her," Jeanie said. "I know another mom who did that too."

Eric's eyes flicked between us. He cleared his throat. "Right ... well ... like I said, I'll see you around."

I stepped forward. I opened my arms and pulled Eric into an embrace that caught him a little off guard. I went up on my toes and kissed his cheek.

"Thank you," I said. "You're one of the good ones, Wray. Don't let anyone else tell you different."

He blushed. He took an awkward step back and nodded toward Jeanie.

"Back at you," he said, then walked back up the hill.

Jeanie waited until he was out of earshot. "You know that man is smitten …"

"Stop," I said.

She sighed. "Come on. You're bullheaded. You know that? Just like your mother was. Your father too. I know you hate this place as much as Todd Menzer does. But I feel the spirits talking to me today. Just like Mrs. Menzer did. Let's pay a visit to your mother. You don't have to say anything. But I've got a hunch she'll know you're here."

She slid an arm around my waist. Jeanie's eyes misted with tears. I shook my head. Nope, I thought. I wasn't going to let her get me.

She did though. I felt a lump in my throat as we made our way down the hill, past the pond, and across a little footbridge.

I laid the small bouquet of daisies I brought on my mother's headstone. They were her favorite. And Jeanie was right. She always was. My mother knew I was there.

Epilogue

THREE DAYS after Sean Allen Bridges's funeral service, I met the wrecking crew out at the charred remains of my lake house. It had taken almost eight weeks for the insurance investigation to conclude. In the end, it had been nothing more nefarious than old wiring that had started the blaze. A spark kindled behind the walls in the dry heat. It wasn't Pruitt. It wasn't Billings. It was just old age. I finally had the go ahead and the funds to start the rebuild.

Matty, Joe, and Vangie came. We stood across the street leaning against Matty's truck as the bulldozers came in to level what was left of the house.

All up and down the lake, the scene drew spectators. The temperature had finally cooled below eighty. The morning air held a crispness that heralded autumn's true arrival. Finally.

One of the trucks backed up, its warning beep cutting through the tranquil morning. In one fell swoop, I watched the remaining exterior wall cave in on itself.

Marbury licked my ankle. He'd gotten almost twice as

big as his mother now. His shiny black coat had settled into a warmer brown. He had a lopsided stripe from the tip of his nose to the crown of his head. Madison barked from Vangie's arms. She fed her a treat from her pocket, settling her.

"Don't you worry," I said, reaching over to pet Madison's head. "You'll have your own room in the new place. And a doggie door."

"She'll be living the high life," Vangie said.

I was in a fight with the township over my rebuild. I hadn't yet told my siblings, but I just bought the empty lot next to mine. When I was through, the new Leary lake house would be the biggest on the whole east side.

"What do you suppose Dad would think of this?" Matty asked.

"He'd hate it," Joe asked.

"Oh, I don't know," Vangie said. "I think he'd get a kick out of it."

She had a glint in her eye. Joe and I passed a look over Vangie's head. I knew she'd been in contact with him even though she hadn't wanted me to know. Since she came back to Delphi, my sister started seeing a therapist. It was good for her. She seemed happier and more settled than I'd ever seen her. She was turning into a great mom. I was proud of her.

Nate Redmond, the crew boss, came around the trucks toward us. He came on Joe's highest recommendation. They graduated together and Nate's father had given Joe his first construction job over twenty years ago. He had something tucked under his arm.

"Cass," he said. "One of the workers found something buried next to the foundation earlier this morning. It's got your name on it."

I shot a look at Joe.

"Thanks, Nate," I said. It was a heavy metal box. It

might have been army green at one time. Now the thing was dusty, rusted, and dented.

"I'll be damned," Joe said, taking the box. He turned it on its side. I could hear the contents inside of it shifting. Joe tilted the box so the rest of us could see what drew his attention. Words were carved in what remained of the paint.

"Clan Leary—April 14, 1922."

"Wow," Vangie said.

Joe handed me the box.

"Thanks, Nate," I said.

"No problem. We find stuff like that all the time. Probably a time capsule or something. You find the weirdest stuff in those."

I laughed. "I'll bet."

Nate gave me a salute, nodded to Joe, then headed back to the crew promising to have the site cleared no later than tomorrow morning.

"It's locked," Joe said. "I'll get some bolt cutters."

I held the box against my chest. "Not today," I said.

Joe gave me a sideways glance.

"You sure?"

"I'm sure," I said. I put the box in Matty's truck bed. I took Joe's hand in one of mine, Vangie's in the other. She caught my eye and seemed to know what I was about without me saying. She linked her hand with Matty's.

"We'll open it when the new house is done," I said. "I've spent enough time looking into the past lately."

Joe narrowed his eyes, then broke into a smile.

The four of us stood there, hand in hand. My brothers, my sister, and me. The dogs sat sentry in front of us as we watched the last of the old lake house disappear into the dust. It opened up to a spectacular view of the lake. Far across the water, the top of the treeline was already beginning to change color. I let the cool air fill my lungs.

I couldn't wait for them to see what I had in mind for the new house. I knew my brothers and sister would all stand with me just like this, just like always, as we watched it take shape together.

Up Next for Cass Leary

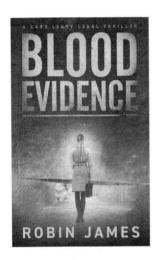

CLICK TO LEARN MORE

Cass's new client needs help finding her birth parents. What should be a simple case takes a grisly, ripped-from-the-headlines turn the further Cass digs. Meanwhile, Cass's own long lost father comes back to town bringing chaos in his wake. Don't miss Blood Evidence, coming fall 2019.

Keep reading for details on how to grab an exclusive ebook copy of *Crown of Thorne*, the bonus prologue to the Cass Leary Legal Thriller Series.

Newsletter Sign Up

Sign up to get notified about Robin James's latest book releases, discounts, and author news. You'll also get *Crown of Thorne* an exclusive FREE ebook bonus prologue to the Cass Leary Legal Thriller Series just for joining. Find out what really happened on Cass Leary's last day in Chicago.

Click to Sign Up

http://www.robinjamesbooks.com/newsletter/

About the Author

Robin James is an attorney and former law professor. She's worked on a wide range of civil, criminal and family law cases in her twenty-year legal career. She also spent over a decade as supervising attorney for a Michigan legal clinic assisting thousands of people who could not otherwise afford access to justice.

Robin now lives on a lake in southern Michigan with her husband, two children, and one lazy dog. Her favorite, pure Michigan writing spot is stretched out on the back of a pontoon watching the faster boats go by.

Sign up for Robin James's Legal Thriller Newsletter to get all the latest updates on her new releases and get a free digital bonus scene from Burden of Truth featuring Cass Leary's last day in Chicago. http://www.robinjamesbooks.com/newsletter/

Also by Robin James

Cass Leary Legal Thriller Series

Burden of Truth

Silent Witness

Devil's Bargain

Stolen Justice

Blood Evidence

75555030R00193

Made in the USA
Columbia, SC
18 September 2019